Advance Praise for Adrianne Harun's
A Man Came Out of a Door in the Mountain

"I have long been a fan of Adrianne Harun's work, and *A Man Came Out of a Door in the Mountain* has raised my admiration to new heights. Writing with astonishing vividness, Harun weaves her own myths and magic as she plots her amazing tale."

—Margot Livesey, *New York Times* bestselling
author of *The Flight of Gemma Hardy*

"Adrianne Harun's dark, mysterious novel is by turns Gothic and grittily realistic, astute and poetic in its evocation of evil everywhere."

—Andrea Barrett, winner of the National Book Award
and author of *The Air We Breathe*

Praise for The King of Limbo

"[An] assured debut collection . . . offers tales of outsiders, idolaters, the estranged, and the just plain strange. These uprooted lives read like dreamscapes spun from fierce realities, in prose radiating intelligence, panache, and wild humor." — *O, The Oprah Magazine*

"A diverse collection . . . These stories succeed as quirky examples of how strange the world looks to people who are not at home in it."
—*The New York Times Book Review*

"A most impressive debut . . . These stories sparkle like expertly cut gems." *The Denver Post*

"A writer worth watching . . . Harun's greatest achievement is that each story comprises its own separate world." —*Chicago Tribune*

"A witty, sure-handed writer whose work shines with real originality."
—*The Baltimore Sun*

"Magical . . . Adrianne Harun possesses that rare ability to see the world at an odd tilt that makes everything appear new, at times even to shimmer."   —Richard Russo, winner of the Pulitzer Prize and author of *That Old Cape Magic*

"These are eloquent stories about restlessness and longing. In them Adrianne Harun manipulates darkness and light, humor and pathos, the familiar and the strange, managing to reveal the peculiarity at the heart of the commonplace and to transform the extraordinary into something inevitable and real."   —Alice McDermott, winner of the National Book Award and author of *That Night*

"In *The King of Limbo and other Stories*, Adrianne Harun writes beautifully of the world we thought we knew, showing it to us from unexpected angles, and introduces us to her own unmistakable world. Her fierce, delightful stories are like no one else's. This is an enthralling collection."   —Margot Livesey, *New York Times* bestselling author of *The Flight of Gemma Hardy*

"Adrianne Harun's stories are elegant, funny, and well-designed."
—Charles Baxter, author of *The Feast of Love*

"These stories surprise at first, literary and wild, and then get funny, and then we read them for pleasure alone. We can properly expect things of Adrianne Harun."   —Padgett Powell, author of *Edisto*

"Adrianne Harun's stories are elegant, mysterious, and polished. They balance perfectly on the edge between ordinary life and dreams. Her landscapes are places you would love to visit, and her characters, be they hopeful, grieving, or disquieted, are rendered with great sympathy. *The King of Limbo* is a wonderful work of the imagination."
—Jean Thompson, author of *The Humanity Project*

PENGUIN BOOKS

A MAN CAME OUT OF A DOOR IN THE MOUNTAIN

Adrianne Harun's acclaimed story collection, *The King of Limbo*, was a Sewanee Writer's Series Selection and a Washington State Book Award finalist. Her stories have been widely published in such periodicals as *Story*, *Narrative Magazine*, and the *Chicago Tribune* (as a Nelson Algren Award winner) and also listed as notable in both *Best American Mystery Stories* and *Best American Short Stories*. She lives in Port Townsend, Washington.

Also by Adrianne Harun

The King of Limbo and Other Stories

A MAN CAME OUT OF A DOOR IN THE MOUNTAIN

A NOVEL

ADRIANNE HARUN

PENGUIN BOOKS

PENGUIN BOOKS
Published by the Penguin Group
Penguin Group (USA) LLC
375 Hudson Street
New York, New York 10014

USA | Canada | UK | Ireland | Australia | New Zealand | India | South Africa | China
penguin.com
A Penguin Random House Company

First published in Penguin Books 2014

LIBRARY OF CONGRESS CATALOGING-IN-PUBLICATION DATA
Harun, Adrianne.
    A man came out of a door in the mountain / Adrianne Harun.
        pages cm
    ISBN 978-0-670-78610-7
    I. Title.
    PS3608.A788M37 2014
    813'.6—dc23
                        2013035043

Printed in the United States of America
10 9 8 7 6 5 4 3 2 1

Set in Bulmer MT Std
Designed by Spring Hoteling

This book is dedicated to the families of the Highway of Tears victims—the mothers, fathers, sisters, brothers, children, cousins, aunts and uncles, nieces and nephews, lovers and friends—of the stolen sisters.

And to the memory of my father,
the irreplaceable Dr. Joseph Harun

There is a war between the ones who say there is
a war and the ones who say there isn't.

—Leonard Cohen

CONTENTS

CONTENTS

CONTENTS

A MAN CAME OUT OF A DOOR IN THE MOUNTAIN

THE DEVIL'S HOPSCOTCH

In mountain towns, children play a game called Devil's Hop-scotch. Perhaps it's a game that's played everywhere, under different names. It goes like this: One player chooses a marker—a fork-shaped stick, a piece of reddish shale, a furred leaf that resembles the torn ear of a dead cat. The marker is set upon a square in an ordinary chalked grid of hopscotch. And the game begins as usual: A throw. A series of hops. A bend, graceful or teetering to a near fall. The tip of a sneaker crossing a line. Boundaries called and kept. Again. Again. All leading to the final chalked box and a return one hopes is every bit as uneventful as the cleanest advance. But here's the rub: if your marker lands in the box with the Devil's Marker and if you or your marker touch the Devil's Marker, you partner with Old Scratch and have the option to do his handiwork when the opportunity arises. The option, mind you, the option. The problem is, that blasted marker won't stay still. It flips and skips of its own accord, changing shapes as it moves, so that you can't be sure until the last minute, when head spinning, you bend to see, that you've knocked against the devil's marker. Confusion, disbelief—all part of the game, and so, should it be a surprise when a simple game of hopscotch devolves into stone-throwing and bloodied fingers, the weakest children ironically becoming the best devils?

• • •

Adults who have studied the games of children allow that the Devil's Hopscotch makes for an interesting variation, but doesn't alter the concept of play since the possibility of trouble is present in all social interactions. The children, of course, devils breaking out on all sides of them, must disagree.

OUR COLLECTED BREATH

That wasn't the first summer girls went missing off the Highway, not the first time a family lost its dearest member to untraceable evil, but it was the first time someone I loved was among that number—spirited away, it seemed, although I knew better. If Uncle Lud were here, he'd tell this story. He'd know right where to begin so you could see how the devil slipped into town, how visible his entry was, and yet how we bumbled right into his path. All the pieces would make perfect sense then. Fractures would vanish. You'd see the whole of it. But Uncle Lud's not here, and he's left me and a few scattered notebooks to set the shards of the story side by side and conjure demons once again. Even as I do, I want to call out to all of us. I want to yell: *Look sharp!* For as Uncle Lud might say, the devil could find a soul mate in a burnt teaspoon and he sure as hell can choose whatever forms suit his purpose. I can almost see myself, crouching down beside Bryan and Jackie at the refuse station as that Hana Swann strolls toward us, or hollering up at Ursie on the motel's upper balcony while Keven Seven waits for her. *Look sharp!* As if that might have altered every part of the day the devil first arrived to meet us—the bunch of us—in person.

"Ursie's not coming," Bryan said as I swung the gun duffle into the truck bed and got ready to hoist myself in after it. "She's up at the P&P today."

"That's good, isn't it?" I said as I changed course and climbed into the cab. "She's getting more hours."

"As long as she stays clear of Auntie and those mining fellows," Bryan said. "Yeah, it's good. Good for you, at least," he said. "You might actually hit something."

All of us were decent shots, but Bryan and Ursie's mother and dad had made their first hunting camp when Ursie was still in diapers, and Bryan was right. His sister was the best. Once she'd had her turn, the rest of us were left with the odd tin can to aim at. But Ursie was modest. She didn't take time off to congratulate herself after every shot either the way we all did, whooping a little, or as Jackie did, banging the big spoon she wore on her belt against whatever was handy, even my head every now and then.

"Thick-skulled Leo," she'd say, "better rattle those smarts."

Even Tessa, the least accomplished among us, liked to celebrate a good hit, handing out clove gum all round and sometimes giving me a hint of her big warm smile.

"She'll miss the show, though."

"The show?"

Bryan smirked. "You forget already? Jackie's bringing that gal up today?"

"Yeah? Hey, don't start talking about her in front of Tessa, okay?"

We weren't even to the curve down toward town, but I imagined I could already see Tessa, the hood on her sweatshirt up despite the heat, waiting on the corner for us.

"What? You think she'll be jealous?" Bryan said. "Man, you wish. *I* wish. She could be, you know. Why else would that girl come up to the refuse station with us but to hang around with your handsome self?"

"You know Tessa's only coming along to help Jackie."

"Yeah, maybe," Bryan cackled. "Or maybe . . ."

I could see Tessa walking up Fuller toward the corner with James Street. For real now. The hood rising as Bryan's truck slowed. My heart already doing its usual wild thumping at the sight of her.

"Shut up, Bry," I said. "Just shut up."

Before Bryan could fully respond, I was opening the door, getting ready to swing to the ground, making room for Tessa in the cab between us as nonchalantly as I could. She was still more than a block away and I was halfway to the pavement when a loud car horn blasted right beside the truck. I jumped backward, smacking my head as I went, then I smacked it again as Bryan reached across the seat and grabbed the front of my shirt, yanking me back into the cab so that I tumbled onto the truck floor, my face scrapping the tattered seat, my right ear knocking against the gearshift. It wasn't a flattering position, and I was cursing Bryan, until I raised my head and slowly understood.

Beside us cruised an orange Matador, the latest acquisition of the Nagle brothers. Their crony, a skinny tattooed cipher who everyone just called "the Brit," was driving, Markus Nagle glowered from the backseat, but it was GF, the older Nagle, who was reaching across the Brit to slam his fist on the horn as if he were sending us a coded message, which I guess he was.

Bryan managed a half wave, and the Matador shot away, but not before a stone-faced GF took stock of us. I hoped Tessa had noticed the car, that she'd slowed down, even tucked herself away into a shop for a moment.

"Don't mess with them, Leo," Bryan said as I pulled myself out of the truck cab, wincing. "Don't let them notice you."

Not even Bryan, who sold pot off and on for the Nagles, wanted to be on their daily radar. The Nagles were like bad dogs. If you stayed off their turf, you might be safe, but if they got your scent, they'd set you running, and eventually you might find yourself in a fight you had no chance of surviving.

We were both squinting up Fuller Street, hoping the Matador had kept going, that the Nagles weren't on their way back around the block, when I felt Tessa squeeze by me into the truck, and a different sort of pummeling began on my heart.

"C'mon, Leo," she said. "Let's get out of here. Unless you want the Nagles to come shooting with us."

What a thought. It propelled me into the truck even as Bryan tried to speed away from the curb, his old truck shuddering and chugging as we left town behind us.

Since school finished in June, we'd been driving up to the refuse station, our dump, a straight half mile from the turn-off on one of the gutted logging roads no one used much anymore, a clear-cut in what Uncle Lud, in one of his stories, liked to call the Once-Impenetrable Forest of Vast and Unclaimed Riches. The five of us—Jackie; Bryan; Bryan's sister, Ursie; Tessa; and me—had been oddball friends since swaddling days, and as soon as we started school, that friendship had been cemented. Part Kitselas, part Haisla, part Polish and German, Ursie, Bryan, and me fit with neither the white nor the Indian kids, who spurned us in different ways. But Jackie, who held her whole generous nation in her blood, adopted us, and somehow Tessa had always been there, a few steps to the side of me, looking on. We'd ridden all the way to our seventeenth year together, holding one another in sight as best we could. We were still trying that last summer.

Townies had used this stump-marked pocket as a dump until the new refuse station with its sanitation center was built. Now, only the logging camp and the occasional hunter dumped here illegally, and so we claimed it for our own private playground, handing a pair of guns—one a .22, the other a 30-30—back and forth until the air jelled and grew stinky, the mosquitoes and horseflies swarmed, and our fingers slipped on the slick triggers so that we missed the rats and crap crows we aimed at more often than not.

You get a good eye shooting rats. They're fast and low and not as mean as the crap crows, which will turn on you and rouse the others so that the air fills for a moment with the chaotic bursts of feathers and bird crap. Crap crows make a hell of a mess, and their kin remember every offense, spreading news of it far and wide. Crap crows aren't as smart as ravens, or as excessively dramatic, but once they get a good look at you, you can't walk outdoors without one of them or a sympathetic raven dive bombing you. They spread tales, they do. Uncle Lud told me this ages ago, and he was dead right. Bryan got his right earlobe nipped hard that way

Rats, on the other hand, well, the rats just kind of explode in place, and the other rats don't give a shit. They just keep coming.

Early on that summer, Bryan and I managed a bottle or a joint or two, but then Jackie nearly got herself killed at a house party and ended up on probation and up at the logging camp, and the rest of us quietly made a kind of pact. She called us every name she could think of, imagining the worst—that we'd found religion—but we stood steady through her every tirade, and after that the five of us just came to shoot, leveling the guns, imagining

7

we were picking off the enemy one by one. And Jackie came around, her ferocious enthusiasm a sure sign that she had plenty of worthy targets in mind and she planned to get them before they got her.

Sometimes we arrived too early at the refuse station, barreling up the rutted road in Bryan's truck, and unwittingly surprised the bears, who liked to riffle through the garbage, digging their snouts into tin cans, riddling them with their teeth so that an unpracticed eye couldn't tell their marks from the hammered impact of the pellets. The bears barely noticed as we fell back to the truck, swearing under our collective breath, like a group of youngsters who'd arrived at the quarry to find our swimming hole taken over by fallers from the logging camp. Didn't matter. We'd wait: me and Bryan and Ursie and Tessa and Jackie. As long as we were together, we thought we could wait out any kind of trouble.

THE DEVIL'S COMPANION

Uncle Lud says she's been around a very long time. You might say she owns these hills as much as anyone. Legends have been written and children warned about how she burrows under the skin, crawls into your heart, lounges behind your eyes so that all you can see is the broken end ahead and . . . it looks . . . so *pleasant* at first. So you take a step forward. One little step, that's all. And for the first time, you see a clear path. It's all lit up like fireworks, like a heaven's gate, and you can't stop thinking about it. The earth seems to pulse beneath your feet. A wind wraps around you, tugging and pushing. You can't pull away. First, you imagine it's her you want. Her image seeps inside so that you can barely breathe, Oh, but take another step . . . and another and soon you'll see it's all you. It's all about you! And, bless her, she's shown you the way to your heart's true desire.

And you hear, *How brave I am, how strong I'll be*, as your feet stumble toward the cliff ahead.

HANA SWANN

That summer, Jackie was working in the logging camp's dining hall, a bunch of killer shifts. Her only break was right after breakfast was cleaned up and almost the whole crew went out on the crummies until supper. She would catch a ride to the turn-off, where we'd be waiting with Bryan's truck.

A big, tough-looking girl, taller than any of us, even Bryan, whose shoulders were as broad as some of the loggers, Jackie was also surprisingly nimble, although after she started working at the camp and she'd hike the short trail from the turn-off to meet us, you could tell that, big and strong as she was, she was beat when she arrived, rubbing her lower back and cracking her neck. By the time Jackie arrived on those mornings, she was already sweaty, stinking of sour milk and old gravy, even her big arms shaking a little from fatigue.

Sweet, though—the sweetest girl ever. She was always squirreling away food at the camp for Bryan and Ursie, who'd been on their own since their father went up north to the pipeline, and for kids like the Magnusons. The Magnusons' crazy mum had taken those tiny babies to live with Gerald Flacker, who seemed hellbent on starving the bunch to death. Talk about the devil. He'd already slipped Gerald Flacker into his pocket.

Those mornings, Jackie wrapped cold fried potatoes or bits

of greasy meat in paper toweling and if anyone was looking, she'd make out like she was throwing out the garbage, but she'd slip the towels into the plastic bags that lined her deep pockets instead. There wasn't an outright rule about stealing food, but the thing was, the fallers ate everything you put out— a startling quantity, outright tonnage—so anything you held back . . . well, let's just say that nothing was about to go to waste, not even the crusts tucked into her pockets. Jackie would pass her bags on to Bryan at the refuse station, and he'd drive them back into town in time for the Magnuson kids' lunch that day, he and Ursie snacking a little if it had been a while.

Bryan must have appeared like something out of a fairy tale to those kids, a gawky giant in threadbare clothes of his own, his big boots split from wear, a queer hitch in his step. They must have glimpsed him from time to time, hovering on the other side of Flacker's metal hell pile, the flash off the plastic bags he carried in his deep coverall pockets giving him away. If Gerald Flacker wasn't around, Bryan would leave a bag under a rusted fender and hope the kids got to it before Flacker's dogs, who didn't have it so good themselves. My mother, who worked up at the animal shelter, was always after snatching those thin-flanked dogs (so skinny they walked sideways as if tiptoeing toward you) the way Jackie and Bryan wanted to rescue the Magnuson kids. Flacker took delight in keeping his hounds pretty hungry too. A mean-boned man. All of us had a few of those in mind when we took aim those mornings at the dump. Revenge, resentment—a kind of low-level heat that burned constantly within us, tamped down by the silence we knew would be our only protection until we couldn't stand it anymore and the flames burst through. We had seen that happen to others and wondered when it would happen to us, break us wide open so that we would be set free or singed beyond repair.

Jackie would be the first, the rest of us were sure. She was tough and stoic, but beneath it, her sense of fairness was acute, and her pain at every injustice became harder and harder to hide. We could see it in her rising color, her even more pronounced silence when men unrolled their car windows to spit out a few words about what "a big fucking squaw" could do for them. She'd beat up more than a few who had naïvely thought they could slap around her sisters or hurl insults toward her mother and aunts as they walked to the market. The law knew Jackie's address by heart. Warnings had been issued with at least one officer leaning in too closely to make his own declaration, his own deal, a few moments on her knees to buy her way out of trouble. Lucky man, that fellow. Jackie's BaBa arrived in time, his sorrowful, proud eyes holding Jackie tight enough so that she could breathe again.

At the camp, no one was going to discipline Jackie if she whaled on a fellow who tried to touch her or anyone else, and not one of those tough guys wanted to be laid out cold by Jackie, so they let her be. The work wilted everyone, anyway. Half of 'em were always sleeping on their feet the first few weeks, their necks burned by the hot fuel dripping off the chainsaws they carried against their shoulders. They didn't come fully awake even during their time off, when they'd head down the mountainside to get drunk and try to remember how they'd ended up here. A few flat-out disappeared and were replaced almost overnight by one of the continuous train of strangers coming through, every now and then bearing a surprise so startling it seemed lives would change forever. A surprise like Hana Swann.

They were barely into the first week of July when the French camp cook got into a screaming match with the longhaired kid who was Jackie's co-worker, a hitchhiker one of the fallers had brought up to the camp. Almost from the first, the cook had refused to even use the kid's name—he despised him on sight, apparently—pummeling him instead with every insulting term he could. The screaming match that day, a particularly virulent one, disintegrated into a shoving contest (which was no contest at all, the camp cook being two hundred pounds of crazed Québécois fury), and the kid, whom the cook called the *niaiseux* or *plotte*—obscene terms that meant something akin to "nanny-goat pussy"—ended up with a broken wrist and spent half a morning weeping in pain before someone could spare the time to drive him down to the clinic.

Crisse de cave, the cook spat in the kid's direction when the longhaired boy finally wobbled out the door, his thin arms slung around a faller's scarred shoulder.

Great move, Jackie told us, via Glenn Closby, who drove one of the supply trucks.

They're in for it now, Glenn said, until they get another pair of hands.

And the cook and Jackie did struggle mightily through two rough days before they shanghaied a bush bunny from a sunken trailer down the hill to wash dishes. He was nearly as crazy as the cook, though, and it was another full week before real help was found.

Like Jackie and the kid, that newcomer, a young woman named Hana Swann, was hired to do the grunt work, to peel endless piles of potatoes, chop mountains of onions, and blister in front of those massive stainless-steel stoves. Jackie was ready for anything that resembled relief by then. Even so, her first reaction when she glimpsed Hana Swann was to snort. *Little girl like that at the camp. Give me a fucking break!* Minutes later, she watched Hana Swann beating batter in a bowl with a clean impressive fury and decided maybe Hana would last the morning after all. A few hours later, that "little girl" was still easily hoisting heavy pots of oatmeal and urns of coffee, weights that had made the longhaired kid grunt, and Jackie began to feel the shifting. Hana was a worker, all right, despite the looks.

When the men came in early that morning, the dark just lifting, a hush descended, but not the usual thunderous vacuum of men intent upon their food. Jackie was too distracted at first to register the change until the quiet was broken with self-conscious chatter that was equally strange, like a foreign music she didn't recognize, and she and the cook glanced at each other. He shrugged, but like the fallers, Jackie was now openmouthed, marveling at the grace of the new girl, who stopped them all cold. Then Jackie couldn't peel her eyes away. The coffee ran low, a criminal act and all Jackie's doing. With that, one faller reclaimed his bellow and complained. Eventually, the cook woke her, threatening more than a swat of a spoon: *Lâche pas la patate!*

But the cook, too, could not imagine who had hired this fragile-looking girl. He intensified his hollering, embellishing his usual insults and orders, only to discover that the new girl was always a step ahead of him and not at all perturbed by his bad humor.

All that first morning, as Hana peeled and chopped and stirred and scrubbed, Jackie longed to pinch her, to see whether that white, white skin would pinken or, as Jackie suspected, remain unscathed. Her desire was so great that by the time they themselves sat down to eat, Jackie had been stricken dumb.

Kitchen work is back-wrenching labor. Too hard for most. Jackie began to wonder if Hana was for real, if they were dreaming her into being. When the breakfast was over, Jackie was relieved to see Hana pull off the blue kerchief she'd wound around her hair and wipe invisible lines of perspiration off her forehead and the back of her neck.

It fell to Jackie to show Hana where she'd sleep, in a metal shack like those for fallers but considerably more cramped, ("the tin bin," Jackie called it), an arm's length away from Jackie. Hana stowed her gear, a single filthy yellow duffle, leaving it without a second glance as if its loss would mean nothing to her. Jackie wanted to ask so much that she couldn't ask anything, could only wait hopelessly for Hana to tell her tale.

Almost everybody who shows up here has a story, usually embellished and smoothed out. That's one big difference right off between those who arrive and those who live here. Our own stories were unedited—sprawling and unpretty—and nothing could clip and shape and redefine them as long as we stayed here. As long as we were alive. In fact, our stories started out messy, our families telling tales on us as mere infants, cataloging all our peculiarities in the womb and pinning them on us as soon as we arrived so that even our good points became barbs, jabbed back at us whenever we got in the way. In a place like this, the stories circulate over and over and grow flatter with each pass, and it's no wonder townies got hungry for new ones, ones with more drama, which more or less explains our behavior. No one wants bad news, but it's something to tell.

The stories were about all we did like about new people, who were either awestruck or blind or rude or plain damaged, hell-bent on trashing whatever they could get their hands on all the while pretending they were here to help. And, sadly, the most interesting-looking newcomers weren't much inclined to share their stories—not the real ones, at least. All Hana Swann would say is that she'd heard of the job in town, after breaking up with the boyfriend with whom she'd been traveling. Before long, we wanted to see that asshole boyfriend, who was probably just sobering up to what he'd lost. I wondered if he'd become one of those men Uncle Lud claimed to know, who having experienced a vision, haunts the highway hour after hour, hopelessly longing for its return.

We hadn't heard about Hana Swann from Jackie, but from Ursie, whose auntie could not stop talking about the girl she'd seen leaning beside Peak and Pine Motel's coffee machine talking to the camp manager. You'd think Rose Prince, saint of the Carrier Nation, had returned to Earth, Ursie said, the way everyone at the motel had gone on about her. One fellow crashed his car into a brick wall on Seventh Street after a brief encounter with her, they said. He was so overcome. Even Albie Porchier, the motel owner, had reportedly gone into cheerful spasms of terrible courtliness at the sight of her, opening doors and whipping off his cap. And, too, we soon heard how when the French cook sliced his hand in the middle of one of his rants, Hana had not only swooped in with the first-aid kit, she'd conjured up a foul-smelling poultice and bound the wound with poplar bark so the wound had closed tight by midday. The cook's heart had raced so fast, he said, he felt he'd have to stab himself to slow it down. He'd nearly done that, would have, but Jackie grabbed the knife off him. Might have been the result of the herbs, sure, or might have just been the sight of his rough, blood-soaked hand in her unmarked palm that set his heart to racing. Still, the poultice had done its job.

"She knows the plants, then, eh?" we said. "She must be from around here."

But clearly she wasn't. She would have been a legend if she had been. Or, at the very least, we thought, we would have known her weak spot. That's how dumb we were.

Once Jackie made it back up to the refuse station, she was quiet while we conjectured, as if for once she didn't want to share. We asked her if she thought Hana Swann was a saint like Rose Prince, and she only made a guffawing sound. Bryan asked her if she thought the French cook was fucking Hana Swann yet, and Jackie didn't say a word, just frowned, and shot two rats in rapid succession. Bryan wanted a real description. How tall? he asked, how big? His hands curled in front of his own chest. I said maybe it would be better to drive up there in Bryan's truck and wait until the crummies left, then go see for ourselves.

Jackie said, "I'll bring her."

So we waited.

A week later, and there was Jackie, coming down the old road with Hana Swann.

You hear about celebrities, how they have this kind of glow, this presence that makes everyone hush or grin, pawing the ground in front of them. Hana Swann was maybe twenty-four, tall and lean, with a fall of black hair we all recognized and eyes a shade of turquoise we'd only seen up in the high mountain lakes. We did not truly believe people came in her variety. Pretty? Was she pretty? Who knew? Her skin, that particular shade of white, was unknown to us and maybe even a little strange. She was an unblemished person, and while we all had wanted to believe such people existed in far-off cities where people can live in pristine white rooms, cushioned by fluffed-up carpets and over-stuffed silky furniture, up here such a person was a fantastic notion. It was hard to imagine not being riddled by bite marks from mosquitoes, swollen eyes from black flies, bruises from a sudden fall or the back of metal spoon, or burns, gashes, old scars, hickeys, peeling skin, sprawling rashes, the raw, burning edges of a nose that wouldn't stop running.

Hana Swann had none of these. Not even a freckle. I finally saw why the cook had taken one look and dubbed her "Snow White."

"Hey." She smiled, with tiny pearl teeth that transfixed us.

We waited for Jackie to say something. To crack a joke or push one of us around or even just grab the gun off Bryan and start pinging at the dump pile to see what might come out. But Jackie was shy and awkward, tripping on roots and making a lot more noise than she usually did. It was as if she'd just discovered her body was a few sizes too big and was stumbling around inside, trying to gain purchase.

A brilliant day. The cool morning air had slipped away. Our old flannel shirts and hoodies long since peeled off. The dump was already heating up, sunlight burning through the high clouds, crisscrossing the random piles and striking each of us in turn. Soon, we would be blistered by the stench, blind and sweating. Not yet though. In the woods beyond the rutted logging road, great swaths of God's rays formed halos here and there, illuminating the tunneling clouds of mosquitoes that were already claiming the day. Once, when I was in grade three, I'd been up on a trail with my mother and the dogs and a God's ray fell right over us. My mother, who'd been schooled by the nuns, started to kneel, but the dogs pulled her upright. Still, we all were held tight for a moment, even the dogs.

"*No bears?*" That was the second thing she said. Nothing about the scavenger gulls squabbling over the remains of a moose butchering a few days ago. Nothing about the black flies that swarmed around our heads and made us all a little frantic. Nothing about the guns in our hands.

"N-n-not y-y-yet," I stuttered. Everyone turned and stared at me. Even Jackie finally raised her bent neck and managed a weak smile.

"Leo Smooth Talker here," Bryan jabbed.

"Bear got your tongue," Tessa teased as we began to let our breath out. Annoyed as I was by my clumsiness, it felt good to have Tessa joking with me. I ducked my head with pleasure, but not before trying to catch her eye.

The old dump smelled like piss and sulfur and rot, but Hana Swann didn't seem to notice. She leaned against the big lava rock that we often used to balance our guns, and for the first time, with relief, we could see her weariness. Tessa offered her a stick of that clove gum she loved and hoarded from the rest of us, and we couldn't help noticing Hana Swann's hands as she unwrapped the gum, long and white and elegant and, just as everyone said, completely unblemished, as if she'd been soaking them in milk her entire life.

"Thanks," she said, offering Tessa more of that pearl-toothed smile. I was surprised to see Tessa frown a little at that smile, as if she'd seen something in it she recognized and did not like one whit.

Hana Swann waved off Bryan's gun, even as she eyed him closely, reading, it seemed, his particular brand of longing.

"Who are you?" she said. "Ah, Bryan, sure, that's right." As if she'd known about him for ages.

He handed the gun to Jackie instead, who took it in her own trance. Once she began to sight, her new awkwardness seeped away, and when she stepped up to take her shot, we relaxed a little more, forgetting for a moment to glance at Hana and see how she was taking it. Jackie nailed a young rat. The crap crows went ballistic, and we fell back a little to let 'em go, although Bryan managed to hit two who were reluctant to give up their positions in the moose offal.

Throughout all this, Hana watched with a kind of ease as if she'd been with us always. I could feel her eyes move from one to the other.

"Ursie isn't here," she said out of the blue, and Bryan smirked at Jackie, imagining she'd been telling Hana all about us—a telling fact, since our Jackie didn't like to reveal anything personal to many. The thought that she'd described us to Hana kind of thrilled me, and Bryan pointedly wiggled his big eyebrows in Jackie's direction. She pretended not to notice. Instead she picked up one of the tin cans visited by bears and carried it to Hana. Big ol' Jackie looked like a little kid, shy with her treasures. We could see how much she wanted Hana to like this place, like us, like her, and when Hana said *You have a good eye, Tessa* or *Steady hand there, Leo,* we were all absurdly, uncharacteristically happy as if we'd been training for her approval all this time.

Before long, we were almost bullshitting as usual as we traded off taking shots, although even our simplest jeers felt like lines given out onstage. We could feel Hana. She damn near glowed behind us, so that by the time the heat had fully risen, our T-shirts were soaked through, and our hearts were about to burst with the need to stop and stare. Jackie had already quit and was hunched on an old stump beside a patch of late-blooming fox-gloves, her eyes pinned on Hana, who it seemed had gone to sleep while we were aching with her presence. She was still leaning against the big black rock, that bone-white girl, asleep there in the middle of the swill and the stench and the noise of the guns. Yet when it was time to go, and Bryan and Jackie went to the far side of his truck, Hana rose fully awake and followed them, head tilted to one side, watching as Jackie pulled plastic bags from her pockets: biscuits and back bacon wrapped in paper toweling. Without a fuss, the food parcels were placed on the cracked dash-board of Bryan's truck.

"So what's this?" Hana asked.

Bryan shrugged. Gerald Flacker didn't seem worth his breath, and it hurt him to conjure up the Magnuson kids, but Jackie managed an explanation laced with "dickhead" and "fucker" and just about every other adjective we'd ever hurled toward Flacker. And then, all warmed up, she told a story about a back room Flacker had kept for truckers, about girls drugged and branded and raped; about his drugs, his guns, visits in the night; about his private posse of goons, the Nagle brothers and the bald, dead-eyed Brit who accompanied them as they trolled town; and lastly about those two little kids trapped by their meth-head mother in Flacker's kingdom.

"And this is how you deal with him?" Hana said, nodding toward the truck's dashboard. "You sneak around behind his back?"

She didn't say it meanly, but her question cut Bryan to the

core, I could see. She had offered a tease, but clearly she had no idea of what Flacker really was, although for one terrifying second, I thought we'd conjured him, a black-bearded monster, tattoos riding up his neck and across his iron knuckles, a twisted livid face striding straight out of a stunted jack pine. He'd set men on fire more than once, it was said, and stuck around to watch them burn. A swelling heat enveloped me as the vision faded, and I hurried to cut off any suggestions Hana Swann might be about to make.

"Would be suicide to do more," I began. "Anyone who crosses Flacker . . ."

"You got a better plan?" Bryan interrupted, closing the truck's passenger door.

"The best plans are the simplest ones," Hana said.

"This is pretty damn simple," Bryan said. "We bring food."

"How pure you all are," she said, confusing the hell out of us again and embarrassing us too, especially me. I could not help cutting my eyes toward Tessa. Out of all the kids we knew, we were probably the only ones not screwing around. At least, not much.

The morning was spent. We began pocketing the pellets and gathering the guns, none noticing for the moment that Hana had picked up the .22 and was scoping out a shot, but she wasn't aiming toward the tipped piles that had occupied us. No, she was turned in the opposite direction, her eyes scanning the woods behind us. She got off several shots in rapid succession, causing Tessa to fall against me in surprise, an event too unexpected to relish. Before our shouts had fully erupted, Tessa had regained her balance and Hana had aimed the gun twice more, and our thin shouts arced high to pursue her shots into the trees. Even

Jackie looked vexed. We had rules. In weather like this, so hot a spark might ignite the woods, we only shot toward the garbage pile, a containment, we hoped. And we had a rule too about shooting behind our backs. We'd even mentioned those earlier when we thought Hana might shoot with us. Hana didn't seem to care. She'd already flown away into the woods. It seemed she'd barely wandered into the jack pine, scrub alder, and black spruce before she returned cradling something in her arms. The disconnection was too great—the shot, Hana returning as if she'd skunked out an infant. The scene barely made more sense when the infant slid along her arm so that she was holding it by the tail.

"What is that?" Tessa said. "A marmot?"

"Too little," Jackie said.

"It's a marten," I said. "A young one."

"Another A for Leo," Hana said.

"We're not high enough. They live above the tree line, don't they?" Bryan said. "Shouldn't be here at all."

"Would you call this his bad luck?" Hana said.

Tessa took a few steps backward and thrust her hands into her pockets, assuming what a stranger might suppose was a nonchalant pose. The truth is that Tessa is the most superstitious girl alive, placing trust in a collection of talismans she rotates among her pockets, and I, at least, knew Hana had set off one of her alarms, and inside her pocket Tessa's fingers were busy rubbing a white-striped rock or a knot of red ribbon or the silver fish charm I once found behind the Shelter.

"They're protected," I said. "You can get fined for shooting them."

"They're just as bad as rats, really, Leo," Hana countered. She turned toward Bryan: "Do you know they feed on the young of other animals? It's not dead, either. Only stunned. Go ahead, Leo, feel it."

And I did, just for a second, the tiny heart beating a mile a minute. Truthfully, I was more transfixed by the line of red coursing down that white arm, spotting her open palm. I suddenly wanted to catch it in my own hand. I wanted, oh so strangely, to feel the heat of the gun, the stink of blood, on me. If I'd been alone with Hana, I might have even said to her: *Me next. Shoot me next.* Even as I heard the words bounce in my head, I was paralyzed by a desire to find more hurt. It came from her. Like a gift, I thought irrationally. Out of the blue, I heard another murmur that reminded me of Uncle Lud's voice. Uncle Lud, telling a story. I went to take a step backward, away, away from Hana Swann, but I was crazy dizzy, and stopped short. I might have stood there even longer, openmouthed above the marten's wounded side, but Tessa murmured beside me, and in response, Hana pulled the creature away and tossed it, a trapper's nightmare, onto the refuse pile with a nonchalant coldness that finally made me want to run from her.

Jackie and Tessa went over to have their own look at the marten. Hana handed the gun back to Bryan. I turned in time to see her lean in closely, touching his arm with her stained white hand. Bryan, like any sensible person, went stock-still at her proximity— my own heart lurched again—but the crap crows, lulled by the temporary quiet, had returned along with a pair of inquisitive ravens, and whatever Hana said to Bryan was muffled by the birds' raucous reclamation of the moose entrails, their excitement at the new addition of the not-quite-dead marten.

It all happened quickly, and then we were done, more than ready to go, to get away from this spot. As we were climbing into the truck Jackie told us they'd be hitchhiking the highway route back to camp: Hana's plan. A quicker solution, she said.

"Nah, you can't do that," Tessa said. "You know better than that."

"There's two of us," Jackie tried. "It's daylight."

"Hasn't she heard?" Tessa asked, her eyes skittering past Hana.

No one wanted to go over the details: the names of the girls, the tiny children left behind, the rumors of truckers on the highway, chains hanging in the cabs, a silver van with blacked-out windows. Native girls were prey, as thoughtlessly disposable as that moose carcass or the unlucky marten, and we all knew it, regardless of how many times some uniformed dope with his tortured hat got on the television and explained how hard they were trying, how impossible the landscape, how thin the clues and evidence gleaned from family reports they never seemed bothered to fully consider. What we heard was a kind of irritated grumbling: *C'mon, you can't find anyone out there, especially with skin like that.*

"She's been traveling all around," Jackie said, unable to fully keep the doubt out of her voice. "She says she never has a problem."

Bullshit, we thought. A girl like that had to have encountered a few issues on the road. But then the image of Hana striding back toward us—that thin line of marten blood running down her white forearm—returned all at once, and we weren't sure any longer. Bryan and I hardly dared look at her. Her head tipped backward, hair swinging behind her, that long, breathtaking white neck exposed, she was scanning the high hills as if looking for someone else.

"Those hills are full of girls," I thought I heard her say. Although she might have said "gulls."

The comment pierced us. Not one of us moved. Hana seemed impervious to whatever stories she'd heard, whatever truths we knew.

"This is *God's* country, isn't it?" she said, with an odd, faraway gaze that implied God hadn't visited in a while. "And I'm still here, aren't I?"

A marvel indeed, we might have privately agreed.

And for one slender moment, we believed her, and like Jackie, we might have fallen into her cool sureness ourselves, but then a raven called out from the refuse pile, mocking our reverential stillness, our continual stupidity. The light shifted, and we woke up, feeling again the sweat running down the back of our necks, the sun scalding the tops of our heads.

"Lucky," Bryan said, "that's all."

Hana stared past us as if she were already traveling on and we had been left far behind.

From the corner of my eye, I noticed Tessa crossing herself. The concept of luck made her almost as uneasy as the pictures we all just conjured of Hana and Jackie wandering up the highway together. More than anything, I wanted to enclose Tessa in my arms then, to offer her safety. Instead, I settled for interrupting her unease.

"Luck gets spent," I burst out, quoting Uncle Lud to Tessa's amusement. *"And an empty pocket won't hold tears."*

With that, Hana returned to us. Her laugh was a lucent bell, a golden peal I swore I saw arc and ripple in the shimmering air before its chime faded away. Even the trash-talking raven was momentarily nonplussed and fell silent.

"Native wisdom?" Hana smiled.

"German bullshit," Jackie spat. "Leo only looks like an Indian. He's got the heart of a Kraut."

"And the soul of an Irishman," came Tessa's whisper, echoing a phrase my mother once uttered after I recited a poem in a school play.

I opened my mouth to argue, but it didn't matter. Hana sent Tessa an amused glance as she swung up easily in the back of Bryan's truck, nestling beside the old narrow duffle bag I used to carry the guns. Jackie, looking as if she were shaking off her own trance, managed to lumber in beside her, offering us only a faint semblance of her usual grunt. Any possible talk ended then, Bryan driving as gently as he could in that old truck with its worn shocks. We stayed quiet, grave even, in the bouncing cab until Bryan pulled up by the camp turnoff.

Jackie usually swore as her feet touched the ground, offering a "Fuck us all," before she hit the trail, but that day we could see that it wouldn't matter if the cook pitched his usual fit, pissed at the weight of chores ahead, all those potatoes to be peeled; it wouldn't matter how heavy the mop buckets were as she scrubbed away the filth of one more meal or whether a dry gust through a propped-open door ushered in black flies. If bears trampled laundry and upended trash, who would care? Not Jackie. As the girls eased down from the back of Bryan's truck, Hana slid beside my open window and we all jumped. Already we had been starting to doubt her existence, all that perfection, and there it was again.

"Good luck," Hana said, a general wish, it seemed, although Bryan's mouth twisted a little as if he were holding back a response. "Wish Ursie good luck too."

She said the latter in a way that made us all think for a moment that she knew Ursie, knew her secrets, and really had missed her good, sweet company, her crazily accurate shooting. I glanced over at Bryan in time to see a frown break apart whatever was weighing him down, his expression settling into the shell-shocked self-consciousness that Jackie had arrived with that day.

Then Hana was gone, with Jackie and her backhand wave, disappearing up the gravel trail. Hana Swann, easy and bright, her own bruising white ray swelling outward to include Jackie with that new ganglyness. Jackie dazed and in love.

We didn't say a word most of the way down the hill until I finally managed to say what I thought then we must all be thinking: "Gonna be some hurt in that one." Tessa and I sighed as if we had been holding our collected breath for hours, because we already felt the first uneasy pangs heavy in our own hearts. To our surprise, Bryan, usually ready with his own wisecrack, stayed silent. What's more, he turned his face away from us, his eyes scanning the side of the highway as if he spotted something moving along beside us. Tessa and I watched him as whatever he glimpsed took on shape and he struggled to keep the truck in a straight line. Just as fast, whatever Bryan glimpsed apparently shot ahead. His chin went up. He squinted toward the distance.

"Bryan," I began. "Yo, Bry, you playing a game?"

I reached around Tessa and nudged his elbow and only gradually did he seem to come back to us, tossing his head and purposefully downshifting as the truck grabbed another curve.

Tessa and I glanced at each other, and for the first time in a long time, the awkwardness between us was gone. We'd cast it away in our concern. I guess we both must have known then that trouble was not on its way; it was already here. Although how could we have known how many forms that trouble would take? Neither of us was like Uncle Lud, who with his catalog of stories would have warned us all on the spot, would have wrestled the wheel from Bryan, driven straight to collect Ursie and Jackie, and taken a sure road to safety. Was there such a thing? Even in retrospect, I can't imagine where we could have fled.

KEVEN SEVEN

Albie Porchier was in a bad state that morning. Two big fights the night before. Car windows smashed in the parking lot, a few more holes punched in the walls. One fuckhead had ripped out the sink plumbing in Room 11. What the hell was the point of that? He could have used both the new gal and Madeline, but Madeline had gone up to the hospital to get her blood checked again. Or so the niece, that Ursie, said. More likely, Madeline was having one of those days; she had an ailment, unspecified but prone to flare up during work hours. It happened. He hated to admit it, but after a decade or more of owning the Peak and Pine Motel, Albie expected continual failures from his staff. So he was working Ursie hard while he could.

She had surprised him. Seventeen, just out of school, she was Indian all right, a Haisla like Madeline, but also half-Ukrainian, he'd guess, or German. She had that big-boned, Slavic look to her mixed in with everything else. A good gal, he'd decided, maybe too nice and quiet to see what had been left behind in some of his rooms, but a dedicated worker. He didn't need to direct her and stay on her the way he usually did with his maids. Even before he'd come back from the Sub-Rite with the new PVC pipes and fresh spackle, she had swept up the glass in the parking lot and started on the empty rooms, and the curses he'd been about to bark dissolved into a nasty taste he spit into the weeds.

Not a sign of last night's fight remained. The tortured cars had screeched away, and the lumber company's big diesels had followed. In fact, other than Albie's own black Chevy, only a single vehicle, the Econoline van that arrived a few days ago, remained, still parked almost out of sight behind the Dumpsters. Mild fellow, some kind of entertainer, it seemed. A musician maybe. Or a magician. With a silly rhyming misspelling of a name: Keven Seven. Funny, Albie couldn't quite remember when he'd come in, a few nights ago at least. And for some reason, Albie could have sworn the musician had wandered down from the highway bus stop alone, until he noticed the van and felt the vague prick of a recollection: a half-heard conversation, a woman's voice engaged in a bargain of sorts, a duffle tossed onto the curb, a whispered curse thrown after it. Well, how many of those exchanges had he overheard? As he picked up a shard of glass Ursie's broom had missed, Albie no longer wondered at the fellow's need to isolate his vehicle. God knows how he'd slept through last night's ruckus.

After she'd cleaned up the parking lot, Ursie retrieved her cart and vacuum and began on the first floor. She skimmed dirty sheets off the beds and covered their sloping mattresses with rough, clean ones, shaking out each worn, yellowed pillowcase so that it almost snapped in midair before the pillow fell seamlessly into its open pocket. She picked up shredded paper wrappers and the jaundiced ends of cigarettes and empty bottles and sticky glasses and wads of tissues. She averted her eyes from the plastic garbage cans she emptied into her big black plastic bag. She ran the toilet brush around the stained toilet bowls, cleaning as best she could the grime between the cracked linoleum, the thin brown paneled walls. You couldn't get the smell out. Too many men had moved through here and their sweat and farts and piss and cigarette smoke and everything else she didn't want to think about permeated the rooms from the stained blue carpets to the broken acoustic ceilings. Not to mention the creeping stench of damp mold. She sprayed window cleaner, poured bleach, and plowed the vacuum from one edge to another, and at best the stench was furrowed beneath the chemicals, making Ursie a little bit sick all day. She wanted to open windows and call up a storm that would cleanse and sweeten, but the truth was, the men would be back at sundown, ready to go again, and Albie had forbidden her.

"Too many goddamn thieves around here," he told her when he noticed her struggling with a window in Room 6. "You give them the tiniest crack, and they'll take everything."

Ursie couldn't imagine what they'd take from the motel. The televisions were bolted down; the phones didn't work; not even the toilets flushed with regularity. But she had nodded, wrestled the window closed, and wondered privately if she could bring a box of baking soda and sprinkle some on the carpets without him complaining.

Although she'd only been working at the Peak and Pine Motel a few weeks, she'd already developed a feeling around several of the rooms. Room 11 was pure trouble. Two minutes inside, and you could feel a creeping despair press in off those scarred walls until you were choking with it and pissed off, too. Did you deserve this? Was this really your intended life? Those unfortunate to land in Room 11 ground their cigarettes out on the dresser or right into the paneled wall; they slashed at the carpet with pocket knives and bottle openers and smashed the overhead lightbulb and cracked the television once they realized the bed-side lamps were permanently affixed to the tables and couldn't be hurled. They left cracked and putrid vials by the washroom sink and empty syringes on the carpet beside the bed. Ursie would like to burn sage and sweetgrass in there and purge it of all its sour rage.

Rooms 25 to 32, the logging company specials, were full of lies and deceptions and clouded thinking. When Madeline had given her the quick tour, an abiding denseness in those rooms made the air heavy and dulled even Ursie's quickness. Room 2, beside the ice machine, felt the happiest of the bunch, as if its proximity to party ice, the office, and the edge of the parking lot allowed it one foot out of the despair that haunted so many of the other rooms. Albie liked to put the occasional tourist family there, the ones who'd been camping for weeks before the mosquitoes wore them down or the kids came down with a mountain flu. The dad would go down to the café and return with grease-streaked paper bags full of hamburgers or soup and crackers while the mom would cajole Albie, who despised the role of obliging manager, into changing all her dollars into quarters so that she could race to the Laundromat down the road. Bucket after bucket of ice went by until eventually the family was gone, leaving a fragment of their own healing behind in the room among the sweat-stained towels, the empty pop bottles, and the inevitable socks half-shoved between mattress and box spring.

Who stayed at the Peak and Pine? Not many tourists, really, despite the new push by Albie and the *Community News*. Instead, the P&P saw a steady stream of truckers, and the lower-level logging company officials, of course, the ones punished by overseeing the camps. Social workers come to conference with other social workers, deliver new pamphlets the government had printed up after the latest five-year study, to hold PowerPoint presentations not even the elders could follow. And now, more recently, the pipeline scouts, slick talkers who met with the local council and promised not safety or wealth or even good jobs, but instead "a tangible role in addressing the nation's needs" and "compliance with the current laws."

Who else came to the P&P? Men suddenly without homes. Men with "dates." Drunk men. High men. Frantic, desperate men. Furious men. Men whose lives were pallid shreds that nonetheless throbbed like raw nerves. She kept her distance. Her auntie had warned her; Albie had warned her. If her fingers itched when she touched a door handle, if a flicker of tiny shivers coursed down her right side, she moved on, even if she'd knocked and knocked and no one had answered. Someone was waiting. She could tell.

Room 14 had one of the few unblemished doors. If she had a favorite room at the P&P, this was it, because whether it was by design or chance, the occupants of Room 14 were nearly always tidy and contained, arriving and departing with unusual reticence, as if they hoped to erase their passage. Her auntie said that girl Hana Swann had slept here, but Ursie had never seen her.

Ursie had every other room done that morning when she knocked on Room 14's door, knocked again and called "Housekeeping." And the knob cool and still in her hand, she unlocked the door, called again. The cart outside the open door, Albie below in the parking lot, she pushed in the doorstop wedge Bryan had made for her, the one that would keep a hand from easily slamming the door behind her, and began her quick survey: unmade bed, pizza box, beer bottles on the nightstand and floor, but also clean brown shoes lined up neatly by the nightstand, a stack of folded clothes—jeans, a red shirt—on the torn chair. An odd scent, like a pot left too long to boil. A strange, not unpleasant hum in the air and then there between the bed and the washroom door, a man in green plaid undershorts sitting cross-legged on the sour carpet in front of a spread of playing cards.

"I've lost the Queen of Hearts," he said before she could retreat. His hands still moving through the cards, he hadn't even glanced at her.

"All my fault. I was warned, of course. A warning I flagrantly ignored—*for good reason*." He raised his head then and grinned at her. "Silly ass," he said.

Ursie's heart lurched, but she knew enough not to grin back at him despite the infectiousness of that sudden surprising smile. That was the first trick Keven Seven showed her— the way a real smile could transform a thin boy with an old man's face, a boy sitting in his undershorts on a filthy motel carpet, into an irresistible show.

Both her auntie and her brother, Bryan, had warned her against talking to the men at the P&P. Women—*Native* women like Ursie—had been disappearing (only the "remains" of a few had been found). All anyone could remember later was that they'd last seen the gal talking to a fellow up by the motel, down by the bar, outside a party. Nothing good came from cavorting with strange men. Or even familiar men. Get near that Gerald Flacker or his buddy GF Nagle and a girl could be nicked bad enough to carry damage through all her short days.

"I'll come back," Ursie said, but she didn't move, and the fellow didn't seem to hear her in any case. She couldn't take her eyes off him. His looks made no sense to her at all.

He was as slim as a boy with a head full of tousled brown hair tipped with gold. She might even have believed he was a boy but for the long lines etched down his cheeks, the crinkles by his eyes as he grinned. His eyes were clear though, blue and bright. And his hands, those white, white hands, narrow and long-fingered, those clever hands began to make the cards twirl before him. His fingers barely grazed their edges, and the cards all stood up, revolving ever so slightly before fanning back and forth. She swore they danced for him as he bent his head and scanned them once more. She leapt a little with them.

"It will ruin everything, you know," he said, his eyes back on the cards.

"It's that important?" Ursie asked. She hated to see anyone in trouble.

"Life or death, I was told," he answered.

"A card?"

"Not just any card. The Queen . . ."

". . . of Hearts," she finished.

She looked then for herself, lost for a moment in the fluid music of his hands, each card turning and preening like a mask in a ceremonial dance. She thought of the river where she and her brother Bryan and their father fished, the way her eyes learned to scan the ripples and eddies and separate out the proud, fast shot that would be her fish. If Ursie harbored a secret vanity, it had to do with her quick eyes and even swifter reactions, that unnatural surety. Whenever boys praised her for her skills, their awe and envy made her flush as sure as if they'd openly admired her breasts or slipped a hand on her bum—events that had never happened despite a ferocious amount of quiet dreaming on her part. Though she let no one see, she preened at such compliments and grew almost pretty under them. Her mother always said no fellow would romance their Ursie without first taking her fishing or shooting. That was the way to true love with their girl. They'd have to see her, her words suggested, not as a mere big-boned girl, a quick shot, but instead as the marvel she was, with her uncanny ability to ignore the rules of this world and transpierce its narrow limits.

Now Ursie let her breath wind among the cards, mimicking their silver-quick turns before, with one quick motion, she braved the swell of cards and plucked one free.

"Here you go," she pronounced. "The Queen of Hearts, okay?"

She expected relief, but the look on his face was so troubled, so profoundly clouded, she felt pained as if she'd ruined the game. The magic had disappeared. The beautiful boy was now again a half-naked, ordinary man in Room 14, far older than he'd first appeared. The cards tumbled into disarray, stilled and lifeless, nothing more than flattened paper. She dropped the queen back into their midst and began to back away, but Keven Seven was too quick for her. He snagged her wrist with his long fingers.

"That was beautiful," he said. "A . . . a . . . a life-saving move. Do you realize that?"

His face was rapidly regaining its glory. For the first time since her mother died, Ursie felt the wonder she might engender, and she paused in her flight. Her wrist sagged, and her hand slid right into Keven Seven's waiting palm as if choreographed, so that for a few glorious moments, the two of them were kneeling there, holding hands among the scattered cards.

"Curious," he said finally. "Your hand is warmer than mine."

Ursie knew he was right. She had felt the heat grow in her fingertips as the cards had danced below them. Already her hands were cooling.

"But not for long," she said.

"No," he said. "Not for long."

He had the oddest smile—a quick flash, intimate and knowing—as if he were colluding with her. And yet his seeming appreciation for her talents—*for her*—made Ursie less wary than she usually was. After all, she had found the Queen of Hearts, just like that, and he'd seen right away how talented she was in this arena. Most people didn't. Most people simply saw her—if they noticed her at all—as a capable bear of a girl, a potential workhorse who wouldn't flinch at a dirty job, a worker's kid. Most people never perceived the graceful ease of her movements, the unusual sureness. But he did. He got it right away, and look how delighted he was, as if he'd been waiting for her.

So when Keven Seven drew her other hand in and exposed her palms, she didn't shrink away from his slow scrutiny. When he held both her hands, perhaps a bit too tightly to his chest, as if bringing her into him, her heart began a strange skipping that she mistook at first for fear. But when she raised her head and considered again that smile, she knew she wasn't afraid of him. She was curious. Who was this fellow who recognized her so quickly, who knew what she might be capable of?

"Yes," he finally said, "you have talents. I can see that." He released her hands momentarily, just long enough for the cards to somehow arrange themselves in a neat stack between his own fingers, then he reclaimed her, depositing the deck into the open palm of her right hand.

"You'd like this, wouldn't you?" he began.

She had no idea what "this" was, but almost before she'd realized it, she was nodding and the cards had begun a subtle whirling, as if impatient for shuffling.

"You were made for this," Keven Seven told her as he nudged the door wedge Bryan had constructed for her protection to one side. And Ursic, her attention wholly owned by the possibilities within her hands, didn't even seem to notice as the door began to squeeze closed behind her.

HIS PLAYGROUND

Where are we? A simple finger poking around on a map won't do. Neither will an article ripped from a city newspaper a full day's drive away, an article that details another disappearance, another girl, vanished off the notorious highway that borders town. My mother has that article pinned to a corkboard behind the kitchen door as if it's a reminder, an invitation, an appointment. Or some kind of prayer. Yeah, some people might call this God's Country, but others swear it's been colonized by the other team.

You see, here's a place where a singular story won't suffice, if one ever could.

One of the teachers up at the school, Mrs. Brenda Vanderleux, oblivious to my grade-five successes, once told me my school themes lacked "specificity."

"You need to commit, Leo," she told me. She demanded details—dates, names, and places—articles of confirmation, she called them, but the only evidence I had been willing to release were the bones of facts, the "what happened"—a man goes off on a ship to catch a whale, one fellow kills another, a dog freezes to death. That's enough, eh?

You know where we are. You do. Even Uncle Lud, who loves the briery strands of a complicated story—Uncle Lud, whose own stories reverberate with pinched-dog howls and red neckerchiefs tied against whiskers, with crunching footsteps in the snow and taps on the window that wake us from one vigil and plunge us into another—declares there's no need to tell you where we are. You've heard of this place. The news was all over it for a while. And they'll be back, Uncle Lud guesses. That's the thing about places like this. People come here to get lost, but all that means is that they want to do whatever they'd like without anyone interfering, and eventually, someone else is going to get in the way. Conflict, Uncle Lud would assure Mrs. Vanderleux, addressing her other foremost concern, will most certainly ensue.

If we give the name, if we say, here we are in Canada, in Terrace or Kaslo or Avola, or we tell you that here we are hidden away like a bunch of bush bunnies in Alberta, you'll say, nah, I passed through there on my holidays or my aunt lived near Smithers or my entire band's been here for more generations than your family has years, and that's not the Terrace or Kaslo or the Peace I know. And you'd be right. It's none of these, nor is it Victory, Idaho, or Ruston, Colorado, or, heck, Australia for that matter. It has not one thing to do with Omak, Washington, where we've heard they've started up the gold mining again.

The way we see this place is different from how you would if, say, you were a vanload of senior climbers come for a camping trip from the city or the exiled Bavarian wife of the lumber executive constantly comparing our forests with those of your youth or a Kitselas woman working your first job at the Centre after pushing through the community college and nearly collapsing under a daily weight of disregard so that you vibrate with the dual desire to both shake and embrace everyone you meet. Or different, say, than if you are one of those kids common here who begin drinking in the womb and keep it up, starting early in the day, driving trucks as old as Bryan's straight off the graveled, icy logging roads. *You* only know boredom and splintered light and the constant nagging in your heart to *get out, get out, get out*.

No, this place is none of those places, but Lud says he'd lay down ready money that you know where we are. You do.

The town has a mill yard and a railroad, two motels (three, if you count the half-built one on the highway a few miles down), a Greyhound station, a community center with a card room, an animal shelter, a bunch of little sawmills outside town limits. We've got the school and one little museum stuffed with pioneer paraphernalia—the usual rusted traplines, cross-saws, and gold pans—and another new museum, just a couple of rooms behind the shopping plaza, one of those rooms self-consciously marketing genuine First Nation art no one really wants you to buy and take to your suburban house, while the other room boasts a few pieces of real art from real aboriginal artists that no one ever will buy because it's not your traditional black-and-white-and-red-hang-on-the-sitting-room-wall-paint-by-numbers Native art.

We've got Anglicans and Baptists, Uniteds, Catholics, Pentecostals, Jehovah's Witnesses, and Christian Indians and more than a few of the reformed varieties of each, all of whom will be happy to save your everlasting soul and give you a T-shirt to boot. (Well, except for the Anglicans. You have to fill out applications to join them.)

We've got a coffee shop and a bakery, two banks, a garage, a nearly bankrupt car dealer, a thriving Canadian Tire, a 7-Eleven, a narrow-aisled supermarket with peeling linoleum, and a shopping plaza with a Sub-Rite, which is kind of like a Sub-Walmart, if such a thing can exist. You can buy anything from fifty-cent snack biscuits to hip waders to shotguns there. And four taverns, one of them the size of a small bowling alley that pretends to be a "club." We haven't got a bowling alley, of course, but we've got a scabby ball field and a well-worn hockey rink just beyond the community center, which has a four-lane swimming pool so chlorine-rich it can turn blue eyes to green.

We have a health center with an operating room, and we have three dentists (one good, two terrible). An office "park" with six separate offices for mining agents, insurance agents, and agents of the peace —police, that is—and on the other side of town, a couple of liquor stores (shoplifting havens that are robbed at least a dozen times a year, despite the aforementioned presence of peace officers).

The main street, Fuller, is a flat concourse that runs parallel to the train tracks and the lumber mill and the yard. Every other street goes uphill. Just outside of town, even Fuller climbs up and joins the famous highway featured in that newspaper article. We have no less than seven traffic fatalities a year on that highway. Some years a lot more. The highway's trajectory, its every curve, is a nightmare, but that can't be helped. The landscape, the one we claim to prize, forced its shape and won't allow the highway one inch more so it pinches us continually.

In the distance, great snowy mountains ring us; closer in, green glacial rivers swell around and through us, some with islands big enough for an ornery homesteader. In places, the rivers and the forest are like what you'd imagine heaven might be like: quiet and powerful and personal. They course right through your veins and, despite that intimacy, don't give a damn about you either. In other areas, the rivers are ravaging highways, littered with hurling logs or choked by their jams, and the forests beside them are the stuff of dire fairy tales, dense and black and thick with bears. These are better than the alternative, the bleached grave-yards of forests that appear without warning, clear-cuts like old battlefields, still bloody, still carelessly showcasing open wounds. Don't think about complaining, though. (*You live in a wood house, don't you? Write on paper? Read books, eh?*)

We've got weather, the kind that looms like pagan gods, pok-ing and prodding and playing their secretive, torturous games as if suffering could be a prize in itself. Think snow and ice and hammering rain, think fog so thick you lose sight of your own fingers as you're chopping wood, think lightning strikes that set one hill after another into a booming whoosh of flames, and a choking summer smoke that squeezes your chest so that it hurts to curse.

Despite that, the long-standing rumor is that we've got a re-sort coming in, back of beyond. They say it will have wooden boardwalks snaking through the second growth straight to the river, to cabins and fishing boats and a lodge with a fire-resistant metal roof. That rumor's been alive for years.

On the eastern side of town, a homesick Scottish man is building a private golf course, open and green, his heaven on earth.

We've got a five-page weekly paper, a radio station, middling television reception, political representatives, and taxes. We don't have a jail, but we have a holding station with real metal bars and chicken wire you could suicide on if you felt so inclined. If you've got a cell phone, you can wiggle it from here to there and good luck to you. Satellites don't seem to take us much into ac-count. We've got white people and reddish-brown people and a few shades in-between, foreigners, settlers, tourists, mixed bloods, and Natives. We've got alcohol—store-bought and grain—

warm racks of gas-station beer, bargain whiskey sold by the gallon. We've got Oxycontin and crack and meth and coke with needles and lots of weed and homemade pharmaceuticals, guns and knives and fists and boots, fights and accidents, arsons and homemade explosives, amateur sex rings, love triangles, and charging romances, weddings and funerals—we've got a whole lot of funerals.

See, you know us. Or think you do.

THE DEVIL'S POCKET

Bryan still wasn't himself by the time we reached Fuller again. It was a little past noon, a haze coming off the hot pavement. I hopped out with Tessa, desperate as always for a few minutes more, another chance, even though it would mean a longer walk home alone. For once, Bryan didn't glance into his rearview mirror to shake his head at my inability to make a move on Tessa. I could tell he was stuck on Flacker and the way Hana Swann had dismissed the solution he'd come to with Jackie. A dare? A taunt? Whatever it was, Hana Swann was in him now, a fishhook of longing, a branding iron still smoking.

Follow him, I could imagine Uncle Lud saying, pushing me to hold the story tight. *You know where he's going.* And, yes, even then I must have known where the story was heading.

Bryan had hours before he had to pick up Ursie. His sister would be waiting in the motel office for the ride home, sipping one of the ancient, high-necked Diet Bubble-Ups from Albie's relic of a soda machine. Albie had invested in cases of the stuff years ago, convinced the town would soon be rushed by hoity-toity, ever-dieting skiers. The brands—Bubble-Up, Tab, and Fresca—had sounded exotic and ritzy to him. But a ski resort had yet to materialize, and he couldn't give his stock away. Guests remained suspicious of those old brands, believing a local rumor about a government scheme to slim down the populace by slipping health foods into their favorites, and locals berated Albie for even suggesting such bizarre beverages. Besides, most everyone up here has a raging sweet tooth—calories be damned. Diet drinks aren't a big sell. So Albie allowed Ursie and her auntie to help themselves each afternoon when the rooms were finished, and they were usually so parched they did just that. Ursie admired the long-necked bottles and the frostiness Albie's old soda machine achieved, and despite the odd aftertastes, despite her inevitable preference for Diet Bubble-Up, she savored every brand and would spend several considerate minutes before the soda machine each afternoon. Sometimes she was still gazing at the machine when Bryan's old truck with its often-loose fan belt screeched into the lot.

He was rarely late. Bryan didn't like to think about the men returning to the motel and seeing his sister—no beauty, he'd admit, but young and female and unfailingly kind— alone in the narrow lobby. Another nightmare had him arriving late with Ursie nowhere in sight, Albie simply pointing down the road as if a girl taking a long walk home wasn't beyond foolhardy. Bryan glanced at the old watch hanging from the knob on his truck's broken radio. He had time. He should use it for his own scavenging. He'd heard about an untended scrap pile that might have a few hot-water tanks and a bunch of insulated copper wire he could strip and sell. And he had a little Nagle pot he should peddle at the community center before they swung around looking for him again. But first his truck must buck and bounce past Gerald Flacker's place on Charlotte Road.

Charlotte Road was narrow and rangy, but Bryan didn't slow down by Flacker's, and he barely moved his head, even though he noted that Gerald Flacker's flaking brown Chevy two-ton was not in the driveway. He circled around the dirt road that buddied up against the railroad tracks and parked behind the vacant sawmill Flacker's father had run years ago. On foot, he shouldered through the heat-burned speargrass, tinder his boots almost sparked, until he caught sight of Gerald Flacker's own ever-expanding piles of scrap. Supposedly, Flacker made a living off the bent trailers and broken appliances that littered that old clearcut, but it was obvious to Bryan, expert grubber himself, that only a desperate soul could imagine anything useful in Flacker's yard, a five-acre parcel where even the dwellings lay like litter. At first glance, you couldn't even see the moldy mobile home or the sinking cabin made from discarded planks ripped from the now-defunct sawmill.

Bryan waited on the edge of the property to hear if the death dogs had begun howling at his approach. Despite Flacker's mistreatment, they weren't bad creatures, but they were unpredictable since they had no memories, their years of living alongside meth heaven having burned out what natural sense they might have had. Sometimes, they greeted Bryan with wagging tails, a heartbreaking need to be petted. Other times, they would approach him almost at a crawl, their bellies dragging, deep growls building into the rush and snap he had to forestall by flinging bits from Jackie's bag at them.

He didn't hear them today. Most likely, Flacker had gone off to make his deliveries and collections and had taken his tormented pets along as goons. The Magnuson kids were scrabbling in the dirt behind the trailer, playing their feeble games like a couple of refugees with pieces of sticks and torn shoelaces, pebbles hammered on rocks. Bryan didn't want them to see him either. Or maybe he just didn't want to see them. They were thin, shell-shocked kids whose mother forgot them for days at a time, so that their tiny pants and T-shirts were always filthy, smelling of pee and baby sweat, and they'd almost lost whatever route to human speech they'd undertaken before their mama became enslaved to meth and Gerald Flacker. Twins, a boy and a girl. Jackie said they were six, but Bryan guessed three. Little animals. You could call Child Services about the kids—a foster home couldn't be much worse—but Flacker's cousin Mitchell was on the force, and anyone who interfered with Flacker usually found himself in trouble on the road, no matter how anonymous he or she had tried to be. And the roads could be awfully dark and boneyard lonely around here.

Another kind of silence crawled around Flacker's yard. Bryan thought it bordered on hysteria, as if these broken, busted metal and plastic carcasses composed a kind of receptacle for damned souls, and their anguished cries lay a finger's length beneath the surface, just barely tamped down. That perception was enhanced by the Flacker air, which shimmered in the heat as if fanned by a constant and unforgiving fire.

Bryan didn't have to step too far onto Flacker's property to lift the fender on a mold-covered Ford. He put the tied bag partway beneath to hold it steady before taking off down the trail, spinning a handful of gravel against the far trailer to alert the twins, who did not waste time but scuttled barefoot across that treacherous yard with its spiked pieces of metal and broken glass. Their tiny hands edged into the hole beneath the fender, and they wrestled the bag free and stuffed their faces right there, sinking to their haunches, little paws pushing cold potatoes into their mouths so that even as he walked back to his truck, Bryan could hear their infantile huffing and grunting. Smart kids, they'd hide the empty bag—after they'd licked it clean. The rest of the day, they'd chew or pretend to chew on the pieces of paper toweling stuck like leaves to the insides of their cheeks.

Usually, Bryan would drive back along the railway road until he reached the single-lane of Ledge Road with its deep open drop, where he'd crawl along, half-hoping he'd run into Gerald Flacker or even the Nagles. If he did, he hoped he could gun his old truck and plow forward, no regrets. Since his mother died, Bryan had discovered his only real fear was that something would happen to his dad or Ursie or that Ursie would be left alone with no way to take care of herself, but now that his dad had gone up north and Ursie was working at the motel, that last weight had lightened some, and Bryan found himself in new territory, not exactly brave, but missing any true spark for life. He had so little to lose and so many waiting on the other side: his mother and grandmother; his cousin Brent; a little yellow-haired girl named Sharon who'd held his hand all through grade four; Joby from the basketball team; Russell, whom he and Leo had known since they were babies; the Courchats who'd wrecked the family car only last winter. His old friend Dean. Yeah, hell, he thought, Dean.

With school over for good and no steady job in place, Bryan wasn't seeing many new friends on the horizon, and with Ursie working and me on my way to getting jammed up at the mining college if my father had his way, his closest circle of friends must not have looked too promising either. He couldn't count on Tessa or Jackie—he just couldn't. Tessa's family continually sucked her under, and Jackie, loyal and dear as she was, could also turn on him if she decided she'd been wronged in any way, and that was a line they all knew was far too easy to cross on Jackie's bad days.

And then there was his father, who had let him down in more ways than he could count. Just last week, for instance, that letter had come about the house. *You and your sister are guests in* my *house,* his stranger of a father had written. My *house, remember that.* Bryan wondered if the letter had been dictated; it read so cold.

Bryan's father, Trevor Nowicki, had grown up on a farm up north. He'd spent his youth working on the sour gas wells, but on a hunting trip down here, Trevor met Bryan's mother, Junie, and though they'd tried to make a home together up north, people didn't make it easy for a white man with a Kitselas wife, a "squaw"—not Trevor's family or his old buddies or the people in the town. Junie never spoke about it, but the truth was, she couldn't even get a cup of coffee up there. If Trevor and Junie went out, the waitress would only bring the one cup and, if challenged, spit right back at Trevor: "You should know better than to bring *her* in here." He had gone back to working on the sour gas wells, and more than a few times those wells had flared close to the farmhouse they were renting, sickening their goat and cow and making them all dizzy and nauseous. By then, Junie had lost one baby and the headaches had begun to get really bad right about the time they learned about the second pregnancy, and while Trevor refused to connect the dots publicly—God knows, you don't bite the hand that's feeding your community—he himself kept having nosebleeds that privately terrified him, so he caved in and moved back here, where my dad, his good friend, had arrived and met my own mum, who never pretended she would go anywhere else with him, where Bryan, then Ursie, were born intact and healthy, and Junie's sisters spooling around to help and cheer until one by one, they began to slide—and Junie with them, but for different reasons. In those last days, Trevor was still down at the mill yard, and Bryan, who was fourteen and without a license, would drive Junie home from the clinic to find one of her sisters picking through Junie's clothes.

"Whoa," the sister might say, "you look *bad*! Don't they have a medicine for that?"

Junie would barely manage a weak smile as Bryan eased her back into bed. And when her sister would lurch close to Junie to "smooch" her cheek, Bryan would flinch and bite his tongue, noticing how Junie held her wriggling sister tight and whispered, *You be good*, before the sister pulled free and, giggling, left in Junie's last best blouse.

They tried to swarm after Junie died, but Trevor held them off. All three of them—Trevor, Bryan, and Ursie—would come to the door as the sisters began to rattle the knob and thrash their way back into Junie's house. All three wearing the same fierce expression with which Trevor's implacable Polish father had faced every homesteading challenge. Even Ursie, Junie's spitting image, summoned up her father's kin so that her soft brow grew stern and her usual easy laugh could not be enticed by her once-giggling aunts, begging on the threshold to visit and hold them tight, to be to Bryan and Ursie what Junie had been to them. Trevor chased them off, but it was the kids standing beside him without an ounce of their mother's grace showing that made them stay away. Junie's sisters came to believe the Polack, as they called Trevor, had kidnapped first their sister's treasured soul and now those of their sister's children. Only Madeline, the youngest, dared eventually to come back, sneaking through an open bedroom window one afternoon to pilfer Junie's old red high heels and a bottle of cologne Trevor had bought his wife while she was in the hospital that last time. She tried again after Trevor left, but Bryan set her straight.

"We have nothing," he told her. "You want some of that?"

Still it was Madeline who set Ursie up at the P&P. Madeline who Bryan would come to blame for Keven Seven.

His shirt was sticking to his back, and the truck seat was burning beneath him. Bryan felt on fire as he drove up the dirt road that paralleled the train tracks. The coil of desire that had begun at the refuse station that morning twisted in his gut and made him want to cry the way he hadn't managed after his mother died, after his father left. He had nailed Jackie's longing, but hardly knew it was his own, too. That bone-white girl with the Indian hair. *Who are you, Bryan?* Just once that morning, her eyes had met his. She'd touched his arm with the marten blood, and she'd poured right into him as if passing along a set of instructions, but all she had said was, *Just do it, Bryan.* And the weird thing was that he knew exactly was she was proposing. He'd driven away feeling as if he had made a promise, as if he were a heroic soul, not just another lusting asshole, nearly as half-starved and lonely and trapped as the Magnuson kids. And the thought pierced him, pierced and burrowed until he could think of nothing else: why shouldn't he be brave and bold and do the world this favor?

He was nearing the highway intersection about then, and with his usual stellar timing, he arrived as Mitchell Flacker's patrol car was taking the last curve. Gerald's cousin, his "protection," usually took account of the slightest peripheral movement, trained eyes spotting a truck even when it was slowly emerging from a byroad, half-covered in dust. Mitchell Flacker would raise two fingers off his steering wheel, a country wave that let them know they were under observation. Today, Bryan managed a quick swerve into brush, and Gerald's cousin didn't seem to see the truck at all. He had someone in his backseat—a girl, Bryan thought. On any other day, he would have begun fretting, wondering what was up with Mitchell Flacker ferrying around a girl. Creepy bastard. Gerald probably had that strung-out tweaker Cassie Magnuson out on loan with Mitchell doing the dirty work, which would have meant the Magnuson kids had been left out there alone. Upon reflection, that did not seem like such a bad thing. A blessing, wouldn't it be for those Magnuson kids, if Flacker and their mother just outright disappeared, like the girls up off the highway? Hana Swann claimed his thoughts again, and Bryan imagined a wide pit opening, a whoosh like the gas flares his father had once described, Flacker's world engulfed, and Bryan and that bone-white girl strolling majestically alongside the tainted highway. She would be a cool comfort beside him as each of them chaperoned a Magnuson kid to safety.

As he put the truck into gear and began easing out of the brush, the back tires slipped, and Bryan realized he'd put the truck inches away from a precipice. Sweat crept along his scalp and down his neck, and his hands could barely hold on to the shuddering steering wheel until, with gentle lurches, he regained the gravel road. Full minutes passed before he hauled the truck back onto the dirt track, then the highway, headed back into town, the usual sights yet everything seeming altered. The truck's shocks were shot, its suspension barely holding together, and somewhere in the fire and rumble and sweat, in the pure pressure of bouncing along in that hot truck cab with stinging desire filling his hollow gut, the idea finally jarred loose in Bryan, the beginnings of a plan to rid the world of Gerald Flacker. He would kill Flacker. A simple accident. Hell, why hadn't he thought of that before? He'd need some help, sure, but he knew just where to go for that. Didn't he have the brainiest kid he knew as his best friend? As he came into town, he leaned forward and wrestled the wheel onto Fuller, not right toward the P&P, but left, up Lamplight Hill.

UNCLE LUD

By the time Bryan dropped us back on the corner of Fuller and James, the day felt more than half spent. I knew Uncle Lud was waiting. Still I would have given anything to linger away the afternoon with Tessa. Fat chance. She had her own clamorous demands waiting at home, and although Tessa would tease and laugh when we were all together, when we were alone, she shifted away from me, sinking quickly back into an inscrutable girl, the girl who would not be hurt by some boy. And I ceased to be her lifelong friend, instead—owing to an unfortunate incident a year or so ago—morphing into another ham-handed guy with itchy fingers. So Tessa would head toward the railroad tracks alone, while I would turn reluctantly in the opposite direction, always pausing to glance back and watch her in her tight jeans and too-big shirt and ratty red sneakers, her arms swinging and chin high until she reached the last corner and her shoulders slumped, her head began to bow.

Often, I did follow Tessa all the way to her own doorstep, just to make sure she was safe, I told myself. I would watch as her sister's kids fell upon her, every one of them demanding, demanding, and the old man, her grandfather, began calling out for a glass of wrist-warm tea, a blanket, a hand closing a window. That sister would shriek for Tessa to shut those kids—*her own kids*—up. Tessa, surrounded, bore it all just as calm as could be, but all the bounce and quiet electricity of our time together had vanished as if that bunch had stolen it outright. I could imagine how a fellow might rush in and push them all aside, grab Tessa's hand, and run in the opposite direction, away from town, away even from the railroad tracks, that constant symbol of escape, until our feet were beating at air and the mountain itself opened to us.

It's hard to say, given the troubles visited on us, that Tessa had it the hardest, but still I think we'd all say she had—she did. Her parents had thought they'd discovered ease and good times in drink, and then rebuffed and awakened, they drank even more to blur the trash-filled rooms they found themselves in, those big-eyed children always needing something—a diaper, a shoe, another bowl of cereal. Tessa's parents' thirst was legendary and unmatchable, and like most heartbroken people, they were also magnets for trouble, which—it was generously noted—they greeted almost stoically, feigning indifference at the crap that relentlessly came their way through their own doing or not. They didn't raise much fuss when Social Services came along and collected Tessa, her older sister, and their younger brother and deposited them into a rat's nest of foster homes in another town altogether, none of them much better than what they'd been rescued from. Tessa and I had been eleven then, and I'd known full-on heartbreak for the first time. A year later, her father had a car accident and died, and the mother sobered up enough so that Tessa and her sister could come home and watch her die too, the grandfather, no gift himself, taking over. The brother was too damaged. He'd been in one raging fight after another and they locked him up in a detention center. Tessa, an ever-laughing girl who'd mastered the hands-on-her-hip look-down in grade four, assessing clueless ten-year-old boys as if they had potential, that high-spirited Tessa came back to her old friends after that two-year absence pinched and quiet with a tough resignation that reminded us of the old grannies. My heart hurt to see her, but the couple of times I'd tried to kiss her, lumbering over her, as we were walking alone together, she'd flown at me in a fury.

"She should see a therapist," Bryan said when he asked about the scratches on my face. Bryan's mother wasn't sick then, and he fancied himself a ladies' man, taking one girl or another down behind the railroad depot, as if he were working through a list. This was before all his other friends, like that Dean, started becoming fathers and Trevor clamped down. Bryan's father didn't mind the drinking Bryan did then, but he was pretty convinced that if Bryan got family-happy, he would be the one who would have to support them all. Kind of curious, given the current conditions. But Bryan didn't think about all that then. He was always egging me on, which is how I got the courage to try for Tessa in the first place. Bryan was flummoxed by my bad luck, Tessa's reaction.

"They got those therapists up at the Centre now, pretty much free, Ursie says."

Both of us had mulled that idea over for a moment before busting out laughing. We couldn't help but remember Jackie's comments after her altercation with the local peace officers, who'd suggested, not altogether kindly, that Jackie see one of those counselors herself. They'd suggested one in particular, a butter-handed man with anxious eyes and a bad comb-over. He liked to make house calls, his cheap blue car filthy with dust from the backcountry roads.

"Piss on that," she told Bryan and me. "You ever notice that if you look close at it, 'therapist' is the same as 'the rapist'? No coincidence there."

For Jackie, the Bad Man could hide anywhere, even in the middle of a word. Ever after, she would chide anyone she knew who went to see a counselor.

Going off to see the rapist? she'd taunt before following with warnings: *Don't get into his Gremlin, 'kay? Seats got no springs, pedal got no brakes and him neither. Man says he knows hypnosis, then you better run, eh? Bastard's got a notepad, you bet, every word you say going down in a file. Better stay crazy, fucked up, huh?*

Bryan says you know a girl likes you if she gets real loud whenever she sees you, but the only time Tessa yelled around me was when she was chasing me off, so either that meant she has no use for me or . . . oh, hell, I didn't know. Still, it was Tessa who came to sit with me at lunch at school, handing off her sandwich after ever-hungry, big lout that I am wolfed down my own; Tessa, who even last year stood between me and other girls who would let me fondle them, her fists slightly clenched as if she were claiming territory. And for all her sweet look, that big grin and long fall of streaky hair, she still ignored every other fellow as well, even Bryan's toasty friend Dean, who hovered around, believing for way too long in the powerful charisma that had seduced every other grade-ten girl. Dean is long gone these days, but I haven't been one who's mourned him.

Still there were times when I tried to conjure up Dean's ways, looking for seduction tips, anything to keep Tessa close to me long enough for me to change her mind and win her. All the way down the logging roads that morning, all along the highway, I had gazed off into the woods, glimpsing a dance of those golden

God's rays flickering between the trees, and I had felt a roiling building within me, a longing for Tessa that made me almost physically sick. The window beside me was open and blasting air as Bryan barreled down the highway. My long hair whipped around so that Tessa began batting it away from her own eyes. On a normal day, I would have shrunk away from her, holding my hair with one hand, desperate not to bother her. The day of Hana Swann, I half-leaned out the window, gulping air, and when Bryan finally downshifted for the turn into town and I was jolted backward against Tessa, the violence cheered me as if it were one clear answer to my yearning, and for a long moment I leaned against Tessa as if daring her to shrug me off.

When, once on the sidewalk with Bryan's truck rumbling away, Tessa squeezed my arm, I couldn't believe it. She was half a block away before I truly felt her touch, a compression that reached my heart in stages. Although Tessa had vaulted the half-size cinder-block wall by the railroad tracks and was nearly out of view, I found myself leaping blindly across Fuller to follow her.

I barely made it. I heard the squeal of tires, a promised acceleration, and with instincts well honed from my battles with my mother's own terrible driving, I flew across Fuller, tossing the gun duffle ahead of me, and grabbed a lamppost as a car pealed by, its hubcaps scraping the curb. I was making a good show of myself, I was sure, as I wobbled in midair, hugging the metal pole. I caught sight of a Nagle brother, the older one, of course, mocking me from the open window of that flash orange car they were driving that week, a middle finger jabbed toward me.

The Nagles again: cripes, what hopes their clueless mother must have had for them. She'd even gone and christened them Godfrey and Markus, like they'd be real men one day with permanent postal addresses and government-issued pensions. Markus, given a better model, might have had bullied his way into regular company, causing the usual amount of trouble a big white guy who liked to drink might cause.

Bur Godfrey . . . Godfrey was something else. *God-Free,* he used to announce himself in grade school, as if declaring his intentions even at that young age. Along the line, he'd transformed into GF, pretending to be like his famous ancestor, the pioneer G. F. MacFlouggle. The current GF was a rager, a criminal to the core. For all anyone knew, G. F. MacFlouggle had been a rager— and a rapist and thief and gambling cheat—as well. The local bands still used "Flouggling," a curse that Uncle Lud told me covered everything from penny-pinching to pissing in public to stealing a wife. He had a way of showing up when you were most vulnerable, the threat so palpable I still wondered how I'd survived all these years without a real beating, a knife wound, a burning accident. If the devil had Flacker in his pocket, he had GF Nagle on a string and he dangled him continually in our midst.

Bryan had taken over a little dealing for the Nagles after his friend Dean died. In that last note, left down in the basement with him, Dean had suggested as much, even pointing out that Markus was the easier brother to deal with, and a desperate Bryan grasped the opportunity, only much later realizing the trouble he'd invited was the same trouble that had chased his friend Dean to another world. He started keeping guns, cocked and loaded and pointed down, behind the curtains by both the front and back doors.

"If they ever come here," Bryan had told Ursie, "don't you hesitate. *They* won't."

Meanwhile, he'd kept on with the Nagles. He had to once he started. No way they'd let any useful association slide, and Bryan was desperate for money, of course. Which is how he'd come to Flacker's in the first place and seen those Magnuson kids. Me, I would have never gone back. Even as I recognized GF, saw the sneer that came whenever GF was ready to go after a "dirty Indian," I tried to close my eyes. But here was Hana Swann again, that long neck thrown back in laughter, and God help me, I threw the finger right back at GF Nagle.

Still clinging to the lamppost, I saw the brake lights scream on as if my own chicken heart had finally lit up, and I was wondering how far up that pole I could actually climb as the orange Matador circled back, the door already half open, one fist pushing outward. I hung on tight. GF was going to have to pull me down. And he would have too, I guess, if just then Kenny Dargarh hadn't driven by in his fire chief's truck, eyeballing GF and me and the duffle on the sidewalk below me until—and I could see it happen—I changed color before the fire chief's eyes, shading into a tanned white, and Kenny Dargarh recognized me as Karl and Evie Kreutzer's son and Lud's nephew, and then (shading again), more important, he recognized me as the baby cousin of his treasured dispatcher, Trudy Samson, not simply another stoned Indian dangling halfway up a lamppost.

"You're screwed, asswipe," GF was saying, even as Kenny pulled a U-turn and drew his official four-by-four up onto the curb behind the orange Matador. GF took off then, folding himself back into the car as nonchalantly as he could, but not before cutting me one last look.

"I don't forget," he said. "I'll see you again."

As if for good measure, he gave me the finger one more time

as the Matador took off with a screech of tires. Kenny Dargarh grimaced. He'd had his own run-ins with the Nagles, who even on these bone-dry days threw lit cigarettes out car windows and trampled fire-zone blockades. Kenny sent me a quick, beleaguered wave and lingered by the curb with his windows open, listening to a garbled radio transmission until that Matador was well away and I'd jumped back to the sidewalk and managed my own awkward nod.

Despite Kenny's presence, I cast one more look back in the direction in which Tessa had vanished, my heart in tatters, before shouldering the duffle and walking the blocks from Fuller to Lamplight Hill, wishing as always that I had a car of my own. My mother seemed to believe that she was saving me from certain death by keeping me afoot, conveniently putting out of mind the fact that I often cadged rides with drivers like Bryan, whose vehicles had damaged souls of their own, demented by bad roads and worse weather, and were given to startling lapses or lunges that provoked continual near-misses. And if I complained aloud about the boggling inconvenience of not having a car to use, she might make an absurd offer.

"I'll take you," she'd say without a hint of sarcasm, as if I'd arrive at a party down some deserted lane with my mum, whose own driving skills could be judged by the three banged-up fenders on our old maroon station wagon. The back door was almost fully staved in too. Only the fourth fender appeared untouched. A still-pristine radiant blue, it had only recently replaced the worst of them, so bent up, my mother couldn't fully turn the wheel.

Bryan long ago declared he couldn't let me be such a pussy, and he'd set out to teach me how to drive, but he soon tired of being a passenger in his own lurching truck and he, too, rapidly transformed into an old auntie, chiding me about clutches and gear-grinding until we were both happy to go back to the way it was. In a pinch—meaning if Bryan ever was so blind drunk he couldn't drive—I could theoretically take over now, or so we told ourselves.

At home, I kicked off my dust-spattered sneakers behind the back door, emptied the duffle and shoved it behind the boots, pushed the guns back up on the high shelf where my father kept them, and nudged a box of pellets back into the holding cupboard's sticky bottom drawer. For a moment I thought again of that golden light that had pursued us down the logging road and, dazed, I lingered in the utility room. The heated scent of the marten must have rubbed right into my fingertips, because as I pushed back my hair, damp from my long walk up the hill, the spicy scent of fur and blood nearly became visible; it was that sudden and strong. Right in front of me, my father's chainsaw lay on the middle shelf, a reminder that I needed to sharpen it before he arrived home next month from his work up on the pipeline, and idly, I began to run my finger along the blade's outside edge, remembering Hana Swann's lean white forearm balanced against the gun. I was just thinking "sticky" when I noticed the thin ridge of blood on my fingertips and felt the sting. At the same moment, all four dogs began the joyful howls that heralded the arrival of my mother's station wagon with its rattling muffler onto Lamplight Drive. Except for the oldest, Norbee, the dogs hadn't roused themselves for me, and even Norbee had given me only the vaguest of old-dog nods. But all the dogs—one half-blind, one three-legged, one so whipped she wouldn't raise her head, and ancient wobbly Norbee—came out of the shade into the blistering heat to ready themselves for a swarm around my mother, saint to their crippled souls.

While she parked and went through the ritual of greeting the dogs and fussing over their water bowls, I had time to wrap a kitchen towel around my wound—turned out it was only my middle finger that had grazed the blade—glance at Uncle Lud (sleeping, it seemed, in the lounge chair), slip into my room and spread my books over the desk, and turn on the antiquated computer my mother had purchased from the shelter when the town upgraded. By the time I found the Band-Aids and covered my scratch, I could hear her kitchen clatter, followed soon by her always-comical idea of a whisper, a hiss so loud the dogs began to whimper again outside the back door, sure she was summoning them for a treat.

"Leo . . . *hss* . . . lunch."

In the kitchen, tomato soup was warming in the pan, despite the heat. A tuna sandwich already cut in half and waiting on a plate for me. The fan in the corner was flinging air around in a tight circle, but my mother's forehead glistened.

"What page are you on?" she asked as she reached across the counter to pour a long, gliding arc of milk into my glass. The pure swell of it conjured up Hana Swann, and for a moment, I was speechless as if I had no clue what my mother was talking about.

In the fall, I would return to Secondary for my last year. My father planned for me to continue on to the Mining College, where he had once taken courses, while my mother reminded me daily that I was not responsible for fulfilling my father's dreams. Apparently, however, I *was* on the hook for her dreams. Ever since I had won a rash of school awards in grade six—big success

story, me—my mother had been mapping out my future university career, making lists of prerequisites for a dozen professional
endeavors, then laying each before me the way I imagined tasks
were presented to those godforsaken heroes in Uncle Lud's fairy
tales: *climb a mountain; kill a golden phoenix; outwit a sorcerer.* I
would call that unnecessary busywork. My mother calls it preparation for salvation. Really. Salvation. Her greatest fear is that I'll
graduate from childhood an addled drifter, still roaming around
town like the Nagle brothers. If I do, I say it will be entirely her
fault.

"I could have a breakdown," I've told her. "That happens
when a mind is overtaxed."

Whenever I say this, my mother laughs, and if her cousin,
the fire dispatcher, is nearby, Trudy actually snorts and whacks
me hard on the shoulder.

"That's a good one, Leo," she says.

"You can't say you haven't had advantages, Leo," my mother
liked to tell me, acting like she had no clue of the reality of my life
away from home, the steady dance I did in the schoolyard between "dirty Indian" and "the Kraut Brain," always on alert for
the way the bully wind might blow.

Since my mother was working every day at the animal shelter
office that summer, and my father remained up north, I should
have been left alone to ramble through my summer, doing chores
and keeping Uncle Lud company. Instead, I was also charged
with a physics correspondence course my mother had ordered,
another in that series of enrichments she'd sought out. Most days,
instead of even glancing through the course, I closed the door to
my room, flicked on the computer, and went to lie on my bed,
where, in between thinking about Tessa, I filled notebook pages

with the steady stream of stories my mother could never quite follow, stories Uncle Lud was determined to bestow on me before he left us. I kept those notebooks secret from my mother, who was already convinced that my slowness in the physics course must be due to the hours I spent listening, a fact she couldn't quite complain about given the situation. Yet what she didn't realize was that Uncle Lud wasn't the only impediment; I couldn't seem to get past the first section of my physics course. The notion of velocity flat-out stymied me.

"It's sections, not pages," I finally managed to tell her, as I did every day. "Units. Self-contained units. They take a while."

"Hmm," she said, raising an eyebrow. She watched me bite into my sandwich before she picked up her own and said, "There's another dog dead this morning at the shelter. This heat gets to them, even with all the fans going. And an old tom torn to pieces by the school."

"That could be coyotes," I said. "Or a cougar. A bear."

"Yeah, you think so?" she said. "Coyotes and cougars and bears don't break necks, cut off heads and tails, and make an eviscerating art project out of them, do they?"

"At least they're old ones, gonna die anyway."

"Going to die, not gonna," she corrected, then added, "I really hope you aren't the one taking care of me in my old age, Leo.

"I can't get them to listen downtown," she went on. "You'd think it was a regular sport like hockey or basketball."

"Maybe it is," I said, thinking of the refuse station and the guns sweating in our hands.

"Oh, boy," my mother said, "I sure hope not, kiddo. Don't folks cause enough trouble with the usual games? Trudy told me some fellow and his girl cleaned out a whole crew last week in a card game. The crew was lucky that couple caught them before payday. I guess that pair was lucky too. The crew would have ripped them apart later, laid the both of them out right beside that old tomcat.

"Strangers," she said, almost spitting the word.

My mother saw the world from the underside up. Trouble everywhere. Lately, she'd been musing aloud about all the trouble that could befall a single soul alone in the world, which led her into thinking about how the world had contracted, what with the computers and all, so that all of them were now within shouting distance.

"Look at you," she'd say to me, "taking courses from all over."

We could hear Uncle Lud stirring, the wracking cough that greeted his waking beginning like the strangled barks the dogs let loose with when we chased them outside. All that scraping and baying for breath as they moved from the enclosed world into the next.

Without another word, my mother rose and took a glass from the cupboard, a bottle from the refrigerator. She was not one to put sugar on sorrow. No, the doctors had done their piece, now she'd decided she could only fix the pains that arose, nothing more.

"Here," she said, pouring chilled vanilla Boost into a jelly jar, sticking in a straw.

I carried the glass to Uncle Lud and knelt beside him until the first bout of coughing subsided and he could hold on to the glass and take a sip or two on his own. Thirty-seven years old, and he might as well have been a hundred, the way he looked. His fever was back, and he was shuddering. A line of sweat creasing along his brow and his thin hands with their broken nails shaking so that when I took the glass back from him, I couldn't tell what burned more—my uncle's touch or the shock of ice. Both caused a shiver to run up my arm and neck, and noticing, Uncle Lud reached out a single heated finger and touched the side of my throat to ground me again. To ground us both.

Before he got sick, Uncle Lud had towered over me. Each of his visits would begin by hoisting me high in a bear hug. Even a year or so ago, he could lift me straight off my feet. Imagine that: me, the big-boned nerd, swirling through the air in Uncle Lud's arms, my long black hair swinging, my new glasses bumping up and down on my face, and a huffing sound, an adolescent version of a laugh, chafing the air with each turn, like I was an engine desperately trying to start. There wasn't much better, not even when my father, shaking his head, disappeared into the house as if unable to bear the foolish sight of the two of us, already no doubt anticipating the moment Uncle Lud would release me and I would roil in circles, damn near giggling.

Now my young uncle crumpled in my arms—even his bones had shrunk—and as Uncle Lud revived that afternoon, light pouring in around the bedroom shades my mother religiously lowered, I slung my uncle's arm around my neck and helped him into the washroom. Afterward, I maneuvered Uncle Lud into the living room, settling him gingerly in the recliner with that fresh glass of Boost, a new unbent straw beside him. Then I sprawled on the couch in a show of comradely weariness. With both of us stretched out facing the big back windows and the mountains beyond, I thought it felt a little as if we were embarking upon the road trip Uncle Lud had once promised we'd take together, traveling along in the same direction.

Sometimes when we sat like this, we managed to get the BBC on the radio, a transmission that tickled Uncle Lud. He once told me he imagined the BBC announcers as pompous Claymation figures, entertainingly oblivious of their lack of real substance. One quick-tongued, long-winded, double-talking interviewer, Alexander McAfee, Uncle Lud confided, appeared in his imagination as an animated fox.

"Now, tell me," asked McAfee the fox as he interviewed a famous rugby hero sidelined by family tragedy, "would ye say ye've fully recovered or should I say, can one ever *fully* recover, or rather, might one imagine that an accident like this one would instead alter one irreparably? I'd say, it quite must, mustn't it? I guess what I mean is I imagine ye've become a different sort of player, not a regular fellow, but a man now, wouldn't ye say? Perhaps ye are less inclined to be the demon of a bad boy on the field, then, but a true team player, what one might label 'an honest instigator' instead of a rabble-rouser?"

Uncle Lud would cackle with each of the fox's assumptions and self-clarifications.

A fox, he maintained, was in love with the sound of his own voice.

At least a Claymation fox—dressed, as Uncle Lud and I imagined, in a scarlet riding outfit—was.

But that afternoon, the high comedy of the BBC was illusive, a narrow drawer of static that wouldn't come clear. I flicked the radio's knob to a local station, but even the endless stream of Traveling Top 40 proved unobtainable. In its place, a news report about fears of a potentially dangerous fire bleated.

Dry lightning and willfully stupid campers were in season along with the unusual heat and the tindered grass, but I wasn't sure that things would have been different if the heat had held off. Then we might have had landslides or tremors or a spate of death-by-bear. You couldn't live here all these years and not feel as if the mountainside itself had a soul that flared and suffered and must find its own way of exploding.

"You went up to the refuse station," Uncle Lud whispered, more statement than question. His throat, I knew, was always raw these days. I knew too that Uncle Lud wanted to say more. He would say more, I was sure, as soon as he could dampen the dry edge of his throat. I sat up to bend his straw and hand him his glass, waiting until he sipped before I answered.

"All of you?" Uncle Lud asked.

"Not Ursie," I said.

"She'll be okay," Uncle Lud said, startling me. My uncle rarely misread a conversation. "And?"

"And what?" I said.

"Who else?"

How did he know? I wondered. How did he always know?

I almost laughed aloud and Uncle Lud finally smiled, a tiny anxious twist to his old grin.

"A girl who works up at the camp with Jackie," I said. "Hana Swann's her name."

"For now," Uncle Lud said.

I shrugged, and Uncle Lud read the shape of my morning in that gesture.

"Trouble?" he said as if he already knew she was.

I found myself oddly reluctant to share the truth of Hana Swann.

"Ah, no. She had advice for Bryan, that's all. Pissed him off, I think, this girl trying to tell him how to deal with Flacker."

"Did she shoot?" Uncle Lud persisted.

"Oh, yeah, a little," I said. "You should see her with a .22."

I could feel a pressure building inside, a push against the truth. Uncle Lud read it in my face.

"She killed something, didn't she?" he said. "Something besides a rat."

"A young marten," I admitted.

"Did you help?"

"What do you mean?"

"Did . . . you . . . help her . . . kill it?" Uncle Lud managed.

Did I? For a moment, I flat couldn't remember. A part of me imagined I had stepped beside her to steady the gun or that I had been the one to stroll into the broken forest and lift the bloodied creature against me. I glanced down at myself, almost sure I'd see my shirtfront drenched in blood and was both confused and relieved to see only a speck of blood, my own blood, I remembered now, my own tiny accident.

Something spilled inside me, and in a rapid voice that shamed me, a voice that reminded me of my own childish fears, I babbled out how Hana Swann had shocked us all, how she disappeared into the trees, how blood ran down her white arm.

"She's not afraid of anything," I concluded. "She was even ready to walk clean back to camp. Claims she'd never had a problem, hitchhiking on the highway or any road."

"Jackie stopped her?" Uncle Lud said, leaning forward a little.

"Nah, weird thing is, Jackie knows better. Her sister's friend Minette, you know. They haven't found *her*. Jackie feels safe with this girl, I guess."

I saw again the helpless longing on Jackie's face, and the rush of desire that had lofted me over Fuller Street to chase Tessa returned. I found myself rising to my feet, as if ready to run after her again, this time with Hana Swann looking on, grinning even as the Nagle brothers' car came tearing toward me and GF threw open his door.

It came fully into the room with us, a vision of blood, a burst of gunfire, a lonely figure eyeing a stretch of the highway.

In the kitchen, my mother rattled plates and pots to remind us what life entailed. Water ran, cupboard doors slammed. We could hear the pill drawer open and lids pop as my mother began to sort Uncle Lud's next doses. Uncle Lud's chest calmed, and he inclined his flushed head toward mine, taking stock of me, including the unnamed absence I felt and the bandaged finger even my mother had missed. A new hurt crossed Uncle Lud's face.

"Ah," he whispered in his ravaged voice. "Ah, Leo. You saw her . . . didn't you? You saw Snow Woman."

You know this, don't you? he was almost begging. *You have this?*

One of my father's more uncharitable relatives maintains that a great-uncle of my father's did a huge favor for a medicine man in one of the northern tribes and was paid back with a backhanded curse. Not so, Uncle Lud swears. He was *rewarded*—not with rich farmland or timber or a hefty bank account—but with an enduring connection to the band itself, one that led my father to fall in love with a Native woman and my father's younger brother to lose his heart—and soul—to storytelling. So my Uncle Lud, my white uncle, my uncle who should not have known all he did, stockpiled tales the way others amass tables and chairs and cars and suit jackets, all the props of life. This was his fortune, the legacy he was handing to me.

In Uncle Lud's vast story encyclopedia, one form of the devil is a gentle white lady who places a sliver of ice in your heart and makes you desperate to meet her in the underworld. It is an ancient story, dredged up each generation, whenever a spate of suicides occurred. Some bands call her Deer Woman. Others, Night Woman. When Snow Woman finds you, unless you are the strongest of souls, the most skeptical, or the most protected, the world no longer belongs to you. She has found a particularly easy berth in young Indian men, so eager it seems to flash out of this life into any other. Suicide sounds so desperate; it really does. But following Snow Woman can be damn near noble, irresistible. It is, the rumor goes, an act of pure magic: a disappearing act directed by the devil himself. I'd heard the story a half-dozen times from Uncle Lud. I knew it in my bones. But at that moment it seemed as if I'd forgotten every scrap, and as he watched, I reached for a notebook.

SNOW WOMAN

People go missing. That's not news, it turns out. It's how they get lost that's of interest. Vanishing, according to Uncle Lud, has never been an uncommon event. In the backcountry where he and my father grew up, people still disappear at regular intervals, many from choice, chasing a job or fleeing a failing farm or a hellish wife or a demented acquaintance with a grudge and a storehouse of weapons. Sometimes, the law swoops down when no one is looking, and only rumors are left behind.

Other times, plain old stupidity is the cause.

A perceived aura of invisibility, Uncle Lud says, is the third stage of drunkenness, followed swiftly by a more fatal stage: the belief in invincibility. So there you are, weaving home alone in the moon-starved night, shit-faced in the snow, no worries. Who can even see you? That realization sends you spinning from this world, the once well-known path squeezing down to nothing as if viewed through a closing periscope, the road lost for good, and your last brilliant assumption is that if you are only going to waste time turning in circles, why not rest awhile in that grave-shaped gulley, that pillowy hollow of a snowbank.

Gone, gone, gone.

Another kind of disappearance, less common, of course, is almost never talked about except by those who have nearly fallen victim, but even they quickly learn that their stories are best left unexplored. It was only by chance that Uncle Lud happened to be party to a firsthand report.

This happened in a mining town called Wilton's Cross, which used to occupy a narrow slit off the old highway—a dozen houses, a sand-brick church up on cinder blocks, and a company store with two back rooms (one for playing cards and one for visiting one of the three women unfortunate enough to have landed there without a man's protection). The enclave perched just beyond the spray of a waterfall that fell a quarter mile into the river that ran straight through the town under the half block of a boardwalked main street. Wilton's Cross has all but faded away—kind of ironical, when you think about it—but one of the old mining-company roads ends by the stone bridge that crossed into the old town, and though the boardwalk's long gone and most of the homes burned in a fire that swept through decades ago, you can still walk across that bridge, find bricks from the church, and hurl one or two toward the falls for luck, if you dare.

Uncle Lud, then a boy of twelve, was on his way back from a championship hockey game, a seven-hour drive from the farm where he lived with my father; their much-older sister, Joyce; Joyce's husband, Toby; and my grandparents. Toby was the assistant coach for the team that Uncle Lud had barely made, and he had volunteered to drive a few kids to the championship.

The team traveled in three vehicles—a van driven by the coach, a station wagon by a teacher at the school, and one old car by Uncle Lud's young brother-in-law. Uncle Lud, of course, rode in Toby's car. On the way home, he sat up front and listened while Toby painstakingly went over the games, the two they'd won and the one they'd lost. His teammates, two big boys from the reserve, unwelcome in the van and station wagon, were worn out and slept with their cheeks against the windows, and eventually Uncle Lud too dozed off, his head tipping forward as he nodded to Toby's passionate replay.

Some time later, it might have been a few minutes or full hours, he woke from a dream about butter tarts to a heavy bump and a whooshing rumble as if the car had fallen into a hole and Toby was gunning the engine. Behind him, the big boys stirred but snored on. Beside him, Toby was rubbing his tired eyes. He unrolled his window and craned his neck out, and only gradually was Uncle Lud aware that the noise he was hearing was not the car's engine racing—the car had, in fact, stopped—but the roar of a waterfall about forty feet away.

"I need to walk around," Toby declared, and so, Uncle Lud decided, did he.

They left the sleeping boys behind and wandered up the empty road to the stone bridge that led into Wilton's Cross. The settlement was quiet, even then in its last days of pretending to be a town, and no one appeared on the gravel street or peered out a window at them. At the far end of the road, they could see a truck and a derelict school bus framing a turnaround.

"I'm hungry," Toby said, his stomach growling from the cold air's bite.

They'd left home with wax-paper-wrapped packets of Kraft cheese sandwiches, with thermos containers of beef stew and chicken, with great boxes of sugar-raisin cookies and a couple of sacks of old apples from the root cellar. Nearly every bite of it had been eaten before they even arrived at the championships, and then they'd gone on to gorge themselves on the city motel's free breakfasts, slipping stale doughnuts and hard-boiled eggs into their hockey bags as they left. But now Uncle Lud, too, still craving the butter tarts of his dream, was starved and fingering the two dollars he had kept all along in his coat pocket.

"You think there's a store here?" he asked Toby.

Without answering, Toby began to stroll forward, and Uncle Lud followed.

The remnants of a dirty snow covered the wooden steps up to the company store, and though they creaked and buckled, the stairs held and the door opened on the first try, its wavy glass panes shuddering. Not much on the shelves—dusty tins and cardboard boxes with their sides sunken in—but the clerk, a long-faced, unshaven man in spattered coveralls, wearing a wool hat and work gloves in the unheated store, pulled a dusty bag of potato chips from under the counter and sold that and a large bottle of seltzer to Uncle Lud for the money in his pocket. Toby bought the store's entire supply of spicy jerky, all eight of them in homemade wrapping, and was tearing at one with his teeth before they left the store. As they meandered back over the bridge, a breeze off the falls misting their hair, Uncle Lud privately hoped the big boys were still asleep and would stay that way until he'd finished off the chips.

But the boys weren't asleep. And they weren't in the car, either.

"Taking a piss, I guess," said Toby, squinting off into the woods on the other side of the falls. Footprints in the snow seemed to lead that way.

Early afternoon and already dusky and growing colder by the second.

"We'd better rouse them," Toby said after a few minutes had passed. "We don't have time for sightseeing. Damn kids."

He guessed they'd gone on to get a better look at the falls.

Even half-frozen, the falls were a sight. He hoped those boys weren't foolish enough to go exploring. All of a sudden, an urgency came over them there in the fading light, and both Toby and Uncle Lud bolted for the dimming trail, calling out the boys' names.

They followed footprints to a deer trail and were soon trotting along in the gloaming light, twisting with the trail until the footprints disappeared. For a moment, Toby and Uncle Lud paused, their frozen breath aching in their lungs as they cast around for any clue. Uncle Lud saw the broken branches, and they didn't hesitate. They couldn't hesitate. It was that swift decision to beat through the broken branches, sliding and falling, that ultimately saved the two reserve boys, who they finally saw ahead of them, coatless, both still in their red hockey jerseys, perched above them, mere feet from the falls. If it had been summertime, the boys never would have heard them. As it was, the waterfall's muted winter roar kept them from noticing the newcomers at first.

"Hey!" Toby shouted, but the boys didn't turn, and Uncle Lud noticed how brilliant the light was beyond them. Away from the trees, daylight still held sway. He and Toby climbed closer, their every step now more treacherous. As they climbed, Uncle Lud found himself whispering, *Turn around, turn back. Turn around, turn back.* A mantra in his mind, but Toby soon was stock-still, staring at him, because Uncle Lud was singing the words aloud now: *"Turn around, turn back, turn around, turn back,"* and the boys were slowly changing course, twisting away from the falls, back toward Toby and Uncle Lud. As they did, both seemed to come awake, and one almost fell backward in his horror at seeing the falls so close to him.

Uncle Lud continued his singsong, and Toby reached forward to snag first one boy, then the other, pulling them as gently as he could back down the hill into the warren of broken branches they had all ascended. It took them forever to regain the trail, which tried to disappear beneath them, and it was fully dusk when they reached the car, the two big boys shivering and blubbering now in the backseat. Toby pulled blankets from the trunk and covered them. He found an old tarp beside the spare wheel well and pressed that around them too. Then, he and Uncle Lud got back into the car and hightailed it out of Wilton's Cross. They drove a full hour more on the highway before Toby stopped for coffee, and the boys managed to speak.

"What the hell were you thinking?" Toby began.

Tears leapt to one boy's eyes. The other coughed. Toby waited.

"We woke up," the coughing boy said, "because of the light. We thought we were home and you were shining a flashlight to get us out of the car."

"Then we were outside," the other boy continued, "and the light was . . . pulling us."

"I saw it moving into the wood, and I knew we were supposed to follow it."

"She was ahead of us the whole way."

"She?" Toby asked. "Who?

The boys looked shocked and miserable. They were certain—they were . . . sure, yeah, sure—they'd seen the retreating figure of a woman with long black hair.

"Yeah," Toby kept prodding, "a woman? Not an animal?"

"I don't know," the tear-streaked one said. "I don't know. She kept calling me, and I don't remember nothing else until I turned around and my legs began to shake."

"Dumb-ass kids," Toby swore. "You could have been killed."

But he knew and Uncle Lud knew they weren't at fault. They'd felt it too, that yarning tug through the dusky light.

Later, after they'd delivered the boys back to the reserve, Toby asked Uncle Lud, "How did you know to do that, boy? Who taught you that song?"

But Uncle Lud couldn't say, any more than the reserve boys could explain Snow Woman, the will-o'-the-wisp who tried to woo them from this life. They'd have chills for months afterward, even into the summer. A misery set into their bones that even drink couldn't ease. Uncle Lud played a lot of basketball then, and he remembers getting into a pickup game with one of the reserve boys from that afternoon in Wilton's Cross. He remembers how the boy wore two shirts even in the heat, how his hands shivered on the ball, and how when their shoulders touched in a crashing jump, a cold, clean shock ran though him.

When the girls began to go missing off the highway outside town, this is what I thought of: snow and ice, a half-frozen waterfall, a flickering light, a bone-sick desire to destroy. I knew, of course, that Uncle Lud's story had nothing to do with the vanishing girls, that it would be bullshit romanticizing to imagine they'd simply wandered away following a will-o'-the-wisp, the worst kind of rationalizing, and that it was no Snow Woman but a real monster out there. Still, for weeks, even as wailing began and fights broke out and grief saturated another family, I had gone to sleep thinking, not about that lonely road but a beckoning light that could slash across time and snatch away. And I hoped. I hoped.

"You met Snow Woman," Uncle Lud had said.

"Nah," I told him, feeling a cold sweat behind my neck, "that wasn't her. That wasn't the girl we met."

"Are you sure?" Uncle Lud managed, looking even more tired and concerned.

"I'm still here, aren't I?" I said, immediately hearing the echo of Hana Swann in the woods, declaring her own invincibility.

"She's just a friend of Jackie's," I was insisting when I noticed Uncle Lud was drifting off again.

And then remembered Hana Swann's white arm, that laugh, and I thought: Jackie.

The image of her trudging away from the truck beside Hana Swann twined with a fear I hadn't felt before. It was a different kind of heartache from what came over me when my mother first told me about Uncle Lud's illness. It was different from my constant anxiety about being near Tessa. This was raw and consuming. I could feel it roiling in my gut and rushing up my spine. What was I worried about? Jackie was the toughest girl I knew—Hana Swann sure as hell couldn't hurt her—but still here it was: a big, heartless fear that swamped me and yet wouldn't show its face.

As Uncle Lud's breathing eased, I fixed his covers, adjusted the pillow behind his head, and left him sleeping in his chair. My mother had gone back to work long ago, but not before shooting both Uncle Lud and me a glance that said her heart was hollowed out and it might just be our fault. That look pushed me to my bedroom and the old computer, to my undone physics assignments, where I stared and thought of Uncle Lud, of Jackie's sideways glances at Hana Swann, of Tessa. I thought of Trevor Nowicki, of my own father and his increasingly perfunctory visits, of my mother's chronicle of butchered animals, of Tessa's foster families. Gerald Fucking Flacker. I scrolled through screens, flipped pages, lost again and again, until I began to wonder if Disappointment was a scalar or a vector quantity; if Direction could make a human heart go bad; if the Acceleration Equation could illuminate all the ways to avoid disappearing. And in the notebook (mostly blank) that my mother liked to shuffle through, I sketched my first full equation, the first that made fractional sense to me at least:

$$\text{Average acceleration} = \frac{\text{velocity} + \text{desire}}{\text{time} * \text{wasted dreams}} = \frac{v_f - v_i + d}{t / wd_i}$$

The equation looked so right, like the first true thought I'd ever had, that I entered it into the daily log of section problems I was supposed to solve and keep, and I sent it off to the course instructor, a woman named Leila Chen who lived, I imagined, in that distant university city where this course, like the many others my mother had ordered over the years, originated. While Leila Chen frequently sent me e-mails, reminding me of deadlines I hadn't made and offering oblique help in her stilted prose, this was my first missive to her, and I was still in the grip of a kind of euphoric stupor when I heard Bryan's truck grabbing the gravel off Lamplight Road, and I kind of woke up, the way I imagined those two reserve boys did the afternoon they perched on a precipice, a cold ache half-formed around their eager hearts.

Turn around, turn around.

Hey, Leo. Leo Smartass, Bryan was hissing through the screen window behind me, *turn around, you.*

THE FIRST BAD IDEA

"Here's the thing," Bryan declared. "We make him disappear."

I wasn't in the mood to conspire, but Bryan didn't seem to notice. He pulled a chair up beside the desk and began to hover in a way that reminded me of my mother, of an assignment on the way.

"If one girl after another can vanish off the highway without a trace, then why can't the same happen to that fucker?" Bryan said.

"No one knows what's going on with the girls," I said.

Bryan scowled. *"We know,"* he said.

"Here's what I'm thinking," Bryan said. "He has an accident. Let's say his truck skids off Ledge Road—who would find it?"

If Flacker's policeman cousin Mitchell went looking, even if he called out the entire force and sent out the kind of search parties they'd never mustered for the girls, by the time they hit Ledge Road, Bryan said, a "Good Samaritan" might have cleaned up the edge that Flacker's truck had vaulted so that no sign of its slide would be immediately visible.

"They'd need a helicopter. Even Mitchell Flacker doesn't have that."

Days would pass before a more thorough examination would be launched. Meanwhile, Gerald Flacker would certainly have expired, if not from the impact, from the same dastardly care he gave to the Magnuson kids: he'd starve, pinned in the wreckage.

Bryan hadn't worked out all the details, but the gist of this first plan had been that he'd inspire Flacker to give chase on Ledge Road, barreling directly into a trap that they would set and that Bryan would know to avoid.

"How?" I asked.

"We'll steal from him. His drugs. His tools. Maybe even his dogs."

"*His dogs?*"

In spite of myself, I began to imagine the problem in terms Leila Chen might applaud. *If a truck going 40 miles an hour on a narrow mountain road . . .* Almost immediately, however, I was overtaken with my usual issue regarding vector quantities. Direction I could maybe guess, but who could quantify Flacker's rage or Flacker's meanness or this new, near-suicidal determination of Bryan's? Pure magnitude I would call that, and so, I'd guess, a scalar quantity only. And if—as Bryan sketched out this plan—I was along for the ride, would my innate reluctance, my tendency toward inertia and backward movements, deter Bryan's Acceleration? And what about the Force of Desire? Whose would be greater—Bryan's? Flacker's? Or my own hopeless will to stay alive long enough to woo Tessa?

While Bryan yammered on, I made up equations, all variants of $F = ma$, a fundamental that tumbled around in my head continually and never quite made sense.

"Your truck won't make the curve," I finally declared with no real evidence at all.

"Well," Bryan said as he watched my pencil dart around aimlessly on the notebook page, "all right, it might not be the best plan . . ."

"Yes," I agreed. "You're crazy. It's suicide."

Another thought came to me. "Who gave you this idea?"

"It may not be exactly right, but it's something, isn't it?" Bryan continued, his eyes sparking. "It's beautiful, you know. Turnabout is fair play. We finally *do something,* you know?"

"Leo," Bryan went on, "how much can Flacker destroy before someone strikes back?"

Turnabout. Something about the phrase and Bryan's jumpiness, like a spring under pressure, jolted me. My progress through Leila Chen's assignments might have been stuck, but in those early weeks of summer, I'd wandered through the physics course from back to front, reading pieces and scoffing at story problems I'd never halfway decipher, let alone master, and stopping whenever a real story seemed to appear. Now I found myself remembering a lesson—or at least my interpretation of a lesson—about something called Hooke's law, about Stress and Strain and proportional elasticity.

Tit for tat, I thought. Turnabout.

A look of semi-understanding must have crossed my face, because Bryan glowed as surely as if I'd jumped up and agreed to shoot Flacker myself.

"You see?" he almost shouted. "You see?"

"You can't knock him off a cliff," I said. "Or poison him. He's too damn mean. And whatever you did, you'd have to arrange it so you'd be far away at the time. Plan it to the second, so that no one could connect you."

"Okay." Bryan leaned forward, listening.

Displacement, as far as I understood, describes the length of an imaginary path—a description that still strikes me as funny and apt and also completely nonsensical, because how can you measure a route that doesn't yet exist, and wouldn't you have to know for sure where it was you started from? Displacement wasn't only the measurement of that imagined journey, I'd read, it also was a relative point in space. That didn't help me much. One thing I did understand, or thought I did, was this part of Hooke's law: If you placed Weight on a spring, the measurement and relative position of that imagined path would be proportional to the Stress and Strain of that Weight. It occurred to me that if the pressure building in Bryan finally landed on Flacker, just like that Weight on a spring, Flacker might be blasted to the other side of the moon.

"And you'd have to annihilate him," I found myself saying, "otherwise he'd be coming after you. And then there's the Nagles and that Brit. They'll come after you for sure."

Because that was the other part of Hooke's law: Restoration. All that Stress and Strain would be matched and returned, flinging itself right back at Bryan, a hard kind of justice.

Imagine a pendulum in the bottom of a clock, swinging from side to side, every bit of Displacement ultimately Restored. Hooke's law didn't apply to every material or situation, but it seemed to me now to perfectly describe Tessa and me, that constant movement between us, away and back, away and back. I fucking hated Hooke's law, I realized, and the way it was ruling my life.

"Sure," Bryan was agreeing. "It would have to be all of them." He was grinning now.

So, imagine, I thought, Bryan sending Flacker and the Nagles into a nether region and then, whoops, the whole bunch slamming back to Earth, meaner than ever.

Figure that one out, genius.

"No, no, no. Not happening, Bry," I concluded, coming back

to myself. "It'll be the end of the world before those fellows go down. Fire and brimstone and all that shit. No one can calculate past that."

But Bryan was still nodding as if we were both signing on to a plan.

"You're right," he said. "It would have to be complete destruction."

He was in his own hot daze, staring out the open window he'd crawled through as if the world had suddenly become brilliant with possibility. I glanced out with him, but all I saw was the old shed where my father kept his tools and unused fertilizer, his miner's paraphernalia, all the trappings of a man who once imagined he had a life here. The Old Miner's Shed, my mother and I called it, as if it were an actual historical relic. I sometimes dreamed I could spirit Tessa there, that we could hide away in that shack for hours at a time, where no one—not my mother nor that raucous, needy crowd at Tessa's house—would find us. For a long moment, the shed and its possibilities mesmerized me again. By the time I turned back to Bryan, his excitement had hardened into purpose.

"You got another one of those?" he asked, motioning toward the notebook.

In the living room, Uncle Lud began coughing.

"Hey, hey, it's story time again," Bryan said as I got to my feet. "See if your uncle's got a good one about how to get a girl, huh?"

"You still picking up Ursie?" I said, glancing at the clock by my bed.

"Ah, shit," he said, scrambling to his feet. "Is that clock right?"

"Hey, listen," I said. I wanted to talk him out of whatever new scheme he was hatching, but even as I began, whatever argument I'd had in mind fell away, a peculiar lassitude sliding over me.

Let him go, a voice inside me said. *Look how happy he is.* It was true. I hadn't seen Bryan so directed since before his mother got sick, so instead of arguing with him about Flacker or Tessa or even Uncle Lud, I only shook my head and handed him a fresh notebook from the pile of new notebooks my mother added to continually.

"Is that blood?" Bryan said, pausing to swipe at a mark I'd left on the new notebook. He didn't wait around for an answer. He was already levitating back out the window, plunging into the afternoon glare with a new dark radiance, clutching the notebook in hand as if he intended to fill it with his own peculiar equations, ones that would incinerate all notions of relative elasticity and relegate Flacker and the Nagles to an underworld all their own.

AS HE LIES DYING

The stories of the dying have nothing to do with dying. They are all about past adventure. An inexpert listener might think the dying man is holding on to the hem of life, desperate to feel its weight and value, to make a kind of peace before moving onward. But the truth is, the dying man is opening a door for the living. You have to find out *how* to live; that's his parting advice.

See, he says. Look. Can You Hear Me? Hey, I'm dying over here.

A few years back, my dad was inspecting a tailings pond and a load of debris fell off a partially raised backhoe, knocking him about and half crushing a vital organ or two, and in the hospital, after one complication after another and the infection to boot, the staff made ready to summon a white-collared professional to prepare him for the worst and in sober almost meaningful tones, they asked us: "What is his religion? What does he believe in?"

I had felt a moment of panic, sure my dad was about to fail a crucial test, one that would make his survival impossible, but neither my mother nor Uncle Lud hesitated.

"Science," they both said, almost at once. "He believes in science."

Well, that pissed them all off, didn't it? The hospital social worker with her glossy brochures and clipboard and dozen clergymen on call, that brisk nurse with her not-too-subtle silver cross stud earrings—the pair of them disgusted with this family. Only the doctor managed a twitch of satisfaction, and his smug smile soon tinged with anxiety because now, for certain, he was on the hook, no higher power hovering in the wings to assume the blame my father—and presumably our family, as well—would certainly ascribe to the only scientist at hand.

But of course, my mother didn't share my father's true confidence in science, save as a means to my personal achievement. Instead, she believed in grand myths of the kind governed by multiple sets of arbitrary and often unsaid rules. Her Earth erupted from a fiery birth, and both life and death must involve a long passage, through mountain trails and wild river rapids. The elders around here loved her.

My mother parceled out her faith, also giving another portion to the Church, but not explicitly to Church doctrine. A fierce attendant of Mass, a devotee of Our Blessed Lady, she would bang her fist against your jaw for bad-mouthing a pope, but was more than happy to ignore what she called the lesser details and what His Holiness might call Church law. No, it's the Battle Between Good and Evil my mother believed in: the Big Show. She collected candles and incense and rosary beads as if they were ammunition she's stockpiling away for the day the Dark One comes sniffing around her door. The old tribal stories don't get in the way here. My mother has widened the interpretation so that when the Devil comes to call, he might take the form of a lonesome wolf with black cloven hooves instead of paws and long, yellowed incisors. She'll know when he's close by, she says. She heard him once, years ago, pacing around an old shed where a weak-minded uncle raged with drink. The uncle grew calm; they all remembered that—my mother, especially—the high-pitched caterwauling winding down into a quiet that made them all uneasy. And yet they let him be until morning when they found he'd hanged himself in that shed, his hands laced with marks the doctor said were self-inflicted burns. She'd seen the holes in the yard, indentations that no dog, no cat, not even a moose would make. And though they'd raked the yard smooth a dozen times, those marks never failed to return, almost as if they were a bad memory continually surfacing.

Oh, yeah, my mother's faith took the devil into account. *Another reason* she liked to keep watch over Uncle Lud. If he was going, she wasn't letting him go with That One. *Another reason* she liked to keep me busy. If the devil wanted an entryway into our household, who would he choose? My engineer father? Her holy self? My good uncle? Or a weak-willed, socially ignorant pudding like me, a big, gangly, half-sighted, half-breed boy loping up the middle of the road right into danger, his nose in a fifty-cent notebook filled with scribbles? I'd be safe—we'd be safe—she reasoned, as long as I didn't glance up from that notebook or dawdle around, waiting for trouble to snap me up. If she'd known for certain how I used those notebooks, recording all I could manage, she would have realized what I hadn't yet: that I'd already been converted and was calling up trouble with each turn of the page.

As for Uncle Lud, he claimed his faith in listening.

"That's no kind of believing," I countered.

"Listening to who? Listening to what?" I asked.

"But you're the one we listen to," I added, stating the obvious.

Still, there was no arguing with him. No real answers would be forthcoming. Nothing, that is, you could relay to the hospital staff should they be asking about Uncle Lud one day.

"Stories," I would have to tell them. "He believes in stories."

And from the room beyond, no matter how deeply into a coma he might have fallen, Uncle Lud would likely snort. But I would be telling the truth. I was sure of that.

Whenever I talk with Uncle Lud, I am in a huge field. Uncle Lud's talk is a huge field, sky flung 'round us like a fresh cloth sprung from the laundry line, all sweetness and embrace. I lie back and listen, and fanciful though it might seem, we slip away.

We might be on a fragrant knoll, barely above waving flanks of what must be wheat—although I've never seen the stuff growing— the sun skipping between the rasping rows so that some are tawny and brindled, others pure raving gold. And though the vista narrows and widens with each tale Lud tells, the landscape never fails to unfurl itself, so that soon, too, I can see what my uncle sees and I know (I *know*) that there's another route that leads in and out of town, a secret one that's been here all along and is well traveled by other sorts of visitors, less strangers than well-forgotten kin. That road has none of the stark beauty of our highway. Uncle Lud's secret route is meandering and narrow. In places, it tunnels through forests and giant mica-dazzled rocks that from a distance appear impenetrable. But the route is open and once the traveler reaches what he might suppose should be a wall, there it is: a twining ribbon coursing forward, the fields, the lake. Imagine maps laid upon maps, all translucent, all imperative, soul trails enveloping real space, real people.

Light folds and wind buckles in the field that is Uncle Lud's talk.

Look here, Leo, he says, bending down to caress an insect with mottled wings, a crenulated leaf, a tiny sentient stippled rock whose tin and copper colors deepen with pleasure at his touch.

Despite all evidence to the contrary, I can't believe he'll leave us. I can't believe I won't find my way to Uncle Lud. Because even now, I know where Lud will be.

In a deep, wide field in a town overlaid on this one. As long as I remember every story, I'll know just where to find him, and maybe there, too, I'll find what I believe in.

DEVILS MAKE
THE BEST SALESMEN

A man appeared in Uncle Lud's town the year he started Secondary. A man who went door-to-door with a suitcase. He wore a skinny tie and a shiny suit. What he was selling was hidden, locked within the case.

"I'd love to show you, if you have a minute," he told the woman of the house, children clustered around her. "First, might I have a glass of water? The road up to the house was dusty," he added, "so very dry."

While one of the kids went to fetch the water, the rest noticed how the man's shoes sparkled, and they nudged one another. The fellow's hands were smooth and unmarked. They couldn't tear their eyes away as he unbuckled straps, unsnapped locks, and opened his world for them.

Sweets, that's what he was selling. Only one flavor. An astonishment. His suitcase crammed full of gold-wrapped candies that, unwrapped, made them all take a step backward. On the corner of the porch, a hound on a chain growled, not so much in response to the visitor but to the reactions of his family.

"Madam," the salesman said. "Might I offer you a complimentary sample of my wares?"

How could she say no? The sweet was blood-red, varnished, and salty on the surface. The housewife half choked when it hit her tongue.

"My fault, Mister," she apologized. "I was expecting something else—cinnamon, a spice of some kind." Her tongue dried from the salt, even as the sweet beneath it beckoned. Her hand reached involuntarily for another. The salesman held back, eyeing the children, who'd inched behind their mother, clutching her skirts, hiding their faces from his temptation.

Did you dream this? I wanted to know.

A story is not a dream, Uncle Lud told me.

He went on to describe how a dream is a fractured shadow, a cardboard village.

A story, though, Uncle Lud said, now, a story has solid form. You can hang your hat on a story.

The devil doesn't care about character development—that hidden code for moral expansion. The buds and branches of careworn emotional depth are anathema to him. He favors regression, backsliding, the wave-on-wave corruption, the dissolution, if you will, of character. Don't ask for character here.

Eventually, if not that very day, the candy salesman would find the children at the doorway receptive. And they would be struck by how, once on the tongue, the sweet seemed to ripple as if riding an unseen current before dissolving with an audible *whoosh*, a tiny explosion on the tongue that nothing could replicate, although quite a few children would discover as they grew older how closely the physical effect of that tiny sugar rock resembled a popular homemade drug, the only difference being the candy's effect ended with that marvelous eruption, while the drug's explosion dug craters within them that could never be healed. And they would do anything to get more.

"It's only candy," the salesman said smoothly. "Surely, you've tasted it before."

HOMEWORK

That day, the day of Hana Swann and Keven Seven, seemed unwilling to give way to night. It stretched on for hours, coming as it did at the height of summer, the burnt halo of sunset finally seeping away around ten thirty. At the Nowickis', Bryan huddled at the kitchen table drawing diagrams in the notebook I'd given him while Ursie sat cross-legged at the table's far side and fiddled with a new pack of cards she'd brought home from the Peak and Pine.

"They'll bring you luck," Keven Seven had told her. "A certain kind of luck, a type I'd bet you've never experienced before."

And his words had been made true already. That afternoon, as she'd gone to haul her cart and vacuum back into the supply closet, she'd spotted a twenty-dollar bill on the floor. She'd had an uncharacteristic moment of doubt and greed, half-shoving the bill into the pocket of her jeans, where it bunched uncomfortably, but she'd turned it over to Albie once she got to the office. It wasn't hers. She could hear her mother's voice saying as much. But then, out of the blue, the usually tight-fisted Albie turned around and handed back a ten, a tip that afternoon. One of the truckers had left something—for the mess in the parking lot, he said.

"And I notice you've got a taste for that," he said, nodding toward the cases of diet pop. "Go ahead and take a case of it home with you. Good to get rid of the stuff."

Albie looked up to see Ursie's eyebrows narrow, and he caught himself.

"Don't get used to it," he said.

Ursie and Bryan had taken the money right to the Hot Spot and bought a big greasy bag of Spot Burgers and fries. Ursie set the kitchen table, the same way they always had—two plates on the daisy placemats, two paper towels folded into fat triangles—and they'd eaten their supper almost wordlessly. Bryan didn't mention Hana Swann, and Ursie had no words to introduce Keven Seven, whose face, despite an afternoon of close scrutiny, was becoming more indistinct by the second. Like smoke, she thought, imagining a puff rising from her rapidly expert shuffling. She marveled at the energy captured in tiny bits of paper. Paper and ink, that's all the cards were really, and yet look what they could do.

A new letter from their father lay on the counter. Bryan had decided it could wait. They'd given up the phone; they'd had no choice. The only routes their father had to reach them were to write to them (rough slashes on his new girlfriend's pink paper), leave a message with a neighbor, or show up in person. He hadn't done the latter two in a good long time, and his letters were few and far between and rarely, these days, full of more than barely suppressed rants as if with a little help from the new girlfriend, he'd made strangers of his children, only to have conjured an argument with them, and he couldn't let it go.

"He has nothing good to tell us," Bryan told Ursie.

"Maybe he sent something," she said.

It had been weeks and weeks. He'd been clear in his last letter, Bryan knew. He wouldn't be doing that again.

"Or maybe he's coming home." A weird sense of dismay settled on her heart, surprising her.

"You want to open it?" Bryan asked.

"After supper, I guess," she'd said. "I'm starving."

But they'd eaten hours ago, and the letter remained unopened.

On any normal night, brother and sister might have noticed the oddness of the other's behavior, but not that night. Bryan drew and drew, ripped one crumpled sheet of paper after another. Ursie fingered playing cards. Heat pressed in upon them in the narrow kitchen, the bent screen on the back door wheezing, but no real breeze arriving.

Ursie had never held a deck of cards until that afternoon. Her father once pronounced that a girl playing cards was trashy. But she wasn't playing cards, and she certainly wasn't gambling, and he wasn't there, was he? She fanned the deck out in one long line the way she'd been taught that afternoon and swept the line into a pile again to practice her new shuffle.

"Do we have bleach?" Bryan asked suddenly.

"Under the sink," Ursie said.

The cards had a tendency, she was noticing, to tangle as if they were gripped by a peculiar urgency and must rush into place. Her task—she could see that now—was to provide calm, to stroke them so that they flanked one another in an orderly, well-reasoned line that would unfurl with her tender touch.

"Good," Bryan said, keeping his eyes on the charts and diagrams filling his notebook page.

His reply came after a long beat of silence during which Ursie exchanged a series of winks with the Jack of Clubs. She'd completely forgotten Bryan's earlier question, but she agreed with him; it was good. Containment and control: her index finger stopping each card as it streamed from hand to hand. Elegance: the neat, quick rhythm of a riffle shuffle. *All cards have two faces,*

Keven Seven had proclaimed. One is public and conceals all true identity under a cover of uniformity. The other is the secret and true card, a revelation that can alter destinies.

Games depend upon this secrecy, Keven Seven had told her. In this way, they resemble life and death, because, after all, what meaning would life hold if it weren't for its flip side? Like the "imperfect information" upon which a player must stake his fortune, glimpses of death, dealt, could pry open a life and allow the real betting to begin.

Ursie's wrist burned. She could see two even lines of reddened skin on its smooth underside and nearly felt his grip again, saw the white knobs of his knuckles. How hard had he held her?

She set up the cards again for a shuffle.

Again, please, again, Keven Seven had said, one lean hand pressing on her shoulder.

She would like to have conjured his face right that moment, but he turned away from her. For the life of her, Ursie couldn't recall his features. And yet he occupied her fully. Her chest rose and fell with a churning that, for lack of a better alternative, she accounted to him. She would undress later that night to find the bruising blooms of his touch along her shoulders and collarbone, along her upper arms, and most alarmingly, within the velvet undersides of her thighs. And she would, against her better nature, preen a bit, feeling he was with her. His grip was that tight.

He had hopes for her, he said. Better than hopes. A wonderful plan. She was extremely talented, he said, and it wouldn't be long before she could prove it. Did she like games? Of course she did. Who didn't? Who didn't like winning? He'd only seen one other like her, and unfortunately that girl squandered her talent. Ursie wouldn't. Her gift was too great. His eyes followed her imitation of each of his lessons. Her own learning astounded her. She mastered technique, sure—but she possessed that other intangible: she could lead the eye and capture the beholder. Why even he, Keven Seven, said he was entranced.

That evening, Ursie's hair flew back in her cards' own dashing breeze. Bring it on home with a strip shuffle—Running Cuts, it was called—and she loved this best of all. It reminded her of a long time ago when they were a family and out camping and her father wouldn't even start the truck but simply shift it into neutral so that the old truck came alive as if it had a life of its own, meandering down whatever back road they'd camped beside. And she and Bryan and their mother would lope behind it until, picking up speed, one by one, they hoisted themselves into the truck bed—slip, slip, slip—like cards falling back into the deck.

Ursie was sipping a Diet Bubble-Up from the case Albie had given her along with that astonishing tip. Now she wondered if he'd noticed her delay that afternoon and if he'd wondered what she had been doing in Room 14. She felt her lips and cheeks redden. Even her hair had a new swing to it, one that seemed to mimic the back-and-forth of the cards passing between her hands.

"You be good to yourself tonight," Albie had said, a funny hitch in his voice.

"Yes, I will," Ursie said.

"And get yourself in here tomorrow. Don't be like your auntie. Don't let me down, you hear?"

No, neither Ursie nor Bryan had any intention of letting anyone down.

As the night descended in wave after wave of softened, retreating light, Ursie kept shuffling, murmuring as she did, and Bryan, head still down, nodded in agreement to her whispered commands. He had decided he needed to take a drive back out to Ledge Road and Flacker's place that evening, to catalogue the way the light fell as true night approached. He'd take the notebook, sketch a map of angles and instigations. Forget his original scheme. It was a fool's game. He could see that now. Flacker wouldn't chase him. But no mind, that afternoon, Bryan conceived of another, better plan as he realized a potential goldmine of explosives was right under his nose in the miner's shed. It was simply a matter of choosing his time and finding a way to distract Flacker. That would be the crucial move. He'd need to set more than one fire under the fellow, something Flacker couldn't ignore. He would need to distract Flacker into his undoing. And then there were the little Magnuson kids to consider.

The sound of Ursie's shuffling called up an image for Bryan: Flacker, the Nagle brothers, and a couple of fallers squabbling over a card game at The Landing, a fellow rushing out after the Nagles as they careened toward the car owned by that other fellow, the one with the accent. The faller who'd lost the most dared to follow the Nagles, bellowing complaints behind them that went unanswered (unless you could call hawking gobs of spit an answer) while Flacker sat there with his mean grin.

Don't look at *me*, he all but said. I ain't got your money.

He made a snarling point of pulling out his empty pockets for the others, upending a slim wallet, as if he'd just fallen to Earth, not a penny to his name. If a thread of friendship between Flacker and the Nagles had been evident to these new-to-town fallers, they might have stripped him, but Flacker had mightily pissed off GF in only the third hand, so that a well-used buck knife appeared beside him on the table and had gone on to threaten the foul-tempered Brit more than once. Why would anyone believe they were in cahoots?

But Bryan knew the Nagles and their nasty friend acted as Flacker's temporary bank. The thought descended upon him that intercepting Flacker's potential withdrawals, or more accurately, the Nagles' deliveries back to Flacker, might jumpstart some seriously good trouble, at the least create a little distracting traffic long enough for Bryan to do his own damage. Money knocked everyone off course.

No shit, Sherlock, he heard his old friend Dean say as if he were crouched beside Bryan and Ursie in that hot kitchen.

His pen itched in his hand.

Just do it, Hana Swann whispered, clear as could be from beside the screen door, causing Bryan's head to snap up. His eyes scanned the kitchen for her, catching only one out-of-place object, his father's letter.

Bryan had almost forgotten that letter, which remained unopened on the kitchen counter. Ursie, riveted by her cards, certainly had. But as he considered that square white envelope, his father's familiar hand, Bryan realized he didn't need to prize letter from envelope and decipher that scrawl to hear the hiss and spittle of that new, foreign greed of their father's. He could feel a corresponding heat rise within him, a heat not unlike the one Hana Swann engendered, and catching himself, suddenly felt like rejoicing. If a few unread lines on paper could steam him, here in the simple kitchen beside his sweet and steady sister, what might a single anonymous, incendiary note do to the bomb that was Flacker? A concerned observer, who had information—cheap information—that would reveal Flacker's enemies, reveal an angle that had eclipsed Flacker's notice. That alone, that lapse, might be enough to cause the violent row Bryan needed as distraction. He had a notebook. He had a pen. The sketches of a plan taking shape in neat lists. So simple. Even she'd have to admit that. He'd sell Flacker his own destruction.

Flacker, Bryan had discovered during his pot pickup and deliveries with the Nagles, ran a full-scale illegal substance enterprise. Not only did he make meth, he'd jerry-built a still from a couple of dirty pots and vile car radiator condensers to produce a searing moonshine he sold in cloudy milk jugs to kids from the reserve. The reserve had an alcohol ban in place, but no one really enforced it. Even so, the kids didn't have to go near town where they might be seen. Instead they'd carry their milk jugs into the woods or down by the old school or behind the defunct lumber train depot and drink until they were flat-out numb, even at times paralyzed. "Razed," they said, as in, *"Oh, fawk me, I'm razed."* Moonjuice, Wildwood Mash—these were refined compared with Flacker's home-burnt brew, which was just two steps away from antifreeze. It addled those kids, took away their sight and gave them endless gut pains that if they were lucky they could relieve by massive bouts of vomiting as they began to sober up. Give 'em a week (or even a couple of nights) to recover and back they'd go.

It's not that we're stupid, we all could tell you that. Screw that.

No, take any one of the kids from around here and set him down in a leafy city neighborhood with all the advantages and see what he can do. Guarantee you, you'd see right away the difference between your average coddled suburban kid and one with innate smarts. No, ignorance is not a choice here. But what else do they have? Most of the kids aren't getting away, and those who head up to Flacker's know the world conspired against their kind so long ago it's like they're at the bottom of a murky, shit-filled trench, and they might as well splash about until they drown as wait around for someone to outright crush them.

As soon as Ursie went to bed, Bryan put the truck in neutral, coasted out to the paved road, and drove back out to Flacker's place. It was not quite midnight and sitting in his truck below the old sawmill, he catalogued the stealthy parade of loping kids, customers all, heading up from Ledge Road. He could hear the dogs begin even before the kids started to navigate the speargrass up into Flacker's tin yard. Flacker would likely have a jug in hand by then. Maybe he'd even be sneaking up on the kids, ready to give them a little thrill with their razing, the sight of him with all the knives hanging off his belt, his scarred belligerent face suddenly visible in the eerie blink of dry lightning that could not land and scorch him. Oh, no. You want to talk crazy. Let's talk crazy. Or worse, maybe he'd send that Cassie Magnuson out, half-dressed in a T-shirt and thin panties, a jerry-built woman to match the still, shaking so much that bills would be fluttering from her stained hands and she'd have to search for them on the ground. They'd have to leave her like that, crawling and whimpering. They couldn't risk getting caught up in sympathy for her. No one knew what Flacker might do if he caught you down on the bare earth with his half-naked property.

Then there was the meth, of course, but Bryan had only glimpsed that operation. Flacker's meth had different routes to buyers. Bryan knew the Nagles and their cohort, that nasty Brit, were into all sorts of bad deals with Flacker these days. Bryan got the idea too that they were now entrepreneurs of a different sort, peddling drugs they devised and concocted and barely tried themselves before hawking them without a second thought. A gang in Winnipeg was involved, a planning of a complex route of transportation under way, the famous highway an overland express.

He waited a while before he left the truck to stalk a single kid, too high or foolhardy to know he shouldn't visit Flacker's alone. Bryan whistled quick and low, and the boy turned, his hands already flying up to protect himself from Bryan, who, with the hood of his sweatshirt pulled up, was near-invisible in the gloom. What wasn't invisible was the bright white folded square he forced into the boy's hand.

"Make sure Flacker gets this," he said. "And don't say a word about where you got it."

Twice more in the space of an hour, Bryan passed notes to spaced-out kids. Two of the kids ran headlong to Flacker as if their lives depended upon it, as if he'd set up a test for them. One simply wedged the note as a tiny scrap within the bills he gave Flacker and fled as Flacker began his count, leaving half his purchase unclaimed. Luckily for Bryan, the kid had no sense of direction or maybe he didn't want to encounter Bryan again. He fled on a trail a distance away from where Bryan crouched. Not two minutes later, a volley of shotgun blasts rang out over that far hill, right on that poor kid's tail, and Bryan didn't move an inch, thinking of the messages he'd sent, written in black block print:

THEY'RE CHEATING YOU, ASSHOLE
ASK NAGLE ABOUT WINNIPEG
IT AIN'T JUST YOUR MONEY HEADING NORTH

Bryan might have been risking his own life out there that night as much from the weather as from Flacker. Long black clouds streamed overhead as if the heavens were racing above him, and between them, at steady intervals, lightning cascaded, randomly, it seemed, the way he himself struck out, again, again, until with a kind of luck, contact was made. He stayed for far too long that night without knowing why he couldn't leave until finally the lightning made purchase on a far-off hillside with an orange flare that seemed to spring from his own heart. It was as if someone had screamed, a single, sudden renting in the black night that clamored painfully, then disappeared, only to reappear in sharp orange bursts so abrupt and disconnected he wondered if he was imagining them. Each time another appeared, he seemed to come more awake, as if the fire were burning away his own confusion, until finally he was standing straight, upright on Flacker's land, the full plan gloriously illuminated before him. Fear left him then, but not discretion. He waited, past the hours of Flacker's visitors, past the swollen early morning dark when even on that ridge you couldn't see a hand in front of your face. He waited out the deep silence until the night perched on the cusp of dawn and other creatures began a rustling in the false dark. Then Bryan began. He'd walked those trails a hundred times on his way to feed the little Magnusons. He knew, too, the route the Nagles took when Flacker had commanded they arrive without even his cousin Mitchell knowing. And he knew Flacker, too. He did. The Big Man had his own divining spots, places he'd claim to survey his property and listen for any insubordination. Bryan crept from one to another, crisscrossing Flacker land, almost as if he were impregnable to Flacker evil, setting up markers that only a man who felt vulnerable might seek out. It was almost light by the time he crawled, his back stiff from crouching, into his cold truck, putting it into neutral and pushing, until he could hop up into the cab and coast down the narrow lane below Flacker's now-doomed land, starting the engine only once he reached the end of Charlotte Road. The engine surged as if it, too, were experiencing a new sort of elation.

He could have sworn he heard Hana Swann's laugh right beside him.

"Ah, yes, Bryan," she was saying in that bell-like voice, *"You finally do something. Be better than your father. Be like the real man."*

CARETAKING

The animal shelter where my mother worked had its own crematorium and its own executioner, a fellow my mother and her staff had nicknamed "Hannibal," who volunteered for the duty with a suspicious cheeriness. But my mother was a fan neither of the crematorium nor Hannibal. Bones were important to her. If a body, even that of a stray, went straight to ash, she reckoned, it disappeared, and almost immediately, my mother would begin to question whether the animal was really dead or if, perhaps, it had gone missing in another way. It became an extended loss, one that never quite ended. So, whenever she was personally involved in retrieving a dead animal, my mother insisted upon wrapping the body in an old blanket from the Tried and True Shop's donation box and bringing it home. She kept stacks of those blankets in her closet office, which consequently smelled like old people, as if she'd been harboring geriatric refugees. The blankets' colors had long faded into withered grays and dusty browns, into pale pinks and yellowed parchment—flesh tones—and they'd been worn so soft and thin, it's doubtful they'd ever again provide much warmth. They were mere gestures of blankets, but that was all my mother and her lost creatures needed. She'd arrive home with oozing bundles in the trunk of her car and I'd have to help her slide them onto an old blue tarp, which I'd drag past the back deck and our own dogs' camp, well beyond the vegetable plot, to a scrap of land beside my father's tool shed, where my mother had once let a cousin park a tractor he'd hoped to restore until my father had the rusted pieces hauled away. My mother would follow with a shovel, and I would dig another grave while she chose a long flat piece of amber-striped mountain shale as a marker.

The evening of Hana Swann and Keven Seven, my mother arrived with a full stinking trunk, the heat acting as an accelerant on the stench so that I had to wear one of my dad's old red handkerchiefs tied over my nose and mouth while my mother perched a respectable distance away with her latest piece of mountain shale, calling out instructions until I lifted the shovel and paused, and she quieted.

"We'll have supper soon," she said, as if the activity she'd instigated was whetting my appetite.

"Don't go looking at him either," she called back. "He's one of the ones that got torn apart."

Any groans I attempted were masked by the sound of the phone ringing in the house, and my mother took off running. My father's calls almost always arrived at suppertime, a time I was sure he'd chosen to keep the conversations short, and although my mother pretended she rushed to keep the phone from disturbing Uncle Lud, she wasn't fooling anyone. The phone traveled with her all the way to the basement, where she'd tuck herself into a corner or the tumbledown davenport like a schoolgirl before returning, sighing, upstairs.

"Your father sends his love," she said when, chore finished, I came inside.

Of course, he hadn't.

For years, my father, like Trevor Nowicki, had gone up north for work. Early on, he still had his first good job with Suncor as well as sharing with Uncle Lud the task of caring for their widowed, demented mother. Their sister, Joyce, divorced Toby (infertility, drunkenness, affairs, temper tantrums on both sides), and Joyce and her second husband, an actuary, moved to Edmonton for a finer life. But Uncle Lud had stayed on, scraping out a living on what was left of the farm after they'd sold most of their mother's legacy. He possessed, as my mother frequently mentioned, two graduate degrees. My father, who'd gone up to the mining college, couldn't see that they'd done him much good. He tried to get Lud on at the mining offices, but Uncle Lud wasn't interested. Lud had toiled for the government as a social worker and taught grade seven once, as well, and he said that was about enough bureaucratic oversight for one lifetime. Until he got sick, you'd never know what job he'd have the next time you saw him—machinery repairman, drywaller/electrician, mail carrier, bookstore clerk—but through everything he still maintained the tiny herd of dairy cows he'd inherited, and persisted upon producing a pungent white cheese (much prized by his neighbors) that he simply gave away.

My father was just the opposite. He'd found his way early in a molybdenum mine, seeing, as he liked to say, the future there, although he'd easily made the shift over to oil and gas. You couldn't even breathe the words "oil sands" around our house for fear he'd hear a smidge of criticism in an exhale. A long-standing black mark against him as far as my mother's relatives were concerned. All of them possessed epic and mostly cogent rants against the latest enterprises up north, not a one of them seeing that bitumen-rich sludge my father's way—a glorious national resource: "Only Saudi Arabia has more!" My father wore his love for his work in his wide-legged stance and raised chin, his steady prideful gaze. My parents had met in a library, tussling over a

math book both of them wanted, and although my father had lost
the book, he eventually convinced my mother first to date, then to
abandon her own studies and marry him. Unlike Trevor and Junie Nowicki, they had realized what kind of reception my mother,
half-Kitselas herself, would meet back in his small town, and the
two of them acknowledged early on that theirs would be an un-
conventional marriage in this one regard: they'd live apart. He
bought the nicest house he could afford and, for at least the first
years, drove endless hours to spend every break he had with her.

Whatever hopes my father nourished for me had thinned
long ago. Always he seemed surprised by the look of me, a throw-
back to my mother's BaBa, not a sign of her own father, another
part-white fellow, not a sign either of my father's kin save my
height and my nearsighted eyes, which like his and Uncle Lud's
were neither blue nor green nor brown but shifted between the
three, depending on the light. He was hard with me, my mother
maintained, because he worried I'd never find a real place in life,
that like Lud, I'd be swept away by stories that weren't even those
of my kin. Yet, unlike Lud, I wouldn't have an all-white skin to
shield me. My father never seemed to understand his world was
not the only one, and my mother had long since stopped trying
to inform him. Instead, she pushed me toward the Mining College and dreamed along the way that my father and I would recognize each other, that we might one day work side by side the
way he'd once hoped he and Lud would.

I once thought Uncle Lud had no taste for company work,
but the truth is he and my father had had a disagreement, an ir-
reconcilable breach. It happened about the time the late, infa-
mous Wiebo Ludwig was first put in jail for bombing company
equipment. Uncle Lud didn't know Ludwig, didn't know if he

was guilty or not, but he'd had the same problems with his few dairy cows that Wiebo Ludwig had had—miscarriages, misshapen calves, unexplained illnesses—and he sympathized with the man's frustration. My father fully believed Wiebo Ludwig a madman, and had Uncle Lud not been his most dearly beloved brother, they might even have come to blows. As is was, he bore the hurt while making his disappointment clear. But when Uncle Lud's illness became clear, my father began to sit with him again, sweet black coffee in hand, to talk about the missing world they both still knew well, a childhood world they tended, a place where neither of them could be proved wrong at this late date, where they could simply be brothers. It wasn't until Lud's illness took this last sweep downward that whatever pieces had fallen together, whatever grief and guilt my father harbored ballooned unbearably, and his visits home were canceled, one after the other.

"He'll be later than he thought," my mother said as she began chopping an onion in a neat flutter that she soon swept up with the flat edge of her knife and deposited into a spitting frying pan.

"Too much work, the crew too thin. Week after next, he promises.

"It's just hard for him is all," she said as she whirlwinded through dinner preparations. "Hard to get away, that is. And he knows we're doing all we can here."

Which, to be honest, was almost nothing at all. Uncle Lud had been clear in the beginning. He had only months and would not be a pretty sight. Bone and mash and yellow wasting, the skeleton claiming its place. Babble and drool, fetid breath—who knows, he told us, but that he might fill our house with moans and curses.

"No cures exist for this, Leo," he told me. "Don't even imagine that story."

We all thought we knew what he was asking. Never mind that my father had already fought with him about doctors and hospitals and ever-new procedures. Never mind that in the end my father simply would not allow Lud to remain alone in the farmhouse but must bring him home to us. Uncle Lud begged our pardon for such an inelegant ending. My father, it seemed, could not abide the decision. He left Lud to us.

My mother, who daily shepherded the abandoned and the doomed, the never-found missing, didn't pause. She squared her shoulders and drew up daily schedules, as if preparation would make our loss easier, a finish line we would all cross together.

In the past week or so, a change had occurred, Uncle Lud's waking moments diminishing, and the weird thing was that even as he gave way more and more to the dream world that pursued him, his voice claimed more space in my head. I could feel Uncle Lud's stories taking up residence within me, like an audience of fervent actors, ears cocked, eyes wide, chests puffed up with deep cleansing breaths, all those eager heartbeats, ready to pull in and adapt to whatever show would come next. And between them murmured Uncle Lud's unasked request: *Believe.*

That evening, after I changed my burying clothes, I leaned against the half-open doorway of the bedroom where he slept. Under the steady whir of the fan, I could hear my uncle's breath, not labored at all but low and whistling as if he were only lost in a daydream. In my head, I heard Lud's good long, deep laugh, and not for the first time I was mad at him for leaving me behind with only a pile of stories dashed into notebooks meant for scientific equations or even childish poetry.

"You think this is funny?" I whispered.

I was shocked when, without opening his eyes, Uncle Lud replied.

"Not hardly," he said.

"Bryan was here," he went on, his eyes opening. "He has a plan now?"

"Oh, yeah," I said. "Well, he's working on one at least." Unease shot through me. I didn't know, I realized, what Bryan was planning now.

"A good one?"

"He *had* a terrible one," I said.

"You can stop him, Leo," Uncle Lud said. "If he needs the interference."

"Nothing will happen," I said. "Flacker is pure evil, but Bryan doesn't have a mean bone in him."

"Oh, everybody's got . . . a mean bone . . . or two, Leo. It's a fact of life."

The name of the latest girl gone missing suddenly came to mind as if Uncle Lud had placed it there: Carla. Her name was Carla, and her photo was on a slew of new billboards. It was as if she'd vanished and reappeared in black-and-white stills. Unlike a few of the others, no body had been recovered. She'd been hitchhiking from the tiny settlement where she'd ended up, a place with not a single grocery store. No car, not much money. Even if the Greyhound stopped at her door, a forty-dollar fare to buy milk and bread? Did she have a choice? She left a three-year-old son, who, according to his grandparents, kept digging up the yard, first to look for signs of his mother, then once a kind of understanding took hold, to bury her things—a shoe here, her hairbrush there, her favorite sparkly T-shirt in the ground outside his bedroom window, where he sung his good-nights to it each evening in toddler singsong.

"You don't . . . believe . . . me yet, do you?"

I tipped my head to stare at Uncle Lud, but he kept his straight-ahead gaze, drooping eyes struggling to stay focused on the window. He was pushing back in the only way he knew how.

"Yes," he said, as if I were no longer there. "Everybody's got a mean bone. Some have a full set. Just needs someone to come along . . . and twang . . . remind 'em . . . it's there, the same way folks work . . . so hard . . . to keep the good ones in motion."

"You mean like with the Church?" I asked, thinking ruefully of my mother's Quest for Good, her contorted Catholicism.

"Sometimes, the only way . . . to beat the . . . devil is to become one . . . yourself."

"But . . . ," I began.

"Look at that light, will you, Leo?" Uncle Lud motioned toward a proud pinch of yellow glossing up a nearby ridge. "Don't you wonder . . . what it feels like up there . . . right now?"

This was the way it was with Uncle Lud since he got sick. He had always been the most considerate of companions, asking me what I thought, worrying about interrupting me, a kid. But whether as a result of his medications or a sea change burrowing within him, Uncle Lud now drifted from one conversational thread to another as if his illness had unmoored him. I was about to sneak away, let my young uncle return to dozing, when he reached out to hold me back.

"Wait a minute, Leo," he rasped, and I knew he was readying to offer the next story no matter what it cost him.

"Do you remember," he said, "do you remember . . . the door . . . in the mountain?"

Sure I did. Uncle Lud's version of a Pied Piper, the devil arriving in town in one of his many guises. Uncle Lud had personalized this tale—he'd made it true, I thought—aimed the devil right at one of our own, GF Nagle's milder younger brother, Markus.

Uncle Lud waited. Of course, of course, I leaned back with him—and began.

A MAN CAME OUT OF
A DOOR IN THE MOUNTAIN

A man came out of a door in the mountain. An ordinary door that opened and closed and could be left slightly ajar, propped open with a square black rock to allow eventual reentry.

A man came out of a door in the mountain, a flawless leafy camouflage of earthen color and sun splashes, a door so deep within the brush and swallow of forest and rock, creased and folded and bent into seemingly impassable shape that only the most practiced eye could discern the deception.

A man came out of a door in the mountain. But no matter how hard you were looking at the time, you wouldn't have seen him. A whiskered light, a torqued shadow, he set off without a moment's hesitation. His feet found (or conjured) a path that joined an old moose trail. He slipped easily, like spring melt, down the trail's crevices as if on horned feet, winding an ancient switchback, a dizzying course until he crossed first one, then another, of the oldest most neglected logging roads. He had a map in his pocket, but, truthfully, it was unreadable, having been drawn with a charcoal stick still half ablaze so that lines were smudged and instructions greatly muddled. Nonetheless, his fingers consulted the blind, warm paper in his pocket, and he did not waver as he sharply turned right and continued down the hill to the famous highway.

A man came out of a door in the mountain and journeyed downward, through the maze of trees and brush, through slurries of gravel and the timber graveyards, grayed to ash. If passersby noticed him, a single fellow paused on the wrong side, the sloping untraveled edge of the highway, they would not have had a moment's wonder at first. He was an ordinary-looking fellow of a reasonable height and slight build in unremarkable clothes. So nondescript, he simply disappeared against the landscape as if he were another scrub tree. Only later, deep in their sleep might the nagging image return: a figure on the far side of the highway, waiting. A sober man, no car in sight, no thumb outstretched, eyeing the town below as if he owned it and was on his way to collect rent.

A man came out of a door in the mountain. He might have been unkempt, sure. Smelly and a little ragged—well yes, he could have been. There was a good chance he carried visible scars along his face and neck as if the shadows of tree boughs that played across his whiskered cheeks in the forest had etched themselves to his tough skin and marked him like the others. In short, he must have looked like any one of dozens of fellows that lived in the mountain or worked the backwoods, except for his hands, which were smooth and white as if he soaked them in milk each night.

A man came out of a door in the mountain. No one would remember the exact day he appeared or the season. It might have been the cusp of winter, the light beginning to slant in weak white-gold streaks by midday. Or he may have arrived with the spring on the very day the snow shifted into faltering sun-blown rain and great ruts of mud appeared to hold them tight in an utterly different way.

It was high summer, Uncle Lud told me with certainty.

High summer, early evening, not even a glimmer of dusk, when the man crossed. The highway still so hot the tar road sucked at the soles of his shoes. He kept to the cinders as he wended his way down the steep entryway to town and once he reached the end of Fuller, rounded the corner without pausing and strolled the four blocks to The Landing as if he'd lived and worked here all his life and had, every evening, this singular routine: an hour or two at The Landing, whiskey with a beer chaser.

Not yet six o'clock, but The Landing was nearly full, it being a Friday and a payday and a scorcher at that. Fans beat in every corner and gave the illusion of a thin breeze, the *whomp-whomp* of the blades keeping time with each heartbeat so that the very air seemed to engulf each customer in familiarity. The fellow slid into the last available stool at the bar, right next to Markus Nagle, GF's younger brother, a Flacker goon-in-training. He signaled to the bartender, who was agreeable, having the vague sensation that he knew the man and held him in some regard. The fellow offered two low words to the bartender, and a beer bottle and whiskey shot glass were placed before him while beside him Markus observed.

On any ordinary night, a fight would likely have been picked, Markus offering a disparaging remark about the way the newcomer drank his whiskey or the too-familiar manner in which he appeared to be observing the pool game in which GF was clearly cheating or the way the rancid stink—like that of the old pulp mill—emanated from the stranger's unfamiliar skin. Misunderstandings would have swiftly ensued; ultimatums would have been laid; threats made and happily carried out. Markus, nursing along his buzz, reached the backwash end of his beer and his mouth twisted in readiness. The insults were burbling up when the bartender interrupted by setting a fresh beer in front of him. At Markus's quizzical look, the bartender offered a curt nod in the stranger's direction.

"He owes you, he says," the bartender said.

The fellow was occupied with a wooden bowl half-full of peanuts, cracking each shell in one fist and picking the nut out whole with two practiced fingers, and Markus nursed a moment of doubt before his thirst got the better of him and he raised the icy mug.

"We're even then," he tried.

The stranger—but he wasn't really a stranger, was he?—nodded agreeably, and Markus noted the fellow's overlapping incisors, his familiar snaggletoothed grin, and felt the slightest edge of discomfort. Yeah, sure, he knew the fellow, but he couldn't quite remember from where or how they'd left things. Had there been a fight? Well, probably. Fistfights that led to broken bottles and a boot-fucking in a parking lot. That was the way most things ended for him and GF. Who had won? Likely he had if this guy was buying.

Or maybe the fellow beside him had accompanied the two brothers on one of their road trips, the details of which always faded since those jaunts usually began and ended in a hazy oblivion. Often, he had only bruises and a few oddball acquisitions to tell him that they'd been away. The last time, he'd ended up with a black eye, a pink mitten, and a vague memory of puking his guts out beside the open door of an orange Matador while the Brit, GF's newest buddy, made disparaging remarks in that irritating lilt. This fellow hadn't opened his mouth yet, but Markus didn't think he was related to the Brit whose wiry arms were tattooed from knuckles to elbows. Nah, this fellow's hands were remarkably smooth, as if he were a doctor or a priest. Markus squinted at him but could not recall making confessions of any sort to the man beside him.

Then, again, he felt a little itch. He harbored secrets, like burrs under his skin. Secrets he worried over, scenes he replayed, including the ones in which his own brother promised to kill him if he ever opened his goddamned mouth. The stranger beside him wasn't even looking at him. He hadn't said one word, but as he shoved the peanut bowl a few inches in Markus's direction, a creaking noise began and Markus realized it was coming from him as if a shuttered window had come unhinged.

"You're . . . ?" he began and promptly stumbled. "Aren't you?"

"Yeah," the stranger answered pleasantly. "You and I, we're old friends."

Was his name Courtney? Clifford? Something like that. Markus tried a string of them, and to each the man answered. Eventually, Markus settled on Clark, half-introducing his new friend to the bartender, who shrugged.

"Sure," he said, "I knew that."

Clark was a town boy, wasn't he? Or had been. He'd been away. Most of them had been, if just for a few months. Youthful indiscretions, the Nagles' grandpa insisted to his friend the judge. Local lockup was all Markus had seen. There was that smell coming off him, faintly sulfurous, that now reminded Markus of the night he'd received a constellation of scars on his own forearm, a lit cigarette jabbing, emphasizing each demand in a deal gone bad. All those little scars, usually dull and flat, seemed to glisten a little in this particular bar light.

The evening blurred for Markus. Perhaps it was the drink. GF ducked outside with the squirrelly Brit as if they were after someone. Normally, he might have followed, gotten a stake in whatever deal was going down. But tonight he was content to sit at the bar, listening to his old friend Clark recite a tale Markus had not heard for years (he didn't think), and when his buddy rose to leave, he clambered to his feet as well. GF was not in sight. Usually, he would wait for him, sure GF would return by closing to cuff Markus on the side of the head, pour insults and beer dregs over him, and empty his pockets before pushing him out the door.

Tonight, Markus didn't feel like waiting. He rambled down the Fuller Street sidewalk as if he were being pulled along with a leisurely string into an ever-expanding universe. The air had cooled considerably, the streets in their midnight vacancy had grown wide as city avenues, and stars jammed the upended bowl of the sky. What an enormous world this night was! He felt stoned. The nighttime edges crinkled with static, but he could not remember drinking more than a few beers. Coins shone from the gutters, and Markus swooped down on them before Clark could move, waggling his head a bit in triumph as he deposited a tiny bounty in his pockets. The sidewalk seemed the cleverest invention he'd ever seen, the way it dodged the brown grass and chipped curbs and leaned ever so slightly toward the storefronts as if to encourage visitors. If any shop or office had been open, he would have tilted against the door and entered as if on cue. He wouldn't have been able to help himself. But the sidewalk even seemed to know that wasn't likely this time of night and instead led him neatly from the Landing to the curb to the corner of Crest and Fuller and the Craig Hotel.

"You staying here?" Markus asked as they paused.

"Should I?" Clark asked.

He shrugged. "The P&P's cheaper. You could crash with us, you know, but we've been crashing ourselves at a buddy's house. Your family don't got room?"

"The P&P sounds fine," Clark said. *"Dwindle, Peak, and Pine,"* he half sang, somewhat mystifyingly, as if telling himself a good joke.

A good enough answer, Markus thought.

Yet they didn't go straight to the P&P, did they? First, there was the distraction of the cat, an old tom with a piercing, insistent yowl, who continually darted in front of Markus as if trying to turn him around. Twice the damn thing nearly tripped him up, breaking the fine job of the ribbonlike sidewalk so that he stumbled into dirt and gravel. He swore at the creature, causing his friend Clark to briefly flash that snaggletoothed grin.

"Annoying, isn't he?" Clark said.

They'd crossed the street. They lingered by the summer-deserted school. Markus had despised this place and he could feel his old hatred greet him. The building's nighttime walls had borne so much of the rage he couldn't have exhibited during the days. Even in the dark, the unlit crevasses, he could see nicks and slashes, the ghosts of graffiti curses he was certain were his own. He couldn't count the number of windows he'd smashed here or the times he'd pissed on the door handles and chipped thresholds. But then he'd finally peeled free of the place, an institutional boot on his ass, and gradually it had become something less powerful, another place to slow before and spit toward out the car window, another place not to belong anymore and not to give a goddamn fuck either. Hurrah.

And yet, Markus and GF didn't fully avoid the place. They trolled here occasionally. It wasn't uncommon to come across kids hanging out in the dugout behind the baseball diamond with its sagging net, drinking vodka or Flacker moonshine, keeping time with their own private furies. Some girls there, usually. Young, but willing enough. He tried to lead Clark in that direction down behind the parking lot across the weedy playing field.

But the old tom would not leave Markus alone. It had wound around his legs even in the middle of the street and now was trying to block his way along the alley that led to the school's back parking lot. It drove him mad. It really did. Before he knew it, he clutched a broken piece of concrete in his hand, the cat pinched in the tight cradle of his other arm, and he'd shut the thing up but good.

He did not remember asking, but Clark produced a buck knife, and, without hesitating, as if he done this kind of thing every day of his life, Markus went to work, his head hot, his hands shaking with urgency. Man, was he pissed! When he was done, the knife went back to Clark, just like that. He wiped the blade on the ball-field grass and slid it away so neatly Markus couldn't say just where Clark kept it. He bent too, to swipe his own stained hands through the grass, but they remained sticky and oddly sore.

How had they landed back on Fuller, back on that sidewalk, which now seemed far less magical to Markus, more like a rope twisted around him, yanking him forward?

One of them—was it him?—proposed they take a little drive, see if anyone was around walking the streets like they were.

"I got a van," Markus said. He choked the words out as if they'd been hidden within him.

But he did have a van. He'd just remembered it. He'd found it parked off a dirt path with keys in the ignition on their last excursion. He'd gone for a piss. GF and the Brit didn't even know. He'd pocketed the keys and found his way back to it the next night, parked in exactly the same spot, no one around. He'd taken that as a sign and driven the van to the abandoned mill lot, not so long of a walk on a summer's night with an old friend who carried a bottle he shared without the slightest hint of rancor.

"You mind walking?" he asked Clark, catching his own sour breath.

"Absolutely not," his new friend replied.

But first Markus had to dart into an alley for a moment. Was it the beer or the bottle? The damn cat? A smell itched his nostrils, made him nauseous as hell. It was worse than the pulp mill, worse than the putrid reek of his new van, worse even than the constant underlying rotten-egg stench of sulfur. It was all around him, like his clothes were saturated. He pulled off his T-shirt and flung it away from him.

Clark, leaning on the opposite wall, seemed unperturbed as, bare-chested, Markus began first to retch against the cinder-block wall in front of him, then a little too dramatically to flail at the cinder bricks as if battling that adversary he'd been waiting for all night. His hand went into his pocket to find something, a soiled napkin, a scrap of paper to wipe his face, but his fingers met only rocklike fragments. The coins! Of course, the gutter coins. But as he pulled his treasure from his pocket, the brother saw he'd picked up not coins, but broken bits of teeth, one whole yellowed incisor, cracked down the middle, and two sharp sticky nails. Holding them in his bloodstained palm, he heard something snap, some part of him, followed by that distant wheezing again, his own sobs.

"Don't worry," he thought he heard his new old friend say. "You'll get used to it."

THERE IS A CRACK
IN EVERYTHING

In the kitchen, my mother dabbed pork chops with a paper towel before dredging them in flour and milk and cracker crumbs and forking them into a blistering fry pan. She'd never acknowledge the heat. Potatoes boiled, the window behind the sink steamed, sweat ringed our faces, but by God, my mother would put a real dinner on the table. She made twice the normal amount, as if we were having invisible dinner guests, and then wrapped half the supper up straightaway in tinfoil.

"You'll take that to Bryan and Ursie tomorrow, okay?" she said as she put her tinfoil bundles in the refrigerator. She clucked her tongue, and I heard a long conversation in that sound, which all at once berated Trevor Nowicki, mourned Junie, and warned me to keep clear of any trouble Bryan might be sifting through.

For a while, the kitchen churned with purpose. It was the high spark of the evening. Soon, we would eat in a kind of a hush, the little kitchen fan's beat dwarfed by the evening wind arriving through the open window, rising first with a welcome breeze barely tinged with smoke before escalating into a more malevolent, heavy rush that would whip my mother's work folders off the counter and turn the tablecloth inside out. Then we would rush around to ease the western windows down, allowing only a few inches of open screen, so that the heat did not reclaim us.

After dinner, my mother left me to clean up the kitchen while she checked on Lud. By the time I finished, the little television on his bureau would be tuned into a romantic comedy from the 1970s, the sound so low, you'd have to be one of my mother's shelter dogs to hear a thing. Uncle Lud didn't care. Alone, he slept on, not even waking when I wiped the corners of his mouth, which had gone rheumy, with one of my father's cotton handkerchiefs.

I sat with him for a few minutes longer, watching the muted romance on the television and imagining Tessa and me in that TV Land city, leaning against a skyscraper, kissing intently while crowds surged by without a second look. Maybe that's all Tessa needed, I thought: *both* privacy and witnesses for safety. If Uncle Lud had been awake, he would have seen the longing in me and wiggled his eyebrows in my direction as if patting me on the shoulder from a distance. I might have stayed with him longer, watching the old movie and dreaming up Tessa dialogue, but a rustling down the hall made me uneasy.

In my room, my mother was sitting at my desk, staring at my computer screen.

"You need a better password," she said. "I figured it out in two seconds flat."

She went on. "This is terribly slow, isn't it?"

Just then the computer dinged, and my mother glanced down to poke a finger at the screen, where a new e-mail now joined several unread others from Leila Chen, my physics instructor.

"Leo, you haven't opened these."

A new tension was rising off my mother's velour tracksuit, this one needled by my endlessly dilatory tendencies, the constant spectre of failure, which, when it came to me, she read as outright disaster. She reached up and plucked the glasses off my face.

"You want to go blind, you'll keep on like this," she said as she rubbed them clean with a tissue from her pocket. Finally, she handed them back to me and pointed to the screen.

"Aren't you going to read these?"

"It's not important, Mum. Just promotional stuff. They're selling more classes."

Wrong answer.

"Oh, yeah?" she said, her fingers inching back onto the keyboard. "Like what?"

"Nothing I need," I said.

"He's still sleeping," I said, trying to change the subject.

"You wore him out," my mother said. Her eyes finally left my screen and landed on me in a way that felt even more unnerving. "It's not good for either of you. The stories he's telling call up trouble."

"What kind of trouble?" I wanted to know. I was on Uncle Lud's team. Even so, I could not help thinking about Snow Woman and Marcus Nagle's friend Clark. I wondered if with the stories' constant retelling, Uncle Lud was summoning visitors.

My mother shook her head.

"Keep to your lessons, Leo," she said. "These stories aren't yours to keep, no matter what Lud says. It's too much.

"And promise me," she said, turning back to the screen, "that you'll check these e-mails. Tonight. See what they're offering. You never know. Maybe you could get even a little more extra credit this summer."

I thought now about my impulsive e-mail to Leila Chen and wondered if I could have already failed, cast outright from a course I'd barely begun.

"If you promise me *you* won't," I said, reaching around her to click out of the e-mail screen.

Although she still seemed loath to leave the computer and the answers it might promise, my mother slowly relinquished her grip on the mouse and stood, but not before casting one long, sharp look at the notebooks stacked far too neatly on the floor beside my bed, as if she were conducting an inventory.

For the next ten minutes as she shuttled back and forth to the living room, the kitchen, then the washroom, each time finding a way to pass my bedroom door, I pretended great interest in the blue screen before me. But it was only after her own bedroom door squeezed closed and I heard the sibilance of another television voice that I made good on my promise. As if to emphasize the trouble I was in, the sky outside my window flashed with a lightning strike that briefly sucked all the color from the room, and when I focused again it was not on the computer or the dreaded e-mail (an e-mail I would immediately need to stick in the spam file in case my mother went snooping with a new password in mind), but on Bryan's bedazzled expression as he plotted his attack on Flacker. I felt a little jolt and noticed the loose Band-Aid on my finger. My mother had finally noticed it at suppertime. My efforts with the shovel had opened up the cut, and although I didn't feel any pain, I was bleeding again. Fortunately—coupled with my father's predictable remarks over the phone about my clumsiness—the burial provided an excuse my mother not only believed but felt responsible for. I'd slapped on another Band-Aid, but in fiddling with the keyboard, that too had become loosened and once again, a thin trail of blood was running between my fingers, staining the computer's white keys as I opened the most recent of Leila Chen's e-mails.

Give up, I said to myself before I'd read a single word. *Just give up.*

Even as I contemplated how relaxing, how freeing, it would be to let the world go, my finger tracing a line of fresh blood over the keyboard, another nagging voice arrived in my head, loudly interrupting.

Oh, c'mon now. Utilize some positive energy, my father demanded. *Don't waste your energy whining, son. It's the fellows with energy, the fellows who create or corral energy who make this world turn for every single sucker, rich or poor. Don't you forget that.*

Energy. Cripes. If you'd asked me to define Energy before all this, I would have conjured images of Red Bull cans, of Norbee as a heavy-shouldered pup, leaping through the screens after an imagined cat, of Tessa's powerful, infrequent grin and its corresponding widening within me, of Uncle Lud racing ahead on a bike down Lamplight Hill. I would not have thought of coiled springs or gunpowder or equations primed and pickled by laws that only a few might ever hear of, let alone "know," like the Law of Conservation of Energy, which states, according to my course plan, *that energy can be neither destroyed nor created and that it is the same in a closed system. Energy that is absorbed into a system must always be equal to the energy released.* It made me uneasy to think about Energy the way I thought the physics course defined it, always present, a lurking swirl of potential or kinetic. One course problem after another, all rife with key words—*objects of mass, transformation of energy, initial velocity, blah, blah, blah*—flailed me because the ultimate questions of the physical world would end up being about Energy—what had it done, what could it do, *where it was.*

Dear **Leo Kreutzer** . . .

Leila Chen's e-mails always began formally. Sometimes I

imagined my distance-learning instructor meeting my mother, the two of them, side by side on the couch, engaged in trading calendars etched with schedules for me.

You see here, **Mrs. Kreutzer,** Leila Chen would say, here is where **Leo Kreutzer** must deliver **Section B,** take his midterm exam, engage in final project.

She'd likely snap open her own laptop to prove her own diligence, spooling out her steady reminders.

I've done my best, she'd say. You can see for yourself.

And my mother would nod sympathetically, unable, she would tell Leila Chen, to understand how I'd managed to overlook my instructor's many kindnesses.

Oh, so easily, I would say.

Dear **Leo Kreutzer.**

The first few e-mails I opened were, as usual, her now-familiar, terse two-line reminders:

Dear **Leo Kreutzer, Student ID# 889355,**
Week Three (Four, Five . . .) is upon us, and we have
not received the completed assignment pack. If you
have excessive problems, contact me at your earliest
convenience . . .

Excessive? Well, I was pretty sure my problems—Energy aside—weren't *excessive*, and lacking a good reply, I'd managed to leave Leila Chen's e-mails unopened for the most part. They'd been easy to push aside, up until now.

But this latest e-mail, the one that announced itself to my mother, was of considerable length, and remembering my own hasty submission earlier that day, I braced myself:

Dear **Leo Kreutzer, Student ID# 889355,**

I am to inform you that the answer you have provided for **Question 16 (Section A-4)** illustrates the obvious thought and the overall understanding of how an equation might work. However, as my scoring booklet testifies, the equivalent with which to score your answer is missing. And, too, given that this is the only answer you so attach, you must know the score—even if said answer were to be considered perfection—would not rise above the necessary passing grade for the **Section A-4.** And more, questions unanswered for **Sections A-1, A-2,** and **A-3** remain.

At my advisor's suggestion, I "double-checked" your enrollment status. I see you listed as an "independent, non-matriculated, non-degree-seeking student." Perhaps, Professor Blankenship suggests, said designation confused you into believing requirements are less stringent to you than other participants. My job is to tell you now, **Leo Kreutzer,** that is not the case. To receive the grade and the possible "transferable credit," your efforts must stretch wider. My advisor, Professor Gordon Blankenship, PhD, has suggest I work more closely with you, perhaps on a problem-by-problem basis, at least until you are "out of the woods." He believes, you see, that you are in the woods. I do doubt that. (I think you are outside said woods, perhaps in the distant meadow, observing from the great distance both the woods that draw you and road that leads to your future.) He also believes this would be a good practice for me in dealing with a certain kind of student. Again, you should know that I do not think you are "a certain kind of student." Perhaps you are, as Professor Blankenship also hinted, lazy or delayed, the product of the "less-than-rigorous Northern school system," or, worse, perhaps you are playing games with me. Perhaps you, a snooper, have learned something of my own personal history. I should inform you, if that is the case, that while your intentions may be honorable, said attention is not appreciated.

But, perhaps, after all, none of the above is accurate. You may merely—*merely* emphasized—be attempting to take the leap ahead. I do not have access to all your academic records, but assume you did study the math and science courses previous. If so, you must know that advancement relies upon step-by-step execution of even most familiar problem sets. Professor Blankenship recommends ("heartily," he says) that you return to **Section A-1** and begin once more.

Our department and positions such as my own rely, of course, on full enrollments and student successes. Still, I must confess (and I will trust your better nature here and believe you will keep the comment confidential), I must confess that I do not believe you should either begin again or proceed. Instead, **Leo Kreutzer,** my advice is you must take another course, another route, that is. Physics is clearly not, as one of my other professors said, the "bailiwick" for you. I myself formerly studied poetry as you may know (it seems you *do* know) and completed a full year in therapy (yes, surely you've discovered this) in preparation for another program in psychology and social work before discovering the gift for the sciences. (I did not mention, you'll notice, my months in the Religious Studies Department. That bears no relevance to said discussion, regardless of what your research might have told you.) No shame results, regardless what the family and society infer, to change gears, to take chances, to invoke the probability in your own life and leap into lesser-known abyss. I tell you, **Leo Kreutzer,** young love may be your motivation for the equation submitted, or revenge or despair or mischievous recklessness, but despite all potentials, your cause will not be served by the wrong path.

Should you choose to persist despite this best advice, the suggestion is made for you to begin again, in the straight path as Professor Blankenship denotes. As per, I will then put aside any grade and too begin anew.

We—Professor Blankenship and I—await your decision. Time, you must realize, may be a relative construct, but in this case, it is also a crucial aspect of your equation for success.

Most sincere,
Leila Chen

Ring the bells that still can ring
Forget your perfect offering
There is a crack, a crack in everything
That's how the light gets in.
—*L. Cohen*

Forget your perfect offering. Yeah, yeah. Okay, Professor Chen. But tell me how I'd break the news to my mother. *That's how the light gets in.* Would I ever have the courage of Leonard Cohen, to explain to my heartbroken mother that my physics course was, in fact, an impediment to my light-filled, imperfect future?

Forget your perfect offering.

Hey, hey, I wanted to call out, did you hear that?

Forget your perfect offering.

What a concept. Tomorrow, I could leave Uncle Lud to my mother's cousin Trudy and her morning blender and run down Lamplight Hill straight into town to Tessa's door and wait for her, couldn't I? We'd walk to the corner of Fuller, and along the way, I'd say everything, imperfectly, my hands barricaded in my pockets, and when we reached Bryan's truck, Ursie would be with him, but instead of joining them up front, she and Ursie tilting their heads together, Tessa would climb in the truck bed with me. We'd let Jackie and Ursie do all the shooting tomorrow, well away from Hana Swann and the motel, and Tessa would stay beside me as I persuaded Bryan that Flacker could not be beat, as I mapped out a full strategy for avoiding Flacker and the Nagles the rest of our days. And afterward in the bouncing truck, Tessa's hand would claim mine. I'd stretch my arms around her and hold her tight to me, the distance between us finally breeched.

LAUNDRY DAY FOR THE DEVIL

There was once a woman who had twelve daughters. The girls ranged in age from six to thirty-six, and of course, they weren't related by blood; that wasn't the way they counted sisters in this family. Only one of the middle sisters, a girl of seventeen, could look forward and backward and relate her family's history with any clarity. Her mother had given birth to three girls and then had taken in her crazy cousin's two daughters and a pregnant girl who'd been at school with the eldest. More girls were born. Years later, the girl who'd been the baby of that daughter's school friend came to live with the family too, and a few more girl cousins moved in for a while. The middle girl herself went once to live with a relative and claimed a couple more sisters that way.

Oh, yeah, try and keep track.

Over the years, the sisters multiplied and divided. They reconfigured themselves into new extended families, then looped back into this one, often holding the hand of yet another sister. Through tragedies and joys, they kept track of one another, and even the thieves among them were never denied a home to steal from. One sister died in a truck accident. Another drank herself to death. One hitched to Idaho and married a fellow who started a church. That was a birth sister; Saint Audrey, they called her. Of the others, one was in jail, but it wasn't her fault at all. A debt she'd claimed for another had led her there. One sister was a nurse, the kind who came out to your house and gave examinations. A success was the near-eldest, a pretty, heavy-browed artist who taught at a university but had no luck with men. A family of tough, big-hearted women who looked out for one another. All of 'em loved one another fiercely. No matter where they traveled or who they almost killed or married, enough of them returned or stayed to keep the house, full and crazy and close—real close.

Throughout it all, the mother cared for them. Across the wide backyard, she strung a clothesline long enough to hang twelve dresses. Twelve empty dresses hanging limply or flapping madly. Twelve skirts tucked tight or flitting inside out. Each laundry day, the woman pinned up the clothes and gathered them hours later, smelling of hay and the thin piney northern sun. The filled basket at her feet might have been heavy with gold, the woman prized it so much. No one else could touch it. But one day, Uncle Lud says, the woman went to the line with her empty basket to find a man in a suit, leaning against the far pole.

"Can I help you, mister?" the woman called out, clutching her empty basket. "Are you lost?"

"I may be, ma'am," he said, bowing his head to light a cigarette. "I surely may be."

Warily, keeping distance between them, the woman pointed and waved and tried every which way to send the fellow toward town, short of striding toward him and pushing him. And he did soon leave her. But first he must help, he declared, as thanks for setting him on the clear path. With almost physical pain, the woman watched the fellow unpin the dresses on the far side. He moved so quickly, her outstretched hand couldn't touch a one, and soon he was right beside her, dresses looped over one arm. He laid them across her basket, and when she bowed her head to bundle them inside the basket, the fellow loped away, past the kitchen garden, out of sight around a corner of the house. She did not hear a car engine start up, and she hurried indoors where daughters were cooking, daughters were gabbing, daughters were fussing on outfits to go to town. For the first time in memory, she latched the door behind her. Only then did the mother untangle her laundry, dress by dress, to find each bearing a tiny stain, a constellation of cigarette burns, or an irreparable tear. One dress was missing altogether, a sister's stolen dress, a stolen sister's dress.

COLLATERAL DAMAGE

Yes, an ordinary summer's night, a Tuesday like any other. A dry tempest, the mountains glowing beneath a bruised, turbid sky, an occasional truck screaming up Fuller Road onto the highway, the distant sound of bottles hitting pavement, and echoing outward, the too-familiar siren of monotonous, perfunctory screams, rising complaints joining the chorus:

Somebody shut that kid the hell up!

Even Tessa—quiet, superstitious Tessa—wouldn't escape the devils' wanderings this time. For her, the night began when her eight-year-old nephew, Brice, fell into one of his fits. Tessa says the kid's got a real medical condition caused by her own sister, who spent most of that pregnancy so drunk that she didn't even notice her labor pains until her feet were knocked out from under her and she lay flat against a wall in a growing puddle as if tossed there by one of her boyfriends, which in a way she had been. Brice was born within minutes and really has never stopped hollering, reminding everyone that he's a wronged child. He's a big kid for his age, almost aggressively affectionate when he's not crashing down the walls, and Tessa wears bruises as much from his attempts to have her hug and cuddle him as from his rampages.

That night, he took issue with Tessa when she tried to get him to bed and aimed a steel-tipped boot that nailed her face hard, missing her eye but opening her left cheek so that she had

142

to wake up the grandfather to keep a still-roaring Brice from kill-
ing the other kids, and then call her sister at the bar where she
worked for a ride up to the clinic. Her sister groused but showed
up fifteen minutes later, shaking her head as Tessa, her head
spinning, crawled into the tattered backseat and her sister
gunned and swerved toward the Health Centre.

"First, your 'accident' with the teakettle," her sister said,
grimacing at the bandage that covered Tessa's blistered palm.
"Now this. You'd think you wanted to be hurt."

Earlier that afternoon, Jackie's mother had come to visit Tessa. It
had been almost a week since the family had had word from
Jackie up at the camp. Jackie's mother knew something was
wrong almost the moment Hana Swann arrived at the camp, as if
she'd actually witnessed that bone-white girl materializing at the
dining hall's battered screen door. Folding laundry, an old plaid
shirt Jackie liked to wear, Jackie's mother could not get the sleeves
to lie flat. Twice she bent and folded and smoothed, and twice the
folds undid themselves, slowly unwinding as if the arms were
opening themselves to her, beseeching.

She had an emergency number for the camp and fretted
through one whole day as she waited for another sign. When
none immediately occurred, Jackie's mother tried to quell the
nagging images that appeared like Technicolor plates on her bedroom wall. More than once, she rose from her sleepless bed and
banged a flat hand on that wall, which seemed to be conjuring up
fears all on its own. The hours of utter darkness were brief, but
Jackie's mother never slept right until the sun rose again and the
wall lost any opportunity to display the worst. She knew Jackie
slagged off for breaks with Tessa and the others, and the after-

noon after Hana Swann's appearance at the refuse station, Jackie's mother decided to walk up to Tessa's grandfather's house.

Although it was after noon when Jackie's mother knocked on the door, Tessa had only just returned from shooting with us at the refuse station and, still quietly reeling from the visit with Hana Swann, she was struggling to help her two nieces change out of their damp pajamas and into T-shirts and shorts. Soppy bowls of cereal covered the kitchen table except for the corner where Tessa's bleary-eyed older sister was shakily applying a deep lavender nail polish while also obsessively eyeing a pink plastic toy beside the nail polish bottle. She barely managed to leave off both tasks to greet Jackie's mother and shout for Tessa.

A grubby pair of boys' underpants lay on the empty chair beside the door. Jackie's mother pushed them aside and sat down to wait for her daughter's friend, feeling the wisps of her own confusion gather into clouds the more time she spent in this disorderly household. She could hear Tessa consoling a weeping child, then commanding the lot of them to play outside. Jackie's mother barely had time to raise her knees and shift to one side as they clambered past her to get to the door, one boy knocking down an empty chair as he bullied past and not one of them walking a straight line, either because they'd just been shoved from the side or because—and Jackie's mother feared this was more likely—balance was not a family trait.

She stood and hugged Tessa when the girl entered, despite the bundle of dirty clothes the girl held. As Jackie's mom released her, Tessa snatched up the underpants and rolled them quickly into her tight bundle, which she deposited in a basket by the back door.

"Please," she said, even as she began to stack cereal bowls

with one hand and swipe at the oilcloth on the table with a dish-rag, "please, sit down."

Her sister, who'd yet to manage a civil greeting, seemed to take Tessa's cleaning as an affront.

"You wouldn't have to do this now if you'd stick around during the morning," she began, "instead of leaving me alone with . . ."

The pink toy beside her buzzed, and she left off her complaining and snatched it up, forgetting about her wet nails.

"Shit," she said as she surveyed her damaged polish. Then, "Hey. Hey? Hello? Anybody there?

"Piece of crap phone," she said, shaking it. "Only gets reception in the washroom," she explained as she fled the room.

"No, no." Jackie's mother shook her head as Tessa put the kettle on to boil anyway.

"You want something else?" Tessa asked. "A Diet Coke?"

From the back bedroom came a resonant thump, and Jackie's mother knew whose Diet Coke she'd be taking.

"No, honey. I've got a question, that's all. You seen Jackie lately?"

"Well, yeah," Tessa said. The table was cleared now except for her sister's bottles and a handful of strewn cotton balls. And somehow, too, Jackie's mother noted, Tessa had managed to fill the sink with soapy water and stash away the Sub-Rite brand cereal and the nearly empty jug of milk—milk, Jackie's mother guessed, that had originally arrived powdered in a paper sack and been reconstituted with too much water; the stuff was so thin, it looked blue in the jug.

"She was at the refuse station with us this morning."

"She okay?"

"Sure," Tessa said. "Yeah, she looked good. Tired, you know, but good."

The girl cracked open an ice tray and filled a clean glass with ice and water and gently presented it to Jackie's mother, who sipped at it while she waited to hear what was behind the clouded look Tessa was wearing. Maybe, Jackie's mother thought, it's nothing. Maybe now I'm worrying her.

"She hasn't talked to any of us for a week or so, that's all," she said, hoping to relieve Tessa's worry. But the girl's face remained burdened. Finally, she offered Jackie's mom a single telling fact.

"Well, she's got . . . she's got . . . a new friend."

Jackie's mother felt the kick of that swift revelation. A boyfriend. A fellow up at the camp. Sure, that would make sense. It was about time some fellow tamed Jackie.

"A good guy?" she asked Tessa. "You meet him?"

"Ah, no," Tessa hurried to explain, "not a boyfriend. Another girl cooking up there. Good company, I guess. Like a sister."

Old fool, Jackie's mother chastised herself. Bumblehead, Worry Queen. You'd think a woman with a dozen daughters would know when to worry and when to disregard the vagaries of laundry magic. Jackie was their own good girl; of course, she was in no real trouble. Jackie's heart was a tender one, that was all. And when she fell hard for a new friend, she was consumed by that new passion and the world fell away.

The older woman downed the glass of ice water Tessa has set in front of her and snatched Tessa close for another quick hug as she left. That girl needed hugs. Surely, it was the weight of this household the girl was bearing, not any bad news about Jackie. Jackie's mother noticed Tessa's new curvy figure and the worry lines starting on her forehead and wondered when this little girl had become such a woman. A hard-pressed woman without even a man to blame. Just that blasted sister. As Jackie's mother closed the door behind her, she heard the pink phone squeal again and the kettle whistling, but she did not hear Tessa's agonized gasp as, an image of Hana Swann swimming before her, the girl inadvertently poured the thinnest stream of boiling water into her own palm.

Mere hours had passed, and now Tessa was hurt again.

"I've told you," her sister said. "Just smack him when he gets bad. Smack him and drag him out to the shed. Get that old padlock out. You remember how they did it."

Tessa didn't have the energy to argue with her sister, nor much chance. Her sister dropped her at the Health Centre's emergency entrance but no way would she stay with her.

"I'd like to, but people are waiting, you know?"

Her sister didn't even get out of the car. She lit a new cigarette as Tessa fumbled her way, barely managing to close the car door behind her.

"That's okay," her sister shouted as she leaned over to slam the door properly, and Tessa staggered up the ramp and into the clinic to take her place beside the steadily growing clientele of the maimed and bruised, the punctured young men emerging from the bad end of bar fights. A lethargic woman at the desk passed her a slim pad of gauze loosely packed with another thin wad of some kind of frozen gel and an actual piece of ice, and she pressed it over her swelling cheek and waited and waited and waited.

Across the room, Markus Nagle, a bone jutting out of his own arm, dozed fitfully, slumped in one chair, his long legs stretched across the aisle. He was stoned. He was drunk. Still stoned, still drunk. As far as he knew, he'd been wrecked for the previous five days, had worked hard to get in that state, and would have liked to remain that way, but the night had nattered on too long, his wallet had unaccountably slimmed, then fattened, he'd almost certainly indulged in a goddamn fight he barely remembered, and now he was feeling the corners of his drunkenness slip away against the waiting room's bright, flat lights. He could feel the fall into sobriety rushing toward him, and it pissed him off so that even as he managed a few unconscious moments, he grumbled, and when his eyes did open, they were full of disdain. He hated this waiting room, which he knew too well, which was always, depending upon his own condition, chill-inducing or hot as hell, which was designed for another level of torture as if to illustrate for you, you stupid dick, that due to your complete lack of judgment, your unfailing bad luck, not only had you incurred a peculiar, searing pain—an injury that promised the loss of work and yet more public humiliation—you had also somehow invited the hospital staff to join in and ramp that experience up just a little bit.

Welcome, the place seemed to say, *let's screw with you a little more.*

The chairs, uncomfortably hard, were interconnected by long metal bars behind the seat backs so that you couldn't move them around and, say, get an extra foot away from some weeping monstrosity whose head you might have plowed in a mere half hour earlier. They crammed you in here, and although the Health Centre itself wasn't that big, the waiting room had been positioned so that you couldn't see into the reception station, so unless an aide dashed by to park another gurney in the queue or to motion someone out of the room, you had nothing to gauge your own progress. The magazines were crappy too—ripped and stained *Celebrity Digest*s (with mustaches and swear words and well-endowed body parts scribbled over the pretty people) and pristine *Golf World*s. Who the fuck looked at *Golf World* around here? The place stunk of bleach, which from Markus's experience was a surefire sign of cover-up. One nurse stalked up and down the corridor outside the waiting room, seemingly doing little more than reading a clipboard. Markus despised her and probably told her so every time she clattered past the door in her white clogs.

But of all the Health Centre's nasty tricks, the long, wobbling strips of fluorescent lights enraged Markus the most. He had once been escorted directly from the examining room to the holding center for shooting out the entire row above him, sending glass and sparks hailing over the room. He was shaking bits of glass from his hair for hours, his scalp stinging continually, but he'd been too satisfied to care. He liked to imagine that grand flash of blue light bursting out of the waiting room and engulfing the reception desk and the fat white girl planted there. And for weeks he'd felt a singular sense of heroism as if he'd saved other vanquished souls from that at least. He was pissed to realize they'd replaced the light fixtures since the last time he'd been in here, making not a single improvement in the process. Now one long bulb spasmed above, making him downright nauseous. He was tempted to start anew, but he couldn't raise his arm. And so it was with particular pleasure that he watched Tessa set down the ice pack she'd been pressing against her cheek to pivot onto the highest edges of her paralyzed chair and use the corner of her bloodied shirt sleeve to unscrew the hot lightbulb and give them all ease. He would have applauded if he could have; his relief at the absence of that pulsing light was so great.

After that, he could not take his eyes off the corner where Tessa slumped, her head tilted into the hand holding the gel pack, her eyes closed, the dead gray fluorescent tube beside her. She seemed to Markus a kind of heroine in disguise, and he marveled again at how, slight as she was, she scrambled up onto the chair arm in her little red sneakers and balanced so neatly. The sight of her relieved a pressure in his heart he hadn't realized he felt before. She cleared his vision.

With the gallantry so common among the continuously drunk, he resolved to do his own good deed before every last bit of his edge vanished and he felt too crappy to care about anyone but himself.

"Hey," he bellowed. "Hey, you there. Hey, Nurse!"

In his experience, nonstop caterwauling always got attention, and he wasn't wrong here. When the clinic nurse finally rushed to shush him, her breath caught at the newly dimmed room and even in those shadows, she recognized Markus.

"You," she said, shaking her head, but he would not shut up.

"We need help here," he hollered, resisting an impulse to punch the chair the nurse stood beside.

Across the room, a woman began to wail and another bar-fight survivor held his head in his hands and cursed them all. *Shut, shut, shut the hell up.*

The nurse could see the direction in which Markus was propelling the room, and she knew the two big aides she could count on to break up any brawls were out in the aid car, so she sighed and went to help Markus to his feet. To her shock, he pushed her away, pointing instead to little Tessa, now curled into the well of her chair, her hair wet and matted on one side from the melting ice that had been slipped into the gel pack. One foot, the unlaced sneaker half off, hung over the chair's edge, and Markus saw now that someone had written all over her sneakers with a broad black pen. Somehow, this made him even more insistent, even though Tessa hadn't even raised her head to acknowledge this latest brouhaha.

"*Her,*" Markus commanded. "*Now.*"

"But your arm," the nurse began, gesturing toward the visible bone, which she hadn't given a rat's ass about before.

"*Her,*" Markus repeated.

The clinic nurse could barely get Tessa to her feet. Together, they staggered toward an examination room. Her stunt on the chair had fully depleted Tessa, and she struggled to stay upright. Her head drooped as she was maneuvered from the room, so that she never noticed Markus's satisfied grin. He might have been a little disappointed at her lack of reaction, but he didn't show it. Instead, he crowed to the rest of the waiting room—all those busted, stoned, dead faces—crowed in the last full glory of his ebbing drunkenness. And later, as he crawled into his own examination room, right before the doctor pressed on the bone and he passed out, he caught a glimpse of Tessa, her face a bruised mash, and heard the aide beside her, say, "That one. That was the fellow." And later yet, when Markus, with his arm set in its new cast and a decent handful of painkillers in his pocket, pushed himself back down the corridor and into the cool relief of dawn, he thought he might be dreaming when she slipped off the concrete wall where she must have been waiting for him.

"You need a ride?" his muddled tongue managed.

"My sister's coming," she said, taking a few steps away from him.

"I don't see her," he said.

The van he'd found had gone away. He remembered vaguely

handing over the keys. Not to his brother. Another fellow. A friend, he guessed. His brother wasn't waiting, of course, but that was no problem.

"Car's right here," he said to Tessa.

In fact, the lot was half-full. In the old days, they would have had their pick. He succeeded in nodding once toward the backlit parking lot before something broke adrift inside his head.

"How can you drive with a broken arm?" she asked.

Practice, he thought, a whole lot of practice. The words chugged, but never emerged. His eyes would barely open, and his left hand scrambled weakly in his pocket. His fingers briefly met and caressed a wad of bills (money he'd sworn to his brother he had hidden away) before they found the slim metal rod, his near-favorite and most handy tool.

From her perch by the hospital entrance, Tessa swiveled in place to follow his struggle as he crossed the lot and paused finally beside what must have been the oldest car there, an ancient Toyota parked directly under the sole light.

A slow wave was surging through him. No, one wave after another. Not pain, not the pleasant discomfort of drunkenness either. Some other unknown elemental disturbance that had been dispensed with the pain med. As a very young boy, Markus had spent a summer's week on a fishing boat and he'd never forgotten the glimpse he'd had of a sailing yacht, cruising at high speed past the battered and stalled gillnetter his father pretended was their vacation. Now, a couple of quick moves, the ignition bypassed, and the car was running. Markus felt elated, redeemed, as if a separate being, one as beautiful as that glorious sloop, was sailing through his veins, ghosting on an orphaned wind all of his making. A disconnection. He felt himself slipping and soaring.

"You can't drive."

The girl's words tippled beside him. How had they got to the ground? Bits of gravel clung to his palms.

"Just wait, okay? My sister . . ."

"Your sister's not coming, baby. My brother's not coming. Nobody comes for us, do they, baby?"

Did he say all that? He didn't know. He didn't know.

He danced with her, through air, through a tepid surge of water, through the open passenger door of his newly purloined Toyota. She eased his legs inside, set him right or nearly so. She tucked the wad of bills he hadn't known he'd dropped back into his pocket. He leaned his head back against the car seat and began to cry. A slurping, huffing bout that, even drunk, should have humiliated Markus, but instead comforted him. What a weeper he was, what a grand and wonderful weeper. A tentative hand reached around his shoulder, and he leaned into Tessa, feeling the rough edge of her own bandage press against his tears. He was shivering, too, in a bad way, coming down from the drink and the pain meds beginning to show their own evil edges.

"Where," Tessa said, "where do you want to go?"

Markus suddenly remembered a white strip of sidewalk, another night with another companion, and before he quite realized it, he'd become a ventriloquist.

"The Peak and Pine," he said, his stolen voice tinny and assured, "sounds just fine."

Somehow Markus managed to crack the window, and air whistled beside his raised, pursed lips as if the night itself was astonished to see the pair of them traveling together, that soul-damaged man and the battered girl who could not leave even a hoodlum in distress.

Tessa did not own a car and drove her sister's wreck only when she had to on those nights she was able to spirit away the keys to avert sure disaster. At her best, she was uncertain behind the wheel, endlessly second-guessing distance and speed. And should she ever have to drive, she knew enough to equip herself with a pocketful of good-luck charms: an old (heads-up) penny she'd found unscathed on the railroad tracks, a sprig of dried forget-me-not, a silver fish Leo had won in a grade-six bazaar and tucked into her hand before running away as if he were being chased by the staggering frenzy of his own pent-up, pigeon-toed desires. She had none of those talismans with her in the clinic parking lot, but she had no choice. The car's engine was running. Markus was moaning. And although Tessa had hardened her heart in a way Ursie, for instance, would never achieve, she knew she couldn't leave Markus like that. The nurse had dressed the burn on her hand as well as tending to her face, gliding a numbing gel over the growing blisters before taping a fresh piece of gauze over her palm. She could barely bend her hand around the steering wheel. Her legs trembled, and her foot jumped on the pedals so that the car's progress was jerky and belabored. As lightning sliced across the hills above town and the brief shock of illumination seemed to crumple and compress the landscape, poor Tessa's heart leapt as painfully as if she'd achieved the crash she feared. She drove even more slowly then, as slowly as she dared, the lightning punctuating every turn, bursts of blue light that engulfed the wretched car as if determined to expose—and demolish as well. When they reached the P&P, she braked right in front of the office door, leaving Markus snoring openmouthed while she went inside alone.

Albie Porchier's night clerk, Vincent, was also asleep, and

Tessa had to go around the empty front desk into the back room where Vincent dozed on a cot, his hands folded across his chest like a corpse. His habit was to stay up a full hour past the last bar's closing time, waiting for potential stragglers before setting his alarm to allow him a few hours' rest. He'd been awakened in the past by such niceties as a beer poured on his face, a jab in the gut, even the blunt side of a knife once edging across his temple. (That last was Albie himself proving some damn point.) Most of the night's receipts were stuffed in a locked drawer under the front desk. He had another thin envelope of actual cash wedged under his ass. He liked to think he'd trained himself to jump to his feet at the slightest tickle in the air. But Tessa shook him again and again, recoiling each time to wipe her good palm on her still shaky legs, and when she finally did rouse him, he gasped and cowered against the back wall. Tessa did look a mess, her little face half-engulfed in bandaging, her wrapped hand raised like a spectral mallet, but she ignored him. She wanted to finish up here.

"Fellow outside," she told Vincent in the tough-girl voice she'd learned from Jackie, "needs a room and some help in. I've got to go."

Vincent was suspicious. "What fellow?" he said.

Tessa backed out of the door, and Vincent tentatively followed her into the tiny reception area.

"Right there." She pointed. "In the car there, right in front of the door."

"You paying?"

"He is. He'll pay you. I saw his money."

"Not you."

"And you'll have to help him too. He just got back from the doctor. He's got a broken arm, I guess."

Vincent was coming round now. He recognized Tessa from the high school. "You could have at least parked the car."

"There's no key," she said. "He didn't have a key. I can't turn it off."

Then Vincent understood.

"Shit," he said, peering out the glass door toward the slumped figure. "That's Markus Nagle, isn't it?"

"Wait," Tessa said, seeing his face closing. She ran back to the car and slipped her good hand in Markus's pocket, removing the bills wrapped in a rubber band. She clumsily peeled off three and tried to stick the rest of the money back in his pocket, but Markus rolled and moaned and the bundle would not stick to him, so for the moment, she shoved the roll of bills into the front pocket of her own jeans.

"Here," she said, thrusting the three loose bills toward Vincent, who was watching her every move as if reluctant to believe in the money. It was more than the nightly rate. He knew that. She must know too. But Tessa didn't say a word when Vincent simply took the cash and put two bills into the locked drawer and the last into his own private envelope.

He grabbed a door card from a boxed stack and swiped it through a machine two or three times, swearing until a beep sounded, then he swept out the door in front of Tessa, slid into the driver's seat, and drove the car to the lot's back edge.

Once Tessa heard the engine stall and die, she began walking. The P&P was on the far edge of Fuller Street. Not too long a walk home. Fifteen minutes, if she walked fast. And she would. The dry lightning that had chased her from the Health Centre had moved onward far back into the hills, and the street ahead was glazed with darkness that seemed almost fluid. Security lights offered shafts of illumination she'd sooner avoid as she navigated the blocks home. Any other time, she would have run the whole distance, lithe, unstoppable, but whatever they'd given her at the Health Centre had numbed her limbs and left her with a racing heart, and she wasn't sure how far she'd get. One side of her face throbbed uncontrollably. If she could just lie down. She wiggled her hand into her pockets, disconcerted by a wad of paper. The center receptionist had thrust a handful of tissues at her as if she'd been suffering from a runny nose. If she had the fish, she thought. Just Leo's silver fish. She wouldn't, couldn't, think about it; she'd just go. She squared her shoulders, shivering a little now in the near-dawn air, and had nearly made it past the P&P's parking lot, that line of stunted pines, when she realized both her shoes were untied.

She shouldn't be cold—at home, they'd all be flinging the sheets off them and peeling off their thin nightclothes to find relief from the heat—but she could not stop shivering. The laces would not come together in her hands and she'd just managed to grasp them for a third failed try when she glimpsed a movement ahead of her and to the right.

For one absurd moment she thought it might be the help she'd been hoping for.

"Leo?" she whispered, straightening and peering into the dark.

She saw him then. A figure only a few feet away, standing clear of the parking-lot lights within scrawny pine seedlings Albie Porchier called landscaping. A slim form with a tiny coal in his hand, a cigarette, she guessed, that he was pointing in her direction. Her vision was messed up—the sidewalk ahead had a wave to it—and her heart continued to bump and grind as if out of control.

"How tired you look," a man's voice said, clear as could be. His lips might have been right beside her ear. Leaves rustled. A shoe tapped.

Tessa caught a glimpse of a shiny swath of hair—metal-colored in the black-and-white coloring of night—a granite face of lines and angles that she believed she recognized but could not place. It might have been a trick combination of his cigarette and the motel sign's light, which could only reach so far and began petering out here in streaky lines, but she could have sworn a halo of smoke surrounded and obscured the figure. She *smelled* smoke. Beyond the outline of his form, town faded away into pitch. This had the unsettling effect of seeming as if nothing existed beyond him. The wound on her cheek began again to tremble as if calling out. She pressed a palm against her bandage to shush it and sang out with the sudden pain. The face before her reacted as if he too had been stuck with that quick stab, that electric jolt, but then he smiled as if that pang translated as pleasure.

Behind them, Vincent had managed to extricate Markus, whose now-familiar moan rent the night air behind Tessa. A kind of inquisitive bellowing followed as Vincent cursed and tried to hush Markus. The sound might just as well have come from her; she felt it strike deep in her belly. And even as the figure before her advanced with eerie certainty, she fled. She ran straight back to the P&P, feeling a damp breath on her neck, the man's smoke pinching her lungs. She flew so fast, she ran right out of one shoe, leaving it among the wood-chip mulch that bordered the motel's walkway. She arrived at the door Vincent was opening, oh, brilliant embrace of light, the blinding fluorescence, just in time to ease under Markus's good arm and stagger with him into what, at that moment, surely must have felt like safety.

"Yeah," Markus crooned, "oh yeah, baby."

His eyes would not fully open, but a dumb smile crept onto his face and stayed there even as he drifted away again.

Vincent dumped Markus on the bed, ignoring his new cast—hadn't they all seen worse. That was as far as he planned to go, it was clear.

"Keep him quiet, will you?" he told Tessa.

"He'll have to be out of here by eleven tomorrow, unless one of youse pays for another night," Vincent told her, as if she were in charge.

Oh, sure, Tessa thought. Once Vincent scuttled away, she locked the door and put the chain up and, after a moment, also pushed the single unbolted chair against it. Vincent's remark had reminded her of the money in her pocket—not tissues, stupid!—and she tried to squirm it back into Markus's pocket but he'd rolled onto his good side by then, and his broken arm covered the other pocket. She thought about sticking it under his pillow or setting it on the nightstand, but what if he didn't see it there? She pushed the money back into her own pocket for the time being.

Oh, to go home. She wanted desperately to go home. She tried the phone, imagining she could call her feckless sister, but the line was dead, and she couldn't—she couldn't—face the man outside again. A charge was still racing through her, but the screaming pain in her cheek was much diminished. The room swooned thick and sour with the day's heat, but she didn't dare crack a window, imagining a familiar wrinkled hand, grayed to ash, suddenly clutching the sill from the outside. A fan switch on the wall produced no result.

She held her ear against the door, and in the brief, heartrending interlude before Markus began to snore, she heard footsteps—

oh, the lightest, most assured of taps—passing in the open corridor. Markus was already insensible to the world. He wasn't going to hurt her tonight. Gazing at his tousled hair, the white gleam of his pale face, that openmouthed, uncluttered expression, she felt oddly sure of that. First sign of dawn, she'd get out of there. For now, all she could do was wait. She flicked off every light and curled up as best as she could in the room's only chair, the vinyl bucket with a long, curved crack in its back she'd managed painfully to drag against the door. She was determined to wait out the hours to sunrise, but was so exhausted she soon fell into a deep hole of a dream, one that might have carried her well past midday if, sometime around eight that next morning, a heavy banging had not begun on the door—a violent, boot-kicking frenzy that not only yanked her by the back of her neck from the nightmare ravine she'd fallen into but also sent her flying, a rag-doll weight, from the slick vinyl chair against the bed with such force, she continued banging first against the night table, then the wall beyond, until she came to rest (if one could call that broken pose "rest") directly beneath the stained bedspread that Markus in his restless sleep had thrown to the floor. The entire action occupied mere seconds. Whoever engineered the broken door, the soaring chair, apparently missed Tessa's own flight. Neither did anyone notice her landing. Momentarily, the fall crushed Tessa. Even so, she had the presence of mind to reach out two fingers and snag the bottom edge of the bedspread and draw it closer as she swiftly rolled beneath the bed that was the only defense between her and whatever new rage had catapulted her to this spot.

"Hey, asshole," a male voice boomed as the bedsprings above her bounced inches away from her stiff, sore face. "Wake up. Where's the fucking money?"

THE NEXT BAD PLAN

Half eight in the morning and Norbec and his pals were howling like banshees. In the kitchen, my mother's cousin Trudy was shoving raw eggs and brewer's yeast and, with tongs, the bristled ends of nettles into a blender as my mother hustled down the hallway to stand at the end of my bed and shake one of my toes hard until I jolted awake in pain.

"Leo," she said. "Get up. Go stop that racket."

No use to complain, to point out whose dogs they were. No, my mother had no use for any arguments I'd give. My mother wanted me up. She and Trudy had the blender tonics to fix and, with any luck, to get down Uncle Lud before she'd go to work. And more: she had to bathe Uncle Lud with downy cloths dipped in warmed-up holy water; make up the bed beneath him with fresh sheets dried with seven dryer sheets then hung out on the line just long enough to get wind-blown and sun-soaked, sweet-smelling and soft enough, she reckoned, not to chafe his newly delicate skin; and, last of all, murmur her secret, incantatory, and customized Catholic prayers into the open nest of his two hands. She had no time to waste on any nonsense arriving from my direction. So she monitored the hallway, her crossed-arm pose hustling me from bed to washroom to kitchen and straight out the back door before I was fully awake.

Outside, Bryan crouched on the old picnic table, mere yards

away from the howling dogs, who gradually shushed at my approach as if ceding this dangerous intruder into my care. If Bryan glanced in my direction as I slid on the bench beside him, I didn't notice. Bryan's attention seemed pinned on my mother's animal graveyard. Norbee, who longed for nothing more than to dig in that semi-sacred spot, wandered to the end of his chain and stared with us toward the newest grave, heaped high and decorated, as all the others, with a nice flat hunk of mountain shale.

"I never noticed all that before," Bryan said. "Is that what they call a rock garden?"

"Not exactly," I said. "It's my mother's . . . project."

"What's she growing?"

"You couldn't knock?" I said.

Bryan seemed to come more awake then. He cocked his head toward the driveway, where Trudy's Monarch sat behind my mother's dented station wagon. Well beyond, the tailgate of his old truck was visible. He'd parked all the way at the end of the driveway, pointing downhill for a quick getaway.

"Didn't want to bother your mother and her cousin."

Trudy scared the hell out of Bryan. He was convinced from local rumors and folks who knew her from the fire station that she could read minds and see the future. She'd once summoned a fire truck to an old sawmill a good five minutes before a blaze actually sparked. The truck arrived as the manager was beginning his frantic dialing for help. Bryan had been there. Fucking eerie, he said. No, Bryan kept his distance, oblivious to how he was riling Trudy and my mother by stirring up the dogs.

"Scared she'll read your evil mind," I tried to joke, "this early in the morning?"

I yawned, stretching out on top of the picnic table and taking a deep breath. That simple act undid me. I flew up and bent over into a hacking fit as if I were a pack-a-day man. I finally managed to catch my breath and shot Bryan an accusing look.

"What've you been doing out here?" I said.

Bryan shrugged. "It's not me, man," he said. "Check it out."

He gestured toward the southeast and the dying hills studded with the reddish-brown boughs of dead jack pine. I could see now how heavy and low, how beleaguered the sky was, as if it were straining to contain the smoke we couldn't fully see rising from the hills. The mountains to the south and east had all but disappeared under that lowered sky, the two pressed together. Even while folks had been eating themselves up alive with all kinds of new self-inflicted sickness down here in town, a mass of pine beetles had been at work in the forests as if to show them how destruction's really done. It doesn't take much, we'd learned, to ignite catastrophe among the weak. I could taste ashes, and I wondered aloud how long it would be before they closed the camp down the other way and Jackie would be back in town, taunting both the police and every local hoodlum she could before their own possible evacuation alert arrived.

"Looks like a bad one, eh?" Bryan seemed weirdly pleased. "That will empty the hills."

"Jackie," I said, shaking my head. I could guess what she'd have to say about Bryan's plan.

I laughed as if I had heard her voice, crooning from an open car window in the made-up accent she used to mock: *Hey gangsta, hey baby. Where's da boyz at, eh? Gone ta do a roundy wit out ya?* Bryan's old friend Dean had been a wannabe. That was before he had all those babies and succumbed to Religion—which warranted a new epic tattoo (Jesus on the mountain) to finish the

sleeve on his left arm (his two babies' names and likenesses decorated the other arm)—and spent every free moment he was not
at a meeting playing video games in the basement or selling for
Flacker and the Nagles. Jackie sometimes felt guilty for how she
got on him, considering his piss-poor prospects. That didn't stop
her from getting up into even crazier faces, like the Nagle brothers, who everyone knew were using Dean. She didn't like that
Dean sold pot for them at the little kids' school and really hated
that Bryan took over for him sometimes. She didn't know the half
of it, but she guessed, and she put on her Big-Bad-Girl-Don't-
Piss-Me-Off act the moment they entered the vicinity, spitting on
the sidewalk like a guy. At least once, they actually understood
she was ranting at them.

"You gonna get yourself killed one day, bitch," GF Nagle finally said to her when he saw her alone at the Sub-Rite. "And it
ain't gonna be a pretty passing."

"Jackie's already left the camp," Bryan said. "I saw one of the
fallers getting coffee this morning at the service station. She's
probably sleeping away the day in her own bed. I would be if I
were her."

Looking up toward the hazy hills, I inhaled another harsh
breath, and my eyes teared as if the fire had already begun to race
toward town. With the camp closed, I realized, and Jackie already
back in town, Hana Swann must be here as well, all gleaming and
subdued. I couldn't imagine such a sight on Fuller Street. Thinking of her made me glance at the Band-Aid on my finger, my trig-
ger finger.

"I'll grab the gun," I told Bryan.

"Leo," he said with a sigh, "you are the dumbest smart guy
ever. Didn't you see those hills?"

But Tessa, I wanted to whine. *What about Tessa? How will I see her today?*

"No way we're heading to the refuse station today with that fire. Ursie doesn't even know how long she'll have to stay. We heard all the camps have to close. She thinks she might be up at the P&P through the evening, getting the place ready for the crowds," Bryan said. "Auntie will be there, though. She'll bring her home tonight. Even stay with her if I'm not back."

"Back from where?" I said.

"Listen, your dad still go fishing?"

"Not in a while." I grimaced, waiting for the joke. My father's idea of fishing was to dynamite a section of river and scoop up whatever surfaced with a net, a technique that never failed to elicit downright ridicule from Bryan and Ursie.

"I need to borrow something of his from the shed then, yeah?"

"You'll get it back before he gets home?"

"Oh, sure," Bryan said, sliding off the table.

Not that my father would notice much even when he did get home again. Years ago, he might have inventoried that shed on every return, practically counting the nails and the spray cans. It had been a long time, though, since he'd showed much interest. He kept a few tools in the mudroom—old tools he designated for my use—since he'd kicked most of the chores my way, leaving detailed lists about firewood and caulking guns as if he imagined my mother and I were totally ignorant.

Bryan was already fiddling with the shed door by the time I found my feet again, an empty sack he'd been sitting on clutched in his hand. As Bryan retrieved the hidden key and unlocked the padlock, Norbee starting going apeshit again, and I had to go over and fill the dogs' water bowls and throw a handful of kibble into the grass to shut him up.

By the time I came back, Bryan had already locked up the shed, key hung back on the cup hook, and he was hoisting his sack of borrowed goods into the truck bed. The set of his jaw reminded me of those months Bryan would leave school midday to take his mother to her doctors' appointments.

"You ready?" he said.

"For what?"

Bryan climbed into the truck without answering, and a moment later, I followed, slumping onto the tattered bench seat even as the truck rumbled alive and began hurtling down Lamplight Hill. Something else was different.

"The truck's not screaming anymore," I said.

Bryan nodded. "I tightened the fan belt finally. Yesterday.

"Stealth mode," he added, laughing.

We passed the corner of Fuller and Craig—vacant, of course. I knew I was being stupid. Tessa would have looked up toward the disappearing hills and known right away none of us would be heading to the refuse station. She was always miles and miles ahead of me. But I wanted her beside me so badly for a moment I was sure I glimpsed her racing down a side street toward our corner. I swiveled around and peered out the window, coughing again, so overcome I didn't notice where we were heading, until the truck jumped the curb and Bryan manhandled it, backing it into a space right in front of the Sub-Rite.

Ours is the sort of town that can feel empty even as cars snort through intersections. The Sub-Rite's parking lot almost always felt desolate despite a steady trickle of squabbling kids and dazed young mothers weaving through the lot to dodge the whey-faced, unshaven men in trucks that couldn't ever seem to stay in the empty, narrow lanes. Nobody paying attention. It's an illusion, of course. We are *always* watching one another. All of us in our private worlds, peering out as if no one can see us, but *we've* got the front row, you bet. As Bryan came to a stop, I could imagine him gearing up that minute for a nasty bit of business and half the parking lot taking full note of it.

Not that anyone would try to stop him.

"Ah, c'mon," I said. "Don't tell me you got another plan?"

"Sure do," Bryan said, "I'm going shopping. A few last particulars."

He pulled a couple of plastic Sub-Rite sacks from behind the seat.

"Your dad send something?"

Bryan grimaced. "Yeah, you bet he did, Leo. And Gerald Flacker invited us over for a beer and party snacks."

"You wait here," he said as he hopped from the cab. "Don't let this sucker stall, or that mob will probably loot it."

"I might loot it myself," I told him.

Then I watched Bryan saunter between the clusters of Sub-Rite shoppers, all of them seemingly in a hurry, flat blind to everything but the ashy clouds above and their own fiery demands.

My mother had chased me off before I could so much as pinch a slice of bread. I rummaged through the pockets of my jeans looking for something—gum, a Tic Tac, anything to silence my stomach's long, unwinding growls. Although I knew better, I even started to search Bryan's glove box and found only a wad of notebook paper folded into thirds. They looked like the notes my mother used to write to me, inspirational letters that she'd slip into my pants pocket or beneath my keyboard, winsome, pep-talk notes like girls wrote to one another in a school yearbook:

Never give up, my son, she'd write. *Be true in Your Spirit.*

Life is hard, Leo, she always seemed to add, *but you are a Strong Boy with a Fine Mind.*

Oh, yeah. Oh yeah, I thought.

Dumbest smart boy ever, now slumped behind the wheel of a truck he can't drive, revving the stalling engine and waiting for his best friend to finish his petty larceny. I could barely bring myself to unfold the papers, and when I did, I was stunned to see each page covered with a string of taunts, all aimed, it seemed, at Gerald Flacker. But Bryan couldn't be so crazy, could he? Didn't he know what would happen if the Nagles happened to catch sight of these? Or, what if Mitchell Flacker stopped him, unraveled these notes, and called him out? The back of my neck began to sweat.

It was only then that I noticed just how packed the parking lot was. The road, too, was streaming tight with cars and trucks. Too early in the day for this crowd or this heat. The truck cab was sweltering as if it, too, were under unusual pressure.

"Get over here. Get over here now!" a woman screamed as two kids loitered by the bubblegum machines. "We got no time for that."

She didn't seem to realize that she and her overburdened cart were smack in the middle of the main thoroughfare, holding up an ever-growing line. And no one had time for her troubles either. One truck began to weave around her, coming danger-ously close to sideswiping another car. A motorcyclist revved up the side, nearly hitting one of the kids. And the mom didn't even notice. Finally, everyone actually in his own world. A perfect situation for what I finally realized was Bryan's intent. I let the truck stall out, manhandled the gearshift into first, and followed him into Sub-Rite.

It was the Nagles who'd taught Bryan how to shoplift.

First and only rule: *It all belongs to us. Or should.*

You could say a lot about the Nagle brothers, but you'd never call them shifty. They claimed space; proud beyond all reason of themselves. Even—maybe especially—when they were in the thick of a bad piece of business, they cocked their heads up and chests out. It was their calling, their world; it fucking belonged to them.

Up and down every aisle. No Bryan. He must have been practicing every bit of Nagle wisdom, I thought, because he was flat invisible in that crowd of equally purposeful shoppers. I couldn't find him anywhere. One of Jackie's sisters was working a register, scanning items with a speed that seemed downright violent. I might have taken my chances and asked her for help if I hadn't finally glimpsed Bryan through the clouded gray front glass of Sub-Rite. He was outside already, crossing the parking lot with that borrowed headlong white-boy gait, as if all the bits of knowledge he'd gleaned from his criminal brushes had attained perfect reason: a skill set for a mission I couldn't imagine he'd really go through with. Not one head turned upward, and no one chased behind Bryan either as he tossed four full plastic bags nonchalantly, one by one, into the bed of the truck.

"You know I have to," he told me once I caught up to him.

And even though I'd disagreed mightily, I couldn't say a word. She was standing there again in front of us, holding out that white forearm with its trace of stolen blood that was, in actuality, a coursing river of a dare, and there was no turning away for Bryan. I could see that. Self-destructive though the path might be, it was the only one that made sense to him.

And it made no fucking sense at all.

What Bryan hadn't figured on in his initial plan, what he realized last night once he'd gone back, he said, was that getting rid of Flacker had to involve getting rid of the Flacker operation, not just the man himself.

"You're crazy," I said.

"Be crazy not to," he said.

A great wail of sirens began outside the Sub-Rite, even as overhead a bird-dog plane led what might already be a low-flying air tanker over the hills. Could the fire really be that close? If so, Bryan wasn't kidding; this fire was swift and serious. Perversely, I was pleased. No way he would try a stunt in the middle of a town emergency. A police cruiser inched past the lot. Bryan looked right past it. Even when the sirens began again, rippling across downtown, he didn't flinch. No one did but me, because clear as could be, I had heard another call.

"I need to go home," I said. "Right away."

OUT OF THE PAN,
INTO THE FIRE

Albie Porchier couldn't believe it. Broad daylight and they were brawling. Thanks to Christ the head logging boys had left at dawn to assess the eastern-ridge fire. But there were others to think of, weren't there? He cursed as he noticed the entertainer's van was no longer in the back lot. Had they already chased his newest regular away? Ursie had run to tell him. She had rolled her cart to the upper rooms and was cranking through each task at an even higher speed than usual, anticipating an early finish and the progress she'd exhibit for Keven Seven, when the first crash pierced her and she flew down to the office, leaving the door to Room 18 wide open, her vacuum cleaner fallen to one side.

"It's Room 11," she said, rushing into the narrow lobby where Albie was training a new clerk, a thin-lipped white girl named Tracy.

Albie managed a quick glance at the computer over Tracy's shoulder. Even so, he couldn't quite believe his eyes. Vincent was a moron, but even he should have known better than to check in a Nagle brother. You had to steer that shit back out to the highway, out of town even a breath, toward the half-ruined chain motel that had obliviously sprung up in this wasteland of a town and immediately gone to seed with bedbugs and fleas, fire and water damage. A Nagle brother stood more chance of harming himself there than doing much more damage to the place. For all the Peak and Pine's failings, Albie *maintained*. He had a contract with the two lumber companies and an understanding with a few oil outfits as well. Bad enough the occasional drunken parking-lot brawl. He did not need the likes of a Nagle brother, the real promise of murder and mayhem and, hell, full-bore destruction.

"You two stay right here," he told Ursie. "If I'm not back in four minutes, call the police, Tracy. And get in the back room there, and shut that door tight. Don't want them taking anything out on you if they see you in here on the phone."

Tracy bolted straightaway, forgetting the phone and locking the door behind her.

"I'll be fine," Ursie called after Tracy, who did not answer. Ursie grabbed the phone and crept to the front windows. And she would be fine too. She was as tall as a man, and although gangly with thin, broad shoulders, she could lift astonishing weights. Her endurance was mighty. Should a crazed Nagle brother burst through the office door, she decided, she'd nail him with the fire extinguisher.

Still, she intended to do as she was told in this much-needed job and would have if she hadn't stuck her head out the door and glimpsed a single red sneaker in the corridor not far from Room 11's door. It looked familiar. Along the sneaker's side were loopy black marks that looked a lot like the autographs she and Jackie had provided one bored evening at Tessa's request. That girl believed in the strangest things, like that if she had Ursie's and Jackie's handwriting on her shoes, their very names, she'd hold them close to her and keep them both safe. She would always be able to sense where they were, no matter what, and they'd always know how to find her, too. She'd made them spit onto their hands before they signed as if they were eight-year-olds making a pact to never kiss a boy.

Crazy, yeah, but who knew? Tessa was as serious about her beliefs as some of the elders were about the old stories they told. Ursie squinted and could just make out a splotch of yellow paint just like the one Tessa's nightmare nephew had splattered on her shoes the day proud Tessa first wore them home.

Ignoring Albie's scowl, she ran lightly behind him to snatch up the little red shoe he hadn't noticed.

"Ursula," he growled, and she flew back to the office with the shoe, which she knew for sure now was Tessa's. There were her own initials *UMN*—Ursula Marie Nowicki—right next to Jackie's tortured scrawl—*Jackie Lisa Ann Morey—Queen of the Forest.*

A man's voice boomed. Albie's voice slapped back, a little bee. Another man let out a high-pitched howl, and Ursie picked up the fire extinguisher, readying herself. But now the men were leaving with more shouting and fists banging. Someone kicked a metal wastebasket down the corridor. Rolling along the concrete walk, the bin ratcheted like rounds from a rifle. Another shoe— not Tessa's—flew by the window of the office. Car doors slammed, an engine screeched, and Albie, white-faced and sweating, returned to the office.

"Did you call?" he asked.

She shook her head.

"Well, they're gone, but they did their damage. Broken glass all over the carpet. Mattress slit open with a knife. You ever wonder why God made guns, Ursula, you have your answer right there. One of 'em had his arm in a cast and he was still whaling at the other. No point in calling the police now. I'd just have them back later tonight taking revenge."

He noticed the shoe in Ursie's hand and couldn't help chastising her.

"You've got to be careful around here, girl. I know you thought you were helping by grabbing that, but you should have waited until they left to tidy up. There's tons to do, no worries there. Once Madeline gets here, let her take over the laundry cart. And you vacuum up the glass in there. That's about all you can do right now. I won't have a chance to get more spackle until the idiot Vincent comes in this afternoon. I'm pretty sure I've got another door lock in the supply closet. At least the hinges are still intact."

"I'll go right away," Ursie said.

She had to control herself to keep from running. Her hand shook as she entered Room 11, and she had hardly absorbed the breadth of damage—the broken metal chair leg on the shredded mattress decorated with shattered glass and fresh bloodstains—when she became aware of a slight huffing noise and turned to see the edge of another red sneaker protruding from beneath the bed.

"Oh, sweet Jesus," she whispered as she shut the door to the room and lifted the bedspread to see Tessa, eyes wide, half-trapped beneath the broken bedsprings and a slat of wood that had been sheared in two by the weight of GF Nagle.

"Hold on, just hold on," Ursie crooned. As slowly as she could, she raised the corners of the bedclothes and swept the broken glass toward its center, then swept it away in one contained bundle before swooping down with one massive surge and lifting first the mattress, then the broken box spring up on end, and shoving both against the washroom door, exposing finally her poor shattered friend.

Ursie's heart was lurching with all kinds of pain, but it wasn't until she saw Tessa's damaged cheek, the bloom of bruises, the dangling bandages, that Ursie too began to cry.

"Tessa," she wept. "Oh, Tessa, what have they done to you?"

The broken slat had left a long scrape across Tessa's forearm, but it wasn't bleeding. One hand was bent into a fist. The other was bandaged and cocked at an odd angle.

There was no way to reach Bryan, who, Ursie knew, was already out on his scavenging run. She knew that if she called the Kreutzer house, Leo would race to the P&P barefoot over glass, but without a car and a way to get Tessa out, he was of little use to her. And she didn't want to call Tessa's home, not until she knew what had happened, how Tessa had come to be here at the P&P, under the bed in a room rented by one Nagle brother and assailed by another. For all Ursie knew, Tessa's sister could have engineered the encounter, set her up as surely as she kept Tessa captive through her worry for those kids, her fear her sister would leave them and they'd be sent away to foster care just as Tessa had been. Tessa would kill herself first, and her sister knew it. No, Ursie didn't trust that sister. But if she could just get Tessa home to her house—hers and Bryan's—she could clean her up and let her rest and wait to hear the truth.

Albie had gone into the office, but it wouldn't be long before he'd return with his toolbox, ready to piece the room back together. Ursie didn't have a lot of options. He'd blame Tessa as much as the Nagles. Gently, she gathered Tessa into her arms, feeling her friend's brittleness, that unfamiliar surrender. The girl couldn't even talk.

"C'mon, Tessa," she whispered. "I'll get you steady."

Down the hall, Ursie knocked lightly on Room 14's door, Tessa leaning hard against her. When he didn't answer, she unlocked the door and eased Tessa inside. She would put Tessa back into the bed still likely warm from Keven Seven, who as usual had left the room as neat as could be. The bed bore only a suggestion of a human shape outlined on the cheap bedspread. Tessa struggled to keep her eyes open, but Ursie shushed her.

"It's okay," she said. "I'll be right back."

Upstairs, she reclaimed the vacuum, packed up her cart, and trundled the whole shebang downstairs again. Never mind that she had twelve rooms yet to do and most of them beyond wrecks. In Room 14, Ursie wrote a note to Keven Seven, the briefest of explanations. He might not, she realized, even return until after lunch. That was when she'd promised to meet him, in that hour before Bryan was due. And her auntie, Madeline, was scheduled to work this morning. She was late, and Ursie had already been covering for her. Once her auntie showed up, Ursie could make a deal: she'd finish the rooms if Madeline would drive Tessa to Ursie and Bryan's. Ursie relaxed as she unfolded a plan. Poor Tessa. Curled into herself, she'd plunged into something resembling sleep. Ursie finished her note and crept from the room, closing the door as carefully, satisfied that, for the moment at least, Tessa was completely safe.

FREE RIDES FOR ALL!

The highway: pretty and peaceful and lonely as hell in the crackled light before dawn. Two girls on the shoulder, the tall one propelled forward as if she can by her own considerable force cover the long miles to the next town. The other girl—her white, white skin glowing—strolls. She could be anywhere. See how she dawdles, stopping to tie and retie her shoes, to gaze toward the heavy, hidden horizon or into the endless black woods beside them. The shadowed shapes of black bears might lumber across the highway ahead of them, behind them. They don't worry the girls. Bears won't linger. The bears dislike the highway almost as much as the big girl does. A raven wakes as they pass and, pissed at the smoky air, blames them. The second girl, the meanderer, taunts back. Wait here, she tells her friend, and chases the raven into the blind woods. When she doesn't return, the first girl goes looking. She calls and calls. She beats past brush and bushes and spindly trees until only the sound of a truck rushing the highway lets her know she hasn't fallen off the face of the earth. She finds her way back to the shoulder, where she is sure her friend must be waiting for her. Finally, alone, she presses forward. She'll walk all day if she must—and *she must, she must*—under that soiled sheet of a sky that refuses to pull away, refuses to give her a chance to take one good sweet, lasting breath.

• • •

Need a lift?

He drives a big red truck, a silver step-van with blacked-out windows, a foreign shit-can, mustard-colored, with a banged-up right rear fender and no backseat or inner door handles. Who but the driver needs one anyway? A practiced motorist, he carries chains and sand and meters of rope and duct tape and quick-ties and syringes and rags soaked in ether and, well, God knows what are in the plastic containers behind his seat. The weather can change at any moment, can't it? The fellow's generosity has no bounds. He brakes for every hitchhiker and stranded motorist. Hell, he even picks up those who are merely shouldering their way home, head down, purposefully oblivious to the slowing, ticking engine behind them. Persuasion is both a subtle art and a clear show of advantages, isn't it? No one is faster or stronger or more strung out, and who else can lift a full-grown woman by the back of her neck as if she were just one of a dozen spitting kittens ready for drowning?

PATTERNS OF ENERGY

For the first time in my memory, my mother's cousin looked genuinely glad to see me. My mother had left an hour earlier and, given Uncle Lud's condition, Trudy had stayed on, waiting for me.

"Yeah," she said. That was all. And it wasn't until after Bryan's truck rattled off with Trudy tailgating down Lamplight Hill, that I realized we'd talked the way Uncle Lud and I often did, a whole conversation played out before we'd opened our mouths.

I heard the sirens. I know you have to go. I'll be here with him.

"Yeah," she'd said, but what I heard was:

I know. I'll be back soon, soon. Don't you let him go without us.

Given the circumstances, there was no telling when my mother would return. All the shelter animals would have to be crated and trucked away if the fire moved west. Hannibal would be all for dispatching them instead, but my mother wouldn't listen to that kind of talk, I felt sure. Yet, though she would make Hannibal wait until the last possible moment until they put the shelter on the move, much had to be made ready. If it hadn't been for Uncle Lud, my mother would have expected me there as well, chipping in where I could.

And then there was Bryan. He needed me too, if only to steer him clear of whatever trouble he was thundering toward with his Sub-Rite sacks and his splintered rage at Flacker.

Meanwhile, Uncle Lud, ash-colored, slept on, and I kept an

aimless kind of watch. He'd been sleeping, Trudy said, since she'd arrived early that morning. There'd been no drinking of the magic milkshake she'd prepared, not much bathing, either, although I imagined my mother hadn't skipped the whispered prayers. Was it only yesterday Uncle Lud and I had sat and talked together? My mother had told Trudy that her priest said Uncle Lud was traveling in a dark wood, and I knew she was thinking of a wood far different from the ones that ringed us, those hills lashed this moment with the flames that heralded their own demise. Neither was she imagining her priest's version: Uncle Lud eventually lifted free of that gloomy forest into the brilliant light of the Lord's embrace. No, my mother's wood, the one in which Uncle Lud had gone missing, was an impenetrable forest of thorny thickets, a maze of paths he might wander in until at last the right one appeared, the one that would lead him straight back to us.

He did not wake either when I went in to see him. I put my ear beside his narrow chest and heard only the lightest wheeze in and out, not much more. I sniffed around and was relieved at first to smell nothing more than the lanolin cream my mother liked to rub across Uncle Lud's dry knuckles. Then I caught another slight but familiar odor.

A few weeks ago, a fetid smell, an itchy stink, had seeped into our house, landing specifically in Uncle Lud's room. It was not unlike the stench in the back shed when the spring rats overtook it and made nests in the walls. My mother marched around the house, poking a stick at the foundation, looking for weak spots. She'd prodded me into crawling into the basement corners while she held a flashlight and her stick. She ignored her long-standing worries about the dogs and laid down poison and sprayed Sub-

Rite's version of Febreze willy-nilly—at the floors, the ceiling, the windows, the back of my head. It seemed as if the smell shifted from spot to spot, as though it hoped to hover out of our reach until we lost interest.

We attributed it next to the dogs, my mother sweeping poor Norbee out of the kitchen and into the yard as if he were dirt in a dustpan. But the smell didn't go away. She scoured the wash-rooms, scalded the linens. She steeped sweet-smelling herbs in a washbasin and sponged Uncle Lud from head to toe. For a while, she blamed his pain medication, which had been increased, but the truth was, the stench wasn't rising off Uncle Lud, who through everything had retained a familiar warm, earthy scent that I fancied was the smell of the farm where he and my father had grown up. Finally, one day not long ago, as she sniffed painfully around his room, my mother bent to the windowsill, where a thin line of soot was clearly visible.

She turned grim. She swept the sill. Cleaned it with bleach. Then she burnt sage and sweetgrass until she'd got her message across. Only then did the smell retreat. It had all but vanished for days, but now, apparently, that demon scent was back again, waiting in the folds of particle-laden air drifting townward from the forest fires.

Uncle Lud didn't stir at all, not even when I transferred the baby monitor Trudy used during the morning to his silent pillow and switched it on, adjusting its static-laded volume before moving on to my own electronic monitor: Leila Chen.

If I could have asked Uncle Lud, he might have counseled that I start anew with Leila Chen, but I would bet that, more likely, Uncle Lud would fall himself into a correspondence with her, one that sidestepped calculus and hurtled right into atomic radiance. The file was open on my desktop, but even as I stared at the screen, I balked and resolved again to tell my mother the truth that day. Yet along with the arrival of a creeping sense of relief came that familiar ding—another e-mail from Leila Chen— and dread returned.

Dear **Leo Kreutzer, Student ID# 889355,**

Professor Blankenship suggests I check in with you to ascertain your receipt of my previous email, which I apparently failed to cc him upon and will not do so now, since it is a "private communication" between teacher and student. Is it not? Dr. Blankenship trusts me implicitly, understand, yet certain "procedural assurances" must be produced, such as copies and replies and academic follow-throughouts.

You may note I have not cc'd Professor Blankenship on this email either. This is because upon re-reading my previous missive, I see I was perhaps too harsh to you. Physics is a difficult science and not for everyone, despite the preponderance of links to spiritual endeavors and the like that promise a connection between a zen-like peace, abundance, and the "Theory of Relativity in Everyday Activities." Objects do not have souls, I assure you, **Leo Kreutzer.** Nor do particles have a symbiotic electrical relationship with brain waves or aliens or spirit guides. Time travel is not optional at the moment. These are popular myths that might have seduced someone like you, **Leo Kreutzer,** into pursuing the science. As per our last exchange, I can assure you other fields will lead you to romance and myth far more expeditiously should that be your final goal. As mentioned, I myself have endeavoured forms of poetry and find they satisfy that requirement, albeit imperfectly. You, too, I did conclude, might pursue a more direct course if such is your goal.

On secondary thought, what has become clear to me re your efforts is that you do understand one fundamental: **interweaving patterns of energy,** for true connections really, as the renowned Leonard Cohen may once have written. In second sight, I applaud you for this realizing, which many students never achieve, despite the obvious rote-work of problem-solving. You are coming in a back door, I now perceive. You may be familiar with the legendary Leonard Cohen's Stranger—you certainly now seem to me to at least know he exists. (Do I see a *pattern* here?) Yet curiously you did not mention Leonard Cohen's masterful lyric or the Stranger when you started this course. Still I sense the Stranger's impending escape attempt upon your part. The insightful Leonard Cohen might say you are waiting for the High Card, and **Leo Kreutzer,** with the most esteemed Mr. Cohen in mind, I find respect there. And although Professor Blankenship worries for my dwindling enrollment numbers and your reluctance, I am growing converted to your beliefs, **Leo Kreutzer,** and can only encourage you once more to begin again in your own Stranger ways and learn from top to bottom, from inside to out—with mathematics (of course).

Imperatively and simplistically, I commend the basic tenets to you (taken from **Section 1A**) for your immediate review:

Newton's Three Laws of Motion

1. Every body continues in its state of rest, or of uniform motion in a straight line, unless it is compelled to change that state by forces impressed upon it.

2. The acceleration produced by a particular force acting on a body is directly proportional to the magnitude of the force and inversely proportional to the mass of the body.

3. To every action there is always opposed an equal reaction; or, the mutual actions of two bodies upon each other are always equal and directed in contrary parts.

Begin and end with these, **Leo Kreutzer**. Perhaps you will find more of the patterns here and your path inward even as you problem-solve **Sections 1–4**. Perhaps not.

> With sincerity,
> Leila Chen

For the first time in weeks, I laughed aloud, long and hard, forgetting about Uncle Lud's rest, my mother's looming disappointment. So that was what I believed in: patterns of energy—*patterns*. One line intersecting and influencing another. My laughter was joined by the sudden crackling of the baby monitor, a rise in static that came and went so swiftly I might have imagined it. And despite my best intentions, even as my hand began scribbling down that primer of Energy and Mass, I paused, wondering what Uncle Lud would make of that first section's heading:

Lesson One: The Measurement of Space.

Measuring space, I decided, would be like beating Flacker, an incomprehensible task that not even math could truly solve. Physics, I decided, was fantasy, pure and simple.

THE DEVIL DOES STORY PROBLEMS,
BUT FIRST EATS HOOKE'S LAW
FOR BREAKFAST

He owns a slide rule, although he doesn't need it. He brandishes it the way comedians once flailed whoopee cushions and magicians will persist with top hats. Physics, he would like to tell you, is a fat, gaudy prop, a mass of mathematical indirections masquerading as True Fact, Goddamn Science. He loves his slide rule, loves, loves, loves the way he can prove anything with the right equation. It's a sleight-of-hand performance in which the laws of the universe become particular, in which anyone can play God or demon.

Go ahead, he says, set that pendulum swinging, such a lovely motion at first, *ding dong, ding dong.* Watch it lilt to the right, then, *whoosh,* it's back to the left with exactly the same force and lift. A mesmerizing dance of Displacement and Restoration. One could get hooked. He chortles at his pun. Oh, but not even Hooke himself would claim his "law" with all its pretty Latin (*Ut tensio, sic vis*) and that brief symbolic sigh ($F = -kx$) could prevail under all conditions with all materials.

So he fiddles, the slightest of gestures, and if you glance at the pendulum now, you'll see it has abandoned all grace, all sense of equality. It's fallen into a private dance, one riven solely with endless incalculable loss.

Story Problem: *A wandering soul acts as a spring with a spring constant of 132 N/m (or 112 N/m or 10 N/m or . . . well, does it really matter?). If the Devil equals an Unknown Force and applies an Unmeasurable Weight irrationally and erratically to the spring, calculate the Displacement as the spring bounces from soul to soul, from soul to spirit, from spirit to tortured body.*

Ha, ha, ha. What fun. You want to play? You do? You really think you do? He pulls out his slide rule again, and a car slides *up* a smoke-filled mountain road.

A BRIEF REPRIEVE

It was almost noon when Tessa woke again to a series of butter-soft clicks, the interior locks being eased into place on the door, the chain sliding into place. Every bit of her heart began to loudly sing out, but her head felt too heavy to move and although she tried to open her eyes, the gauze underneath the bandage must have shifted, because now it lay too securely over her eyes and seemed to be crawling over her mouth as well.

She clutched at breath. That smell? What was that smell? Rotten eggs and wintergreen, bruised juniper berries and witch hazel, bleach? Each scent declared itself, then fractured and split apart. Her head fell back as if someone had pulled the bed away from her. But no, now she was being lifted and covered with jabs of ice and flickers of rain and a thin, sheeted shroud and . . . wait . . . wait . . . please, wait.

How much later was it when Ursie unlocked the door with Madeline beside her? The bolt jumped back, a released snap, and yet the door didn't budge.

"Fellow's got his own locks on," Madeline said.

Ursie knocked, a gentle rapping she was sure would let Keven Seven know it was she, but Madeline snorted at her.

"Can't get in that way, girl," her auntie said

"Housekeeping," she sang out.

"Come to do a pickup," Madeline added under her breath, giggling a little. "Pickup and delivery," she sang softly.

Ursie couldn't get her auntie to understand how serious the situation was, how much was at stake. To Madeline, clearly this was just a case of one more fucked-up kid who needed to get home. But it was Tessa. It was Tessa.

When Keven Seven still didn't open, Madeline elbowed past Ursie and put a practiced shoulder to the door. For such a little woman, Ursie marveled, her auntie knew how to jolt a door. The second lock splintered the doorjamb. They could hear the crack and see now the second set of chains.

"Albie," Ursie breathed, casting a worried glance over her shoulder.

"Will be, pissed, yeah," Madeline agreed. But he wouldn't for the world suspect her or Ursie, she knew. She was about to stick her slender hand into the opening when the door slammed shut, the chains released, and the room suddenly opened to them.

"You okay, in here?" Madeline said. As she half fell inside, she was ready to explain how lots of people lock themselves in and get all hurt and need help, but Keven Seven wasn't paying any attention to her.

"I'm sorry," Ursie began. "I left you a . . ."

"An unconscious girl in my bed," he said as Madeline suppressed another snort.

"A note," Ursie said. "I left you a note. I'm sorry. I had nowhere else to take her."

To her surprise, Keven Seven said, "Oh, I understand."

"We'll take her now. Madeline's going to drive her home."

"Why not leave her with me?" he said.

"No, no," she was shaking her head even as she tried to get

Tessa to sit up. Tessa looked even worse, Ursie thought, as if she'd been crumpled up and tossed around again. She must have rolled into the thin sheet Ursie had folded away from her and messed with her bandages, too. She smelled odd, like medicine. Ursie hadn't noticed that before.

"She's clearly not able to move." The deep curls of his voice, that sonorous tone that Ursie had carried home with her and twined within her own thoughts all through the last night, tightened and grew brittle. Even Madeline's clowning around disappeared.

"I'll carry her," Ursie said.

She could imagine Albie's reaction when he noticed the broken lock, and she didn't want Tessa anywhere around that, either.

"Aren't you supposed to be working?" Keven Seven asked in this new, too-tight voice. "I could take her away for you."

What a strange offer, Ursie thought. As if Tessa were . . .

"Auntie gets a break now," she rushed to explain, a lie.

He smiled. He knew lies. They were sweets to him.

"And what about your *break*?" he asked Ursie, causing Madeline to click her tongue.

Ursie paused, but she managed to keep her head down as she answered. "I'll be finished by two, maybe three, I think. I'll come back up and fix that lock."

"Oh, will you?" Madeline said, recovering. "You know how to do that? Ho, ho, don't be telling Albie that, eh?"

"Auntie?" Ursie was pleading. She'd gathered the insensible Tessa into her arms and had reached the threshold, but she couldn't keep the door open wide enough for them to pass through.

"Don't worry," Ursie whispered back at Keven Seven. "I'll fix it this afternoon."

"Sure you will," her auntie said. She recognized Keven Seven; she was sure of it. She knew that glance, casual but proprietary. A boyfriend she'd once had used it just before he punched her in the face.

"There you go, *sweetheart,*" he'd said.

Okay, then. Madeline pushed past Keven Seven to hold the door for Ursie, who she nudged forward. She slammed it three times behind her before she was satisfied the latch caught.

Ursie was heartened to see that Madeline had sobered considerably. She darted in front and led the way to her old car, even pushing off food wrappers and soda cans, dirty shirts and towels, before helping Ursie lay Tessa on the backseat.

"My boyfriend's dog weighs more," Madeline said. "And smells . . . better, too. What is that? Phew! Hope my car don't . . . smell so bad after. Hey, is this gal . . . breathing?"

She leaned her head to Tessa's chest and came up grimacing. A skint of breath, that's all she got, but the girl was still ticking.

"Bastards," Madeline added, to no one in particular.

"Can you do this, Auntie?" Ursie said, catching her breath to lay out a string of instructions. It must have been the preoccupation with cards, because that's how she was beginning to see her day, Tessa's options, as one configuration after another, each one leading to another possible outcome.

"You can get her to the couch? If Bryan's there, he can put her in my bed. You lock the door behind you when you leave. Bryan's got a key with his truck keys. Lock up tight. Maybe pull the curtains closed too? You okay, Auntie?"

"Oh, sure, honey," her auntie said, suppressing another old

image in her mind. "You worry too much, you know? I've done this a lot, a real lot."

Madeline reached through the open driver's window to pat Ursie's cheek, but her eyes were uncharacteristically grim. For the briefest moment, Ursie saw her own mother in Madeline, Junie's steadiness and generosity, her unwavering sorrow at the end.

"Hey, kiddo, that fellow back there . . . he a firefighter or something?"

"I don't think so," Ursie said. "Why?"

Her auntie shrugged, returning to herself. "Smells like . . . smoke, is all. Like one of those jumper boys. Makes my throat all dry and cracked thinking about them."

"You'll come right back, okay?" Ursie said.

"You sound just like *him*." Madeline said, tilting her head toward Albie's office.

And she tooted her horn as she started the car and rumbled through the parking lot's back exit, just as Albie, toolbox in hand, left that front office for Room 11.

"She gone?" he said, shaking his head. "Not to the hospital again, I hope. No daylong doctor's appointments?"

"She went to pick up her medicine. She'll be back in ten minutes. Ten minutes, tops," Ursie said, marveling inwardly at how easy the lies were coming.

"Medicine." Albie grimaced. "Well, she'd better be right back. We've got a crowd coming in. They're closing the camps and evacuating. That fire's moving fast. Just hope they stop the damn thing before the whole town's got to head out to a reception center."

For the first time that day, Ursie noticed the extra weight in the air. She'd assumed the trouble she'd had breathing all morn-

ing stemmed from her anxiety and the physical pressure of car-
rying Tessa upstairs. Now she could see the haziness on the
horizon, the heavy tin sky with flint-colored clouds bearing
down. She smelled the dry smoke in the air and recognized the
strain in her lungs. Jackie must be back in town. Ursie smiled a
little to herself, imagining how Jackie would go after—or try to go
after—whoever had damaged Tessa. They'd have to hold the girl
back, and they would. No one wanted more trouble for Jackie. If
the fire was that close, Bryan sure wasn't up at the refuse station
this morning. He might even be back at home, scribbling in that
new notebook, and ready to leap up and help Madeline with
Tessa. For the first time that morning, she almost relaxed. Bryan
and Jackie would see to Tessa.

"It could be a bad one," Albie said.

He sighed. A full house brought gains—a fat till, for sure—
but also the inevitable pains—the bitter card games, the losses,
the fights.

Hell, he thought. I almost shouldn't bother fixing up. They'll
just break it all up again tonight. He'd have to be here; he knew
that now. If that idiot Vincent hadn't let him down so badly, Albie
might have convinced himself Vincent could monitor a simple
run of card games but, really, who was he kidding?

He glanced up to see that Ursie, his stalwart helper, had already skipped right back to work. He could hear her keys rattling
and soon after, the broken purr of her vacuum promising to set
his world back to rights. Thank God there was something—
someone—he could count on.

EQUATION WITH NO ANSWER

When my mother called out to me for the second time that day, I was asleep, my right cheek resting on an open notebook covered with numbers scribbled sideways and equations squeezed into margins. I had no memory of writing any of them down, and in fact, when I first opened my eyes and glanced down, they resembled the muddy tracks of tiny, fleeing animals. Beside the notebook was a full sheaf of handwritten pages. Those I remembered well. I heard my mother whisper my name from the kitchen, and I knew it was her, knew it was my name, and yet for the slightest second it seemed as if those numbers were calling out, and not necessarily to me.

And too, before my mother's voice registered, it seemed I'd been lingering in the dream middle of a wide-open logging road. Up ahead, Bryan and Ursie trudged as if following a sibilant command I could barely make out. And even farther ahead, far in the distance, I could see Jackie, just the back of her, disappearing. But where, I wondered, was Tessa? And where was I meant to go? Whatever directions the others had been given were overpowered by other voices—Uncle Lud's, my mother's, even an unintelligible taunt from Trudy—and soon I'd eased away from the middle of the path, hesitating, as usual.

By the time I came fully awake and made it to the hallway, baby monitor in hand, my mother was there to meet me. The phone was pressed against her shoulder.

"For you," she whispered, handing me the phone I had not heard ring. "Your lunch is on the table," she added.

Noontime, at least. I'd slept away half the morning since I'd come home. I had no idea how long my mother had been home or if she was staying. Faintly, even as I pressed the phone to my ear and willed myself to speak, I could hear my mother in Uncle Lud's room, the steady murmur of a single voice.

"Does Bryan not have another friend?" my mother sighed when I told her.

"I'll stay if you need me here."

"No, no." My mother frowned.

"What?" I said.

"I meant to tell you Jackie's mother called this morning before I left. She wondered if you were out somewhere with her and Bryan and Ursie. You haven't seen her today, have you?"

"Bryan said a fellow from the camp told him Jackie was on her way home."

My mother nodded. "That's all right then, I guess." She glanced back out the window. "The wind's low at the moment. They might stop this fire straightaway. Hannibal's got the shelter covered. We're ready to go tonight if we need to. But he'll have to manage that, I told him. They all will. Still, if we get an evacuation alert, I've got you lot to take care of—isn't that enough? Trudy made a pack up for Lud, but . . . well . . ."

"What?" I said. I was awake now, but still cotton-mouthed and cranky. The enthusiasm I'd carried back from Leila Chen had twisted and split into threads of panic.

"I called Dr. Miller," my mother said. "It's the pain he was most worried about, but I said I didn't think Lud was in pain.

You don't think so, do you? No, no, that's what I told him. I won't wake him for his medicine. Did he have a sip this morning? When did Trudy leave? Did he wake for her?"

In the minutes before Bryan's truck bellied up the driveway, I held my uncle's limp hand. Could I go with Bryan? Should I? Uncle Lud had grown much younger since the morning, his face softening, a boyish curve to his cheek. I could imagine him up on the farm, racing around the pond on his hockey skates. He might have been twelve. At the same time, he'd also aged greatly in the past weeks. His thatch of blond hair had thinned and darkened to a few brown strands; his ears, exposed, seemed twice as large around that delicate face. The veins in the thin hand I held were gnarled and swollen. I could imagine him ancient, too, prodding me into telling my own kids numerous and twisted tales, a luminous shadow in the room's corner that somehow managed to hold every scrap of light.

Please don't leave, I whispered. *Please, please, wait for me.*

I could hear my mother shuffling around in the kitchen, impatient with both of us, I suspected. In the early springtime, the last time my father had come home, he brought Uncle Lud to us, a half-familiar scarecrow in his passenger seat. They were coming then from another hospital visit, the last one, but I didn't know that then. I'd rushed the door, tripping over Norbee and slamming a hip into the mudroom cupboard, sending a basket of trowels and garden snips flying, an exuberance I always shared with my mother and even Trudy when Lud arrived. That time, though, no one was scrambling at my side, tossing the tools away, as we battled to be the first to reach the car. Instead, I could see my mother gazing out the kitchen window, one hand shielding her eyes as if she didn't dare to look. She was crying. Yet somehow she'd managed to shake away her tears so that by the time Uncle Lud and my father and I reached the kitchen door, she was able to shoo Norbee in a voice that did not quake and reach her arms around Uncle Lud and hold him tight. And he let her. He didn't wiggle once. He knew eventually everyone would have to let him go.

I could feel myself rummaging for some kind of hope, nowhere a suggestion of true escape, only a familiar cycle of promise and disappointment. I had been in a minor season of the former, I realized, and now I feared even that forlorn wave was cresting. At least Bryan had direction and purpose. I was an equation with no answer, just a series of muddied conjectures that would not come into focus.

If you took a good look at me, you'd see. How I favored black T-shirts, which faded straightaway, and plaid shirts whose cuffs were never long enough. Seams frayed on my jeans; sweatshirts lost their shape. And directly after a haircut, my old cowlick reappeared so within hours I was shaggy again. I'd shot up so quickly in grade nine that my orientation was still skewed and, off-balance, I continually knocked into doorjambs and lockers and the fluttery little French teacher well known for darting through the school hallways. Like a five-year-old, I could stumble and fall while standing still in one place. A half-bottle of beer put me to sleep. Despite my horrible vision, my height had interested the basketball coach briefly, just as my big square head and hands had once piqued the attention of a grade-school hockey coach, but any moments of coordination I attained were purely accidental, and both soon decided I would be more liability than asset, although they both talked me into sitting on their respective benches for a season or more to offer some misplaced anxiety to opposing teams who had not an inkling of my shortcomings and might only wonder how the game would change against them should the coach finally send me forward—which, of course, he never did.

Yeah, it seemed to me that I was all bleak suggestion, that I would never be enough to take over for Uncle Lud. Which may be why I decided to go along that late afternoon.

"An hour, Bryan," I had told him. "That's all I've got."

"An hour should do it," Bryan said.

"Don't worry, wussy," he added. "Not a chance you'll get into any trouble."

THE DEVIL PLAYS WITH
A TELEPHONE

Who's calling?

Who *is this*?

That you, Donny?

Hey, now, I told you I'd get it. Is there a need for this?

This is Donny, right? Or Getz?

Screw you, BritBoy, if this is you, don't be playing games with me.

Or is it You?

It's you, isn't it? Fuck you, I'm not coming.

No way, no how.

If this is you, I know what you said. I know what you threatened. I know what I promised, too. It's more than . . . well, I know . . . but . . .

But . . .

You still there? Because I'm here.

You know I'm here, damn it.

Damn it. You know.

I'm here.

HENCHMEN

Illegal. Ill-advised. Unstoppable. And sometimes—a godsend.

That's how Albie Porchier regarded the card games that simmered in his motel rooms on any given night. A crapshoot, no pun intended. To tell the truth, the games mostly occupied those fellows who might otherwise go looking for trouble. Their wild talk and drink were contained to a single room and when the game finally broke up, the men often stumbled back to their own beds. So Albie tolerated them. He turned a blind eye and a deaf ear to the sounds of footsteps in the corridors, boots clanking up the metal steps to the motel's top floor, where the bigger rooms were and where the games tended to originate. Sometimes, he even took a little cut to make all involved feel welcome. The ice machine churned constantly, unable to keep up with demand. Even his damn pop machine saw action on those nights. And as long as he caught the games before they soured, before cheating was discerned and called out and denied, before drunken men fell off their chairs and spattered dignities and empty wallets and spilled booze demanded loud retribution that would, if left unchecked, culminate in wall-battering, furniture-smashing fights—well, everything would be all right. And if sometimes he took pity on a fellow who lost his paycheck or even his whole nut in a game, Albie might stand him a meal at the Hot Spot, but that was as far as he'd go. You got to know what you're getting into when you sit down at the table.

Still, Albie had to stay alert. Bottom line was that any law officer could shut his place down for illegal gambling on almost any night of the week. Shut down the game and shut down the motel. Of course, the latter wasn't likely on a day like today, when a slew of operations and folks on the outskirts were being hustled into town. Still, Albie didn't like taking chances, so when Gerald Fucking Flacker's cousin, Mitchell, arrived in the crowded lobby that afternoon to check out a report of a stolen Toyota in the Peak and Pine's lot, it behooved him to cooperate.

"Vincent was on the desk," Albie told Mitchell Flacker. "I woke him up this morning and read him the riot act. Said Nagle drove in in an old Toyota, must have been hot-wired, because it didn't have a key. I'd guess it was that car right over there." Albie pointed.

Mitchell nodded but didn't so much as write down the plate number. He was an odd duck, Albie thought. More than once, he'd checked into the Peak and Pine himself, after hours, not alone, the patrol car parked in the back behind the Dumpster in the space that old van now claimed.

"Anybody been near it?" he said.

"Not that I've noticed," Albie said. "But of course we've all been working around here."

"I need to check out the room," Mitchell said, "since a crime's involved."

"A crime?"

"Didn't you just say he arrived in a stolen car?"

"I've got a customer about to take that room."

"Not if it's a crime scene, you don't."

Albie elbowed past his new clerk, punched in the code, and swiped a fresh card, Mitchell Flacker watching Albie's face during every step of the process as if Albie might be lying to him. Maybe it was that that made him add: "The girl's already cleaned it, you know. And she's damn thorough. Best maid I've had, I'll tell you."

"Who's that?" Mitchell said. "That Madeline Bone?"

"Ha." Albie almost snickered at the thought of Madeline as meticulous. "No, it's her niece, Ursula. Ursula Nowicki."

"Nowicki? She got a brother? Big guy, more Indian than Pole? Drives an old GMC?"

"Yeah, sure. I guess that's him."

Mitchell put out his hand for the keycard.

"Get that girl down here too. I'll want to talk to her."

He left the squad car parked by the reception door, which did not make Albie happy at all. And mention of Ursie suddenly made Albie wonder. She should have been done with her rooms by now. By this time she'd usually be clocked out and sitting in a corner of the lobby with her long-necked bottle of Diet Bubble-Up, waiting on that brother. But Albie hadn't seen either one of them. He locked the cash drawer and made a quick sweep of the upper and lower halls. Not a door propped open. In the service closet, every cart parked neat as a pin, ready to go the next day.

"She must have left today without clocking out," he stopped to tell Mitchell, who had finished sussing out the room and was now scouring the stolen Toyota.

"That usual?"

"Not exactly," Albie admitted. "But this is not a usual day, you know."

"Call her and get her back down here," Mitchell commanded as he pulled himself out of the car, looking cross.

"She doesn't have a phone," Albie said.

Mitchell scratched the side of his face but otherwise didn't let on he'd even heard Albie.

"I can get you her address," Albie offered.

"We got it," Mitchell finally said. "And we've got a report out on this car all right. From a nurse at the Health Centre." His hand bypassed his radio and went for a cell phone, swearing as the connection broke one more time.

"You got a phone in that back room?" he asked Albie as he elbowed his way past. "I've got some calls to make."

Madeline had locked the doors, just as Ursie had asked, but the truth was that since Ursie's mother had got really bad, Trevor had let nearly every needed house repair go. The house was too small. You couldn't be hammering or running a drill with a sick woman trying to rest. And after she passed, well, who cared all that much whether the sinks were slow to drain and the outside bulbs had burned out. The house fell apart right along with the Nowickis: wood window sashes split, linoleum curled, and, most important, the doors refused to line up properly so that the locks had to be jiggled until they fell (barely) into place. Most of the time Bryan and Ursie didn't bother with them. All GF Nagle had to do that afternoon was thunder onto the narrow porch and the screen door gave up and slumped to one side. Add two good fist thumps on the door to shiver the lock from its tentative purchase, and the door fell open.

Ah, GF was pissed. Little bitch thinking she could roll Markus—two fools. Who knew if Bryan Nowicki was in on it? Flacker's cousin Mitchell hadn't said. Nowicki's truck was gone, but last night he'd called about his delivery. He could use more right away, he'd said. The kid had been unusually eager, as if he needed the money badly, right away, and would do damn near anything for it. GF, who'd lost track of Markus about that time, told the kid to meet them up at Flacker's today. But maybe the kid hadn't wanted to wait. There'd been a strange ease in his voice that set GF—who was used to hearing high-wire fear from his runners—on edge, and now he could guess where that ease had come from. The kid was conning him or thought he was. Well, GF would give him something, that was for sure. First, GF would deal with the sister, who thought she could roll Markus and get away with it.

Despite the heat, Madeline had rolled Tessa up in another thin sheet on Ursie's bed, Junie's old Hudson's Bay blanket swaddled at her feet. GF kicked her in the side so that she half slid off the mattress. He slapped her around a little, paying special attention to her bandaged cheek and swaddled hand and still he couldn't wake her.

"She's on something, isn't she?" the Brit said.

"We don't have the time for this. He's waiting. Better take her with us. She'll talk when she comes around."

A roll of electrical tape was produced; precautions must be taken. Who knew but that the girl would belt out a scream when least expected? It had happened to GF before, hadn't it? Pissed him off so much that just thinking about it made him kick the girl again.

In minutes, he hoisted Tessa as easily and carelessly as if she were a garbage sack and tossed her in the Matador's trunk, blanket and all, in the cleared spot beside the tire wheel well, just the right size.

TURN BACK, TURN AROUND

"This feels perverted," I informed Bryan.

"You're not going to diddle them, Leo," he said. "You're babysitting, that's all. You could be saving their lives."

"With Fruit Roll-Ups and Smashy cakes and butter tarts?" I said, peering into the sacks.

"That's right," Bryan said.

This time, when I had slid onto the truck's front seat, Bryan seemed relaxed. Whatever grand scheme of destruction he'd hatched had obviously been abandoned for another kind of mission. The Sub-Rite sacks were neatly piled on the seat between us, the truck bed behind empty—and this was strange—broom swept. At the end of Fuller, Bryan's truck joined the line of highway traffic heading east, only to rumble off alone onto Ledge Road.

"So, you're not really after him then?" I said.

"You won't have a thing to worry about," he said. "It's simple."

Bryan would use the contents of the Sub-Rite sacks to lure the Magnuson kids into an empty freight car on the other side of the abandoned mill yard.

"Keep 'em safe for a bit," he said.

"From what?" I said, but Bryan wasn't listening.

My morning nap had pushed me off-center and the afternoon's dull glare, the constant drone of overhead traffic headed toward the fires, wasn't helping. Bryan was still talking as he positioned me near the freight car he'd chosen, but I couldn't make sense of what Bryan was saying. I kept missing pieces.

". . . then get back in the truck and start it up . . . otherwise, run like hell—in that direction." He pointed back toward the old mill yard, down those railroad tracks that now led onto a long, open stretch into miles of beaver pond.

"You're kidding."

"If we get separated, I'll find you when it's over."

"When what's over?"

"The fireworks, Leo." Bryan said. "We're all here for the fireworks, aren't we?"

Bryan had sworn no one came near the old sawmill during the day. Just the same, he'd tucked the truck back into the weedy lot down a slope behind the long-closed sawmill. Even if, cruising by, you caught a glimpse of it, you might imagine Bryan's old truck, rusted and filthy, another abandoned relic left by another doomed outfit, a ghost endeavor.

"You'll be as good as invisible here," he'd said as he pulled a backpack from the truck bed.

The thought made me unaccountably nervous.

He left me then, shifting and darting with a feather-soft tread I hadn't known he possessed. He moved from me so quickly, the hand I raised to summon him back was barely in the air before I lost sight of him and that overburdened backpack I was surprised to see crouching on his back.

It wasn't long before the little Magnusons arrived as if on cue, following the trail Bryan had laid out for them, practically somersaulting as they bent to pick up one treasure after another. I didn't think they fully saw me, so intent were they on sniffing their way to the railcar, where Bryan had unloaded the rest of the Sub-Rite sacks, spewing more packages of chocolate biscuits and crisps beside another sack full of soda-pop bottles. Per Bryan's instructions, I watched them edge beside the open door and then, almost without hesitation, fling their bodies upward. Their little chests hit the open bottom edge, their legs scrambled in the air, arms whirling. I boosted them then, shrinking at the momentary touch. They really weren't much more than skin and bone and rag, all animal urgency aimed toward the food. Practiced at disappearing, they seemed, to me at least, to flat vanish into the railcar.

Everyone was gone. The kids. Bryan. And I was, by all accounts, invisible.

A brief wander. A peek, that was all. Wasn't it about time I saw Flacker's world for myself?

The trails went uphill, every one of them, and I hadn't a clue which Bryan had chosen. The little Magnuson kids had emerged soundlessly as was their habit. I ducked my head and headed into the speargrass until my feet found a trail and I started climbing.

When I heard voices, I stopped.

"You still got her?"

"We didn't have time to finish."

"Fuck that. Get it done."

Bryan had told me the Nagles would be at Flacker's now, and I knew his new non-plan involved them somehow. He had grown so calm since yesterday and his wild notion of running Flacker off the road. This new plan of treating the Magnuson kids seemed a whole lot saner if not absolutely safe. From what he and Jackie said about Flacker, the guy would as soon as shoot you for giving a biscuit to one of his dogs as for stealing from him. Beyond the voices, another sound, a shuffling I was afraid had to be Bryan. If Flacker saw him on his property, he'd be dead for sure.

They were yelling now.

"Fucking chopped a head off in Winnipeg . . ."

"Not us. You got . . ."

". . . the rest of the goddamn money . . . pockets for? . . . I got it wrong? I got it wrong? Fuckers won't chew glass before . . ."

The flat blade of cursing chopping the air. I would have turned tail and run away, but I could hear real threats now, and not a whisper from Bryan. On the schoolyard, Bryan used to appear when I was attacked. He'd sidle up beside me and, ignoring the rising catcalls, without fail would be my ally, my protector.

I couldn't leave him alone, and so when I heard the first crack, what I imagined as fist on chin, I threw myself clumsily up the trail, stumbling into the open behind their broad backs.

"Turn around!" I hollered, even before I reached the clearing, feeling for once that I might, like Uncle Lud, actually save someone.

"Turn around!" I shouted, only to see at once that Bryan wasn't part of this fight.

They must have thought I was a bear, at first, or the first of an onslaught of lawmen. The little Brit recoiled and darted toward the orange Matador. GF Nagle, hand on his face, jumped backward too, while tweaky Cassie Magnuson flitted right and left, right and left as if damn sure she'd be the first offered up to any attacker. A greasy, black-bearded giant who had to be Flacker took the opportunity to snatch up a rifle leaning on the concrete steps to his house.

"What is this?" he demanded once he'd gotten a good look at me. He glanced at GF Nagle and the Brit, who seemed even more pissed off.

"You know this fuck?" he said. He lowered the rifle, but his knuckles were still white around it. "What is this shit? What kind of a party are we having here?"

Cassie Magnuson made the mistake of standing still beside Flacker and reaching out to touch his elbow. Flacker pushed her away, squeezing one nipple as she skittered past, then kicking her hard in the rear when she was almost free of him. Girl flew feet while the Brit snickered.

"Get lost," Flacker spat. "So who is this little fuck? One of your runners? You bring him up here with you?"

GF was shaking his head, walking toward me even as the Brit was nodding.

"Yeah, we know him," the Brit told GF. "Little prick was palling around with Markus's girl, the sister, wasn't he? You remember, down on Fuller. That pretty puss in the red sneakers, this stupid fuck run up a lamppost."

Markus's girl? On Fuller? The morning I'd shot the finger right back at the devil's man. A mad rushing began in my ears. I recognized it, and out of hard-won schoolyard habit, I slipped off my glasses and slipped them into my hoodie pocket seconds before a shove from behind sent me flying forward, my chin navigating gravel, a chittering sound beginning as if I'd entered a party and blacked out straightaway. My eyes opened and I threw up all at the same time.

"Get the fuck out of here," Flacker told Nagle. "And take the rest of this mess with you. And get rid of that stupid-ass car. It's like a neon sign around town, Mitchell says. Do a twofer. Nothing left, you hear? And Nagle"—Flacker leaned in close to GF—"get the money to me today or you might as well dig a few more holes. Don't fuck with me."

I cast about one last hopeless time for Bryan before I hit the ground again, my shoulders hitting rock, a steady drag, a creeping stream running behind my left ear into my neck, the gray light splintering as GF threw me against the Matador's backseat and slammed the door.

"We're stuffed," the Brit muttered as he started the car.

"Just drive," GF warned him. "We'll pick up the jeep, then ditch this mess, all of it."

"Markus . . ." the Brit began.

"Don't even fucking mention his name. I'm going to roast his nuts if he shows up again."

The Matador's engine screeched once, then rumbled uneasily alive.

"Yours, too, if you don't get us out of here," GF said.

As to emphasize his threat, a single, magnificent explosion rent the sky behind Flacker's house. The sky split and cracked, raining fire and metal, and an unbearable vibration went through me, rattled my teeth so that I thought for a moment about spitting them out.

"What the . . ." GF swore.

More explosions followed, staccato booms that seemed to travel closer and closer until they shook the road beneath the Matador, which was suddenly moving at high speed. The car actually lofted under the last assault as if pushed from behind, even as the Brit accelerated, so that I was thrown in still another direction, the side of my head banging hard against the half-open window, and in that last bright moment before consciousness faded, I felt as if I had been set free through that tiny, gray gap, flying blindly.

Which way home? I begged the blackened air as I flailed. Which way home?

THE GAME BEGINS

Ursie didn't remember how the men arrived, if they filed in one by one or arrived in one great swell, if they were joking like kids let out early from school or tense like men whose wages would be diminished by the fires as surely as if they'd stayed and fed it five-dollar bills. Or were they simply bored and restless? Who decided the players? Who notified each with the room number, specified the monies necessary to enter this particular game? Not a high-stakes game, no. Not intentionally. But no one would be taking chits here either. Cash. Cash. Cash. Come with your pockets full and your wits about you.

And suddenly they were there. She could hardly believe the moment had arrived.

She had spent most of the late afternoon in Keven Seven's room, practicing. He wouldn't let her clean, but demanded they get to work at once. Work? Whatever that was.

To clean, Ursie wore her usual clothes—jeans and a T-shirt—and over that, a polyester smock with the P&P's logo, a bunch of scrawny pines in front of a cluster of jagged white lines meant to evoke snow-covered peaks, emblazoned over a breast pocket. The smock didn't fit quite right, the sleeves not quite making it all the way down Ursie's long arms. It was a little tight, too, across the chest when it was all buttoned up. But Ursie didn't mind too much. She liked that the smock was long enough and equipped with numerous generous-sized pockets where she could stash clean rags and spray bottles of cleaner so that she wasn't always hopping back to the cart. The color, too, that deep forest green, did nice things for her eyes, she thought. Let alone that she liked the feeling the smock gave her, of belonging to something other than her family. She felt . . . official. So she was more than a little shocked when Keven Seven leaned across the bed in Room 18 and began unbuttoning this uniform of hers.

It's distracting, was all he said.

But what could be more distracting than his smooth hands creeping down the front of her body, slipping buttons free one by one, the edge of his thumb running down the center of her chest, between her breasts, as he finished.

Begin again, he said as he swept the smock from her, not seeming to notice it was his attention that made her stumble, numbed her fingers, and clouded her vision. She had to wait until he sat again, cat-faced and pleased in a chair across the room, thumbing the rubber band on a little bundle of bills, ready for the game.

The time she had spent with Keven Seven that afternoon could not, she realized, be measured. No way could she have learned the lessons, heard the multitude of tales he delivered in allotments of Time.

A hundred combinations lined up before her. A thousand variations. Whole worlds unfolded.

And more:

Listen, he said. *Watch.*

Here is the game of lost souls whom, he said, first played it on the threshold of Paradise: the game of the condemned ones. A game, it was said, that could bring the devil to Earth to collect his winnings.

Some believe it was a clear bargain. The losers gave up their souls, Keven Seven told Ursie with only the slightest suggestion of a smirk.

The truth is the game began as a refutation of heavenly power, commissioned by a famous king whose kingdom was nearly brought to ruin by gaming. He had no choice, that king. His subjects left the grain in the fields to rot. They ignored the plaintive desperation of unmilked cows, the blanketing stench of shut-in livestock, and kept dealing, one hand upon another. Even the courtiers were in trouble, down to rags some of them; they'd wagered so dearly. Worst of all was the queen, who would gamble anything on the prospect of a better hand, as if she could alter her life without consulting God or even her husband. She slipped from her bed each evening, back to the servants' hall, out to the court galleries, anywhere a game might yet be found.

The king went to the cardinal for advice. "Your kingdom is going straight to hell," the cardinal told the king. His subjects had chosen Luck over God, Chance over Fate. The king issued an edict. all gaming must halt. Searches were carried out and cards were destroyed in the public square—pomp of ceremony, bonfires, threatening speeches—but it did no good. His courtiers found other ways to gamble. Eyeing up a cavernous window, split into a hundred leaded panes undulating with light, the courtiers speculated on the number of flies landing on a particular wavy pane within a defined and measured span of time. They laid bets with the flicker of eyelashes, a sideways rub of the nose. The king's spies were at a loss.

A multitude of such games erupted: Who would sneeze first and for how long? On what day and what hour would the royal nephew take his first step? Odds were given on the slightest suggestion. Conversation became impossible, laden with innuendo and the risk of speculation. Not a card in sight and still his kingdom was slipping away. When his own wife grew so distant she would not dare raise her eyes or turn her head, not even blink when he called her name, the king capitulated.

Paradise had already been lost, he decided. What hope had any of regaining it? Forget God! He wanted his wife back. He called on an expert to create a new, even more seductive, game to win her, one that they would play together. The winning card: a portrait of the two of them bound together in the fires of hell, because, truly, hadn't they already taken up residence in that cursed parlor?

Ursie could nearly see it before her, the card Keven Seven called *La Condemnade: The Last Couple in Hell*.

And then, just like that, the card was gone, and she was intent again. She might as well have been alone on the river, making conversation with the wind that skidded between the rocks and made the river jump and froth and the fish bunch closer together. While her hands flew and the cards danced a jig, Time for Ursie rambled and became an old person's gait, slow, meandering. She watched each card claim a place, noticed its companions, conjectured the deck itself into sets. She shuffled and flipped again; the cards were showing off for her now, preening to show their true faces even when turned away from her. That startled even Ursie.

"Oh," she said aloud.

Had her hands ever been so smooth? They were working hands, chapped and careworn before she was nine. But now . . . how beautiful. The skin like caramel. Her shorn nails, whole and glistening.

Perfection, Keven Seven applauded.

He was crouched beside her now, and the word entered her right ear with a little hiss that made Ursie shiver.

Oh how well he knew her! Better than anyone. Better than Jackie or Tessa or Leo or even Bryan. Far better than her father. Almost as well as her mother. Her mother. Ursie tried to conjure her face, but failed. Instead, only Keven Seven's unknowable features drifted before her, until finally he swept up those teasing cards and said, *It's time. It's time.* The dance was about to begin.

For all the weeks she'd been working at the Peak and Pine, Ursie had never actually seen the swamp of grizzled men who called it home. Boisterous at first, claiming places at makeshift tables, sizing up their mates, their eyes skittered past her as she sat, Sunday school straight, on a hard-backed chair against the wall like a hulking refugee waiting for her number to be called. Keven Seven just another fellow in the mix, looking surprisingly unexceptional.

He'd told her to wait until they were all there and ready. And so she did. She'd put away her P&P smock, replaited her hair, stiffened her spine. At the last moment, once the men were seated and quieting, she simply rose and stood behind the last empty chair, enduring the men staring at her. In an ordinary game, the deal would shift from player to player, each choosing the game, but whether it was the careful arrangement of the chairs, the sealed packs set before one place only, the unaccustomed quiet as the men gathered together, it was clear from the start that this game was to be more formal and directed. Even as questions and complaints formed on tongues, Ursie slipped into the chair, broke the seal on a new pack, and began. A rude remark, half-uttered, morphed into a guttural murmuring that rumbled into the room, settling into the empty corners as Ursie began the shuffle.

They couldn't keep their eyes off her hands, of course, and yet what did they see? Dazzled, they struggled to stay with the game, to remember where they were and with whom. The expert counters among them twisted numbers, skipped and recalculated, reduced and revised, until their heads were swimming and they were hopeless in a game for which they'd lost the rules. The veteran cheats, too, the ones who practiced sleight of hand and feigned losses, discovered the usual tricks weren't working. Cards wouldn't flutter to the floor but stuck tight to a hand as if to force an actual move—a call, a fold, a quick burnt exchange in which the player always lost, the new card even less obsequious. Four men tried to remember original rules and basic strategy even as the game itself began to pick up speed.

In waves, the men recovered a little. Beer bottles and flasks appeared to refill plastic glasses. A smoky haze hovered above the room, but Ursie was too intent on her own tasks to notice its origin. The marching of the cards, the dance of dispersion and reconfiguration into the holding of hands, was following the routes she'd learned in Room 14. Her own hands were swift and sure. She did not deal from the bottom of the deck like a crooked dealer. Her fingers picked and chose, awarding each man a singular selection, chosen just for him, all the while, the deck stayed steady beneath and gave the illusion of a simple, straightforward deal as if the fish were arriving on a conveyor belt, laid mouth to tail, one right after another, instead of rising and falling in a constant overlapping stream. It was beautiful, really, how Keven Seven had taken her great gift and adapted it to this singular game. She would have chortled if she could. But not everything was working as planned.

And then Keven Seven made an ace appear where none had been before. Ursie knew this. She knew every card she dealt and the Ace of Spades should still be in the deck under her hand. While players studied their hands and debated silently, Ursie stole glances toward Keven Seven, but he wouldn't look back. He had told her, more than once, that even the slightest glimpse between them would be perceived as collusion.

Look at nothing but the cards. Look at no one, he'd said.

His last bit of advice involved the cold bottle of Diet Bubble-Up beside her.

It will keep you steady, he told her.

And Ursie, who did not drink or smoke, who purposefully averted her eyes from the stacks of crumpled bills Bryan unloaded from his pockets after an afternoon by the school playground; Ursie, who had made deathbed promises to Junie, to stay straight, did not question the open bottle Keven Seven handed her, their fingers interlacing briefly, memorably.

The ace bothered her; it did. Briefly, she felt mutiny flutter beneath her hands, a different sort of energy. In the corner, a man was praying, begging God for relief from one smashingly bad hand after another. He might as well have been cursing. His laments—could no one else hear them?—puckered the air as much as if they were obscenities. Raising her eyes slightly, she caught Keven Seven's satisfied smile.

She sipped. And sipped again. And again. A tart blossom opening brazenly on her tongue. And the bottle stayed cold and full and irresistible. Despite a growing heaviness in her fingertips, she threw her head back and dealt another hand.

CALLING THE DEVIL'S BLUFF

Albie had kept track, noting the men drifting down the corridor, up the stairs, the heady stink of growing sweat. He'd caught the room number with some surprise—he hadn't realized the entertainer knew any of these fellows—and made it a point to get Vincent in at the desk right away, so that he could make the rounds, listening at the thin door.

It was the quietest goddamn game he'd ever heard. He wondered if he'd been mistaken about the room number, but then a fellow had emerged with ice bucket in hand, and he'd heard the faint rumble behind him, the clink of bottles, even the faint but definitive skip of the cards.

Albie slowly recognized the man at the ice machine as French Bert, a burly fellow with a faked hearty laugh that belied the meanness in him. He wasn't laughing now. He wouldn't even look at Albie. Sweat had matted his thin hair to his scalp. He shook his head a few times as if to clear it, touched a fistful of ice to his jaw.

Well, it must be a hundred degrees in that room, Albie realized. Even if they had brought more fans inside, that many men in such a confined space, all of them sweating—sounded like hell itself to Albie. How long would it be before the ruckus began? The first cry of cheating or welching? How long before they realized that someone—always someone and never Albie, thank God—was taking a cut? How long before he'd have to race inside and push the fight outward so that when the police finally did arrive, it wasn't to the sight of an illicit card game but only another parking lot brawl?

Oh, the whole town was on edge, feeling the far-off booms, choking with each breath. Each year, it seemed the fires got worse. Each year, a debate began over whether they'd finally reached the breach, the end of the world. How could you blame a group of lonely, ever-aching men, nursing scars and raw stomachs and shared insults—how could you blame them for taking a few hours of play, dreaming of that big win that would set them up far away from these troubles? Albie didn't, of course. He didn't blame them at all. If in their shoes, he'd be the first one in that room, a full bottle by his side. But he had other responsibilities and what Albie truly wanted then was for these exhausted, fantasizing men to tuck themselves into bed and dream their dreams of new trucks and new lives, ditching wives for girlfriends, backbreaking work for a crack at the more ambitious. He wanted all this striving mess to sleep.

He walked a circle around the Peak and Pine, counting cars, taking note. A dead animal was splayed in the back lot's north corner, a victim likely of the tow truck Mitchell Flacker had sent along for the stolen Toyota. Albie would send Vincent out with a shovel in the morning. The entertainer's van was missing. Fellow like that probably capitalized on times like these, creating a necessary diversion. Despite the heaviness in the air and these few incongruities, all seemed under control to Albie for the moment—until he rounded the last corner and encountered Madeline Bonc fast asleep behind the wheel of her old car.

He banged on the hood and shook his head as Madeline snapped awake, wiping the drool from the side of her mouth with a practiced gesture. His arms flew upward in exasperation. Slowly, she unrolled her window, her eyebrows narrowing with irritation.

"When you gonna let that girl leave today?"

Ursula. She should have been long gone, he knew, and what reason had he to believe she wasn't, but even as he told Madeline as much, he too felt a jolt of disbelief that, coupled with Mitchell Flacker's recent visit, made him deeply uneasy.

"Is she in some kind of trouble?" he asked her.

"Ursie? Ursie in trouble? What did that fellow tell you?"

"He was looking for her, that's all. Wanted to know what she looked like."

Madeline hooted. "He don't got eyes?" Even as the words left her mouth, she felt, rather than remembered, Keven Seven's gaze, and Albie watched Ursie's ebullient aunt fade into a sobriety that he recognized as also belonging to Ursula.

"We got to try his room," she said, fully awake now. Albie could hardly keep up with her as she half ran back to the motel.

"Wait on!" he yelled at her. "His room? Mitchell Flacker doesn't have a room here."

"That police fellow? What's he got to do with the fellow in Room 14?"

He wouldn't have recognized her. Her careful braid had come undone. Her blouse was unfamiliar, a sheer red, unbuttoned right down to her surprising (and shocking) cleavage. Madeline ignored the men, the cards, and went right to Ursie, pulling her to her feet and instigating a tug-of-war, because just as suddenly one of the card players was on Ursie's opposite side, holding her back, forcing her back into her seat.

"You," Madeline said, recognizing him.

"He gave her something too," Madeline said to Albie, remembering Tessa. "Look at her eyes. Smell her."

Ursie's eyes were unnaturally bright and very still, but that might have been from all the attention that had been turned her way, Albie thought. Or not.

"She's working for me," the card player hissed, and it was only then that Albie recognized him as that slight entertainer, beefier now, more muscular. His grip on Ursie's shoulder tightened.

Albie leaned close to the girl and said, "You're leaving now."

Ursie's brilliant gaze ascended toward Albie, then as Madeline waved a hand in front of her, her chin tilted in her auntie's direction as well. Slowly, they watched that artificial blaze wane as Ursie came awake. Her hands dropped to the table and the cards she'd been clutching spilled free. And still Keven Seven held her. She could feel it now, the pinch by her collarbone, the way his touch compressed the whole left side of her as if her heart were failing. Her eyes went first to his hand, that long-fingered white hand, claiming her air. It seemed skeletal against her brown skin, so ordinary and worn now, and made her shudder. She hardly dared to look up at Keven Seven, and when she did, she did not recognize the man.

The other men were also coming awake, grumbling now in the sweltering room.

"Hey, come on now. Let's get back to the game."

"What is this?"

"Who let the squaws in here anyway?"

To Albie: "You'd better check her pockets before you let that girl go."

"She took money off me."

"Hell, she took money off all of us."

"And him?" Albie said, pointing to the entertainer. "What about him?"

But none of them could remember Keven Seven doing anything other than holding his own hand, losing with the rest of them.

"Well, who's running this game, then? The girl? You had the girl running your game?"

They didn't know what to say to that. What they remembered began well after the first cards had been dealt.

Albie nodded at Madeline, who, bless her, understood at once. She pulled at an unresisting Ursie, upending her pockets, patting her down.

"Not a cent," Albie said. Still he knew what was coming.

"Get her out of here," he commanded Madeline in a low voice. "The two of you—out!"

The door scarcely closed behind the two young women before a roar erupted, each man suddenly certain he'd been scammed and someone—was it Albie?—had engineered and profited. An upended chair flew against the window. Drunk and hot and stripped clean of wages, the men couldn't help but fight. The women hurried down the back staircase and into Madeline's old car, which seemed to start on its own. They raced out of the parking lot, neither of them daring to look behind to see if they were being chased. If they had, they might have glimpsed Keven Seven, calmly descending the stairs behind them, ambling into the smoky evening, even as one satisfying crash after another sounded above him.

. . .

For the second time that day, Madeline drove to her late sister's house and unloaded a nearly insensible girl. Ursie waved off her aunt and staggered to the porch.

An uncommon nastiness was running through the girl. She wasn't herself at all. When Madeline tried to bring her inside, Ursie flicked off the hand on her shoulder and scowled.

"It's our place. Mine and Bryan's. You need to go away," she said.

And when Madeline, well-used to drunken rantings, persisted with her help, saying, "Sweet girl, let me just get you inside," Ursie shook her off so hard she sent her auntie reeling, tripping down to one knee, all the while that glittering shard in her eyes.

"Go away," commanded Ursie. "Beat it. Scat! Leave us alone."

So Madeline, her nerves ragged, took off. This time, she was not too rattled to glance in her rearview mirror, and she couldn't help but notice how the porch door lay on its side as if ripped straight from the hinges. She couldn't help but tut-tut to herself those children so brazenly holy about her sister's inheritance, her own Uncle Rainey's old place, and meanwhile, the house falling into bits and pieces. Her tut-tutting amused her in spite of herself, and by the time Madeline reached the main road again, she was cackling with amusement and relief. She'd saved the girl. At least she knew that. And Ursie would remember too, once she came back to herself and Bryan was home and all their friends around them again and all these goddamn fires were out.

THE UNFORESEEN CONSEQUENCE:
SUCCESS

He is well away. He made sure he would be, along with every other innocent. But Bryan knows he's done it. Gerald Fucking Flacker is dying. Bryan saw it happen, the man burned alive. He could practically feel the tight heat in Flacker's chest, the screwing worm. The flaring surge, that thick black rope, would have come out of nowhere, twining Flacker's breath, squeezing the life out of him, so that if he could curse, if he did curse, the howling words birthed in his gut would splutter and rocket alternately like fistfuls of gravel hurled blindly. Only the odd piece might hit and wound with a hot-red edge sharpened by that squeeze, his rib cage tightening.

Flacker moved at speed, but Bryan knew that wouldn't help him. Flacker simply had to run, despite the fact that he was nearly blind by then. He plain couldn't see for the furious flush, which narrowed his vision to one blistering beam. All the edges went gone up in smoke and that was all he was left with, that tunnel of blackening light. He had to smell burning rubber or hair or the hot sear of metal on flesh. From the feeling in his chest, the sheer weight slamming into his nostrils, the stink might have been coming from him. If a man could combust from his own rage, his overwrought spleen exploding and taking down each organ, each sense, one by one in a rapid-fire domino-like shots fired at cans, if a man could die from the vehement swell of his own interior violence, then that, that was what should kill, will kill, *did* kill, Gerald Fucking Flacker.

The first explosion took out the still and might have been survived and explained away. An accident, a nuisance, faulty connectors and imprecise measures, a dozen possible infractions for which Flacker would certainly have exacted retribution from damn near everyone for years; he would have made sure of that. But his private shed, shrine to guns and knives and obscene booty, to file cabinets, envelopes stuffed with cash held stiff with rubber bands like an old-time bank—oh, that was serious damage. Forfeiture of whatever spirit flared and spit within him. And yet even there, some valuables might have been saved, given the thin fortress of metal. He might have emerged piecemeal but mean as ever. Still, when the meth lab camper rumbled and clanked, mere seconds of warning, and the earth itself erupted, Flacker, fully insane now, was hurled upward off his back steps and propelled straight into the flames as if that claim could no longer be denied. He belonged to the devil now, fully and once and for all. All those curses still roiling inside him finally found purchase in that hellhole. Hurled outward in one fierce burst, Flacker's bellow rising and whipping at tornado force even as the furious earth opened in its own fiery rage and sucked him in. Not even ash and bone would be left.

He's dying. He's dying. He's dead.

The house went last behind Flacker like an exclamation point. He, of course, never noticed the sputtering fire under the front porch catching the gasoline spill from a discarded chainsaw, the two-sided leap toward a kerosene heater set against the post and pier foundation and, in a crooked dance, through the speargrass to the oil-soaked dust of what passed as Flacker's driveway.

Da Boom!

Da Boom!

Da Boom!

In one last gesture, Flacker's proud truck flew skyward and rained hard, the hammering pieces just missing the unchained dogs who fled like trained greyhounds up Charlotte Road, a bony flash of grayed flesh and hanging tongues.

In a steel railroad car beside the abandoned sawmill, the little Magnuson kids cowered at first at the thunder, anticipating what would follow, Flacker's sallow face whitening with rage, their punishment arriving. And when it didn't, they hoped. They unfurled from the tight burrow they'd made and turned up their faces like flowers to each sunny explosion. Surrounded by bags of snack foods—Sub-Rite's own store brands of popcorn, pretzels, potato chips, a treasure trove of cake biscuits and sweets, too—and an open, half-full case of tall-necked Diet Bubble-Ups, anyone watching might have thought they'd bought tickets to a show.

Their mother wasn't hungry. She never was. When the first explosion came, the blast had first rolled her down the hill before she'd landed on her feet already running, unwittingly following the same path her children had. She fled. Unusual for her, that flight. Her instincts were dulled, almost nonexistent. She didn't know it, of course, but this quality had attracted Flacker to her in the first place. How he loved a punching bag, and though she would bob and weave like a frantic pup, her timing was woeful and he always found her waiting in the corner, the truth of a situation only dawning when his fist grabbed her hair, knocking her head "to put some sense in it."

Lord knows what pushed her away from the house in the first

place that afternoon. The kick on the rear set her walking and she didn't stop until she was well down the hill. Even so, that last blast might have flattened her as it did her so-called boyfriend, if she hadn't reached the sawmill's tracks by then and flung herself, all the burning bits of her, into the open railcar. She hadn't required the coaxing enticements of Bryan's familiar bags visible at child height as if they'd entered a wild game, an Easter-egg hunt with a raw-boned teenager standing in for the bunny. The surprise of the open rusted boxcar was a gift those addled children didn't even question, and neither did their mother. One shoe was lost; her thin yellow hair singed on the top of her head. She hardly noticed her own two children and their booty as she crouched, hands crossed over her head, shivering uncontrollably, until one of them —it was the boy—scuttled to his feet and ran to hand her a long-necked bottle of lukewarm Diet Bubble-Up as if it were pure medicine, a magic elixir that might cure them all.

The moment Cassie Magnuson appeared at the top of the hill, Bryan knew the Nagles had arrived and that Flacker would be occupied. He'd got what he'd planned, a full-bore distraction, which was the only way he'd managed to get the dynamite in place. He hoped that, like in that old singsong poem his mother used to tell them about a gingham dog and a calico cat, they'd just eat each other up. But justice was slim around here. That's why he was here, wasn't it? He'd done the deed, and afterward, a fine char coating his face, his eyes stung by smoke, he searched, screaming, "Leo! Leo!" until he could wait no longer. Hoarse and blackened, he must have been a horrible sight when he returned to the open freight car. The little Magnuson kids were seemingly impervious to terror, but not to the effects of junk food. One might have thrown up. The boxcar stank of puke. But both were still methodically stuffing their mouths and right next to them was their horrible mother, rocking back and forth with a half-empty bottle of Diet Bubble-Up.

Bryan checked the truck, began calling out again. "Leo, damn it!"

"They took 'im," Cassie Magnuson told him when he returned to the boxcar. "They put that kid away in the orange car."

Bryan felt an unbearable urge to slap her. Slap her or run like crazy. Leo had been right all along; the Nagles had come after them. Instead he roughly hustled Cassie Magnuson and her two kids and their found booty into a van he'd found parked between two firs beyond the rusted millworks, the keys dangling in the ignition. It started up right away, just as it had the first time Bryan had tried it, hours before. Such a soft purr for an old battered van. He all but pushed Cassie into the driver's seat, pretending he didn't smell a thing, and still she stared at him wild-eyed until he did what he imagined every man did to get her attention. He screamed at her.

"Get out of here, you bitch!" he yelled.

His voice was muffled by the roar behind them, but Cassie got it. As if sparked, her bony hands jammed the shifter into drive, and the van all but galloped away, sliding sideways only once before it landed on the loop road. Running, Bryan reached his truck, which mercifully started, and he followed the old van right up to the highway, watched as it merged and began its journey away from town. Bryan followed in the truck as far as the first cut-off dirt road, then looped back toward town to search for the Nagles' orange Matador and the dumbest smart kid ever.

THE DEVIL DRAWS A MAP

All morning, they had plagued him. His brother slamming the back of his head each time Markus began to drift. Even when they were in the car and Markus wanted to howl from the pain in his arm, even when the pain flat made him pass out, his brother didn't let up.

"Where's the fucking money? Where's the fucking money?"

They had to go see Flacker. They had to stay the hell away from Flacker. They had to tell Flacker that Markus was a fucking idiot. That Markus had been rolled. That Markus was a stupid thief. They'd feed Markus to Flacker. Or not. Because who had passed that wad of bills to Markus in the first place? Somehow they decided it would look better if he disappeared along with the money. If he just got the fuck out of town and didn't show his face again. They'd put him in the jeep they kept at the house as a spare. Send him north. Or south. Do mischief on his own. Keep his mouth zipped. Leave them here to take the brunt of Flacker's anger, which would be the equivalent of a hot iron set in his own wounds. Maybe they should give him a taste before they set him free? But hell, they might need that jeep. Why let Markus take it? They didn't need him. Asswipe. They'd find that money. They would. Unless he was screwing with them. He'd better not be screwing with them.

His brother's fists spared nothing, but the last beating was calculated, leaving him energy enough to stagger eventually to his feet. They didn't want him found. They wanted him gone. As if he could go. A pitiful specimen quaking on the roadside, one thumb cocked among that sea of fire refugees, not one of them with a spare inch of room for a broken loon like Markus—unless it was another broken loon, enough of those about.

He wasn't going anywhere anyway.

Markus had to walk the whole way back, skunking through ditches until he regained the outskirts of town, shadowing yards and back alleys, kicking off dogs, and even hunkering down awhile in the baseball dugout to catch his breath and swallow a couple of pain pills GF miraculously hadn't taken from him. He couldn't shake the sound of sirens in his head. They'd begun hours ago after GF had booted him out of the Matador. He'd lain in the ditch, howling, but GF hadn't come back. And just as well. After the pills kicked in, he was able to stumble to the house where they'd crashed the last time and, with his one good hand, make a pile of crappy scrambled eggs, slamming them down right out of the hot pan so fast he raised a blister on his lip. Afterward, almost without thinking, he fled again. Both the jeep he'd hope to use and the Matador were gone now, but GF would be back; he'd find Markus and be more pissed off than ever, sure Markus had lost the money on purpose. But he hadn't lost the money really. It was safe as could be. In an angel's hands.

He hadn't breathed a word of her to GF, not even when the two of them were working him over, GF's boot pressed hard on his chest, its dog-shit stained tip under Markus's split chin. He hadn't mentioned her at all. But he could see her clearly, curled into the chair like a velvety cat, the long sweep of her hair blanketing her shoulder and broken cheek. Tucked up so neat with a red shoe on her as if she were something special. She was, he knew, she was.

Even GF had missed her. That's how crazy-smart that girl was.

He remembers vaguely a wad of bills, her bandaged hand unfurling paper and trying . . . and failing . . . to reacquaint the rolled wad to his pocket, which refused to hold the bills and rolled them outward, a continual expulsion, so that he laughed and tipped his head away. It was such a silly joke: a Nagle who could not snatch money. Still he could not, would not, describe for his furious brother the thin-boned grace of that girl who saved him, who did not desert him, but flew back to his side and saw him safely to bed, poor wracked souls, the pair of them. She had a sister somewhere waiting. A running car. An impatient clerk with a hand out. And she satisfied them all and tucked the sheet around him so that he slept, finally slept, like he hadn't for all his life; he was sure of that. And if GF hadn't interrupted and slammed away every last good dream Markus had, he might have awakened with her hand in his good one, a better, gentler man, A man with hope and promise. No. No. No. He would not give her up.

He must have slept or passed out or maybe someone else had knocked him over. He woke again in the dusky light of that late summer night, coughing from the weight of the air. He could hear cars still moving on the highway, the steadiness like a surf, and they made him unaccountably happy. The town was still here. And so must she be as well. He half ran the blocks past downtown, past the still-humming Sub-Rite, the vibrating strip that led to the neon pine tree pulling him close. The Peak and Pine— what a place that was. The lot was crammed full of trucks, even campers. It occurred to him there must be at least one poker game in progress, but how quiet the place was. Although he knew better, he imagined Tessa sleeping behind one of those thin green doors, the entire motel shushed for her benefit. Which one? Which one? He was wavering in front of a wall of doors, reading their numbers, trying to jog his memory when a familiar voice greeted him and he turned to see his old friend, leaning against a back corner as if he had been waiting for Markus.

You're still here.

I'm always here, you know, Clark said.

Card game, eh? Room for one . . .

It's over.

So early.

For now.

S'okay. I was looking for someone.

The girl with the red shoes.

Yeah. Yeah. Unease tickled Markus. The faint memory of nausea. His arm jolted with pain as if he was truly waking now.

And the roll of cash.

Yeah? How did Clark know? Had she told him? She must know Clark.

Oh, yes. You'll want to see her.

Markus beamed. He wanted to describe her to his old friend, but details eluded him. Her calmness. Capability. Acceptance. How could you put that into words? Better to say "great ass," but Markus felt a deeper, stranger pull toward Tessa. An old-timey phrase came to mind. Heavenly. She was heavenly. She would elevate him, he felt sure.

Heaven is a fortress, you know. Icy, snowbound, Clark said as if in response. *No way in, no way out.*

Markus frowned, sure he hadn't said a word aloud. Had he? And now Clark, like GF when he got a snootful, was off on a rant.

Pearly gates held tight by thunderbolts, pompous know-it-all guards, scads of rules. Hierarchy you would not believe. Crowds and crowds of the most boring souls you can imagine. Only one thought vibrating through those orthodox vestiges: obedience, obedience, obedience.

Markus cracked an uneasy grin, and a seepage began, as if he were losing a vital fluid. His arm ached.

Hell, on the other hand, has no borders. You can find it anywhere. Do what you like, where you like, to whom you like.

Hurts, does it? Clark said, reaching toward him with one thin white hand.

And oh, how it did then. A hot pain shot right to his heart. His legs shook. The parking lot waved and began to disintegrate, and just as quickly, it was over.

A little trick I learned, Clark said as Markus tentatively moved his arm. The sore bone vibration, that endless dull ache within his cast, was gone. He swung his bad arm from side to side. Nothing. He could run with her now; they could leave together.

Guess they took the car away. Markus said. Place is swarming with people.

She's not far, you know, Clark said.

A faint memory of a van stirred in Markus.

His old friend shook his head. *Oh, no. But not far. I'll draw you a map. You'd be surprised at how easy it can be to lose your way on that beautiful highway.*

LOST AT LAST,
IN THE FIERY WOODS

Look at me, Uncle Lud!

Here's a story for you: a true-life tale of metamorphosis, in which your nephew wakes to discover he's been turned into an old cedar log, an elegant golden slab, striated with red, a majestic specimen propped within a circle of stacked, flat rocks.

It's okay, I whispered to my newest friends, those great handfuls of broken sticks, those heady fans of cedar brush who held me high as if I were an offering. The transformation, their humming laments, tells me it's not quite complete. I got the gist. I am a mountain kid, after all.

Hey, it's okay, I assured them, the fire's out.

But even as I made my declaration, jewel-like embers, tiny red pulses below, gained purchase, tickling into flame.

It's a story, I reassured all, just a story. But then my fingers blackened and when I tried to lift myself from this embrace and run away, those fingers, then my wrists, then my forearms crumbled into sooty lines of charred wood.

That's not me, I told Bryan, who was close, I was sure.

Be quiet, Bryan warned, pressing a heel against my side so that the branches below me scratched my cheek as they burst, one after the other, into flame.

Play dead, Bryan said, leaning close to my ear.

I am, I whispered back. Bry, oh, Bry, I *am,* I am so dead.

I woke to the sound of metallic thunder, piercing and steady, beating behind my head. The back of my throat cracked so dry, I had to silently whoop for air, whoop and whoop again, until I finally managed a clean breath and could calm. I had been curled into myself, my face against a backseat window, alone in a car I did not recognize, at least from the inside. My eyes were streaming, too, as if weeping uncontrollably, but it wasn't until I managed to sit up, my head swimming, that I realized I wasn't wearing my glasses. The last thing I remembered was GF shaking his head, and the Brit closing in on the other side.

My left hand seemed to be asleep, but my right hand, sore as hell, went into my hoodie pocket and came out with my glasses, beautifully intact. The skin on my face felt sticky and raw, but I gingerly lifted my glasses into place, wincing as the frame edge touched skin. And now I knew exactly where I was. Crap everywhere. Greasy food wrappers, bits of frayed rope and duct tape, oil-stained rags, beer cans, empty cigarette packages, and that plastic headless baby doll with her fingertips burnt off hanging from the rearview mirror. The smell of sweat and piss and something even more rancid, which seemed to be coming from me. I was in the Nagles' Matador.

The thunder cracked. Started again. After a bit of scrambling and jostling my left shoulder against the door, I managed to get out of the car, falling much farther than I imagined should be possible to reach the ground, where, suddenly aware that whoever had brought me here—GF or the Brit or even Flacker—might be ready to attack again, I crept as fast as I could, bent over into a crawl, just far enough to get a good picture of what I'd escaped and where I had landed. I needn't have bothered. I was completely alone. But where? And where was everyone?

Too close, I could hear a low swoosh like a distant train, and just like that, I knew.

I was on the mountain—on an old access road that had once been flooded out, then cluttered with blown-down branches, a maze of debris that no one would clear since the reason for this road no longer existed, likely miles and miles from home in a gulley filled with dry kindling, a lit match closing in.

And underneath it all, that thunder, which now I began to believe in my dull fancy, came from the car itself, that same old orange Matador that had brought me from Flacker's. The car had been driven up this steep incline and shored in place with heavy rocks dragged behind the rear tires. One of them must have followed behind in another car or the Brit's own rusty jeep, picked up the driver, and finished the chores Flacker had set out—get rid of the car, get rid of me.

The air on the mountain was dense and visible, so utterly strange, dusky and yet, almost as if the air twisted, light would appear in undulating ribbons. I had a moment of disconnect. Leila Chen should see this, I thought, then she'd understand. But understand what? Yes, the air was thick with smoke and soil and sown through with what Uncle Lud would call the mountain's own particulates. Still, visibility wasn't as bad as it might have been. Vaguely, I felt a problem could be proposed and solved here, if I had been smarter, if I had studied. As if to mock my seriousness, a falling branch, not much more than a sturdy twig, knocked me on the head, and I swore I heard Jackie teasing.

Hey there, Leo, better rattle those smarts, eh?

Behind the car's perch, a kind of rough road began, a deeper set of tracks in the dust. The tire marks were large but close together, like those on equipment. Occasionally, Bryan would make an excursion up a service road to siphon gas from whatever rigs had been left in place. The Nagles had taught him that as well. They weren't above stealing a rig to get them back to town. Following those tracks back was the only chance I had. I leaned against the Matador and lifted my shirt against my face and breathed as deeply as I dared. I had no idea how far I'd have to walk—or if I would be able. I might have started running like a scared fool if just then the thunder hadn't begun anew, causing me to snap back into my body, because this time, I knew just where that sound was coming from.

The trunk's catch was partly busted, and at first, I thought I'd have to give up. It had to be Bryan. I was sure of it. No way he would have let them bring me here without a fight. He must have arrived just after they knocked me out. The knuckles on both my hands were scraped and raw and the cut I'd given myself with the chainsaw blade—just yesterday?—had opened again, so that even as I struggled with the trunk lock, blood smeared across the trunk's dusty edge. The sight of it spurred me on. I would slam rocks at the lock. I would pry at the metal until my hands really did fall off, but I wasn't leaving Bryan inside. No way.

"Hey, hey!" I shouted. "I'm trying. I'll get it. Hold on."

None of the trash in the car could help me. I tried levering with a heavy stick. Nothing. Then I remembered something Uncle Lud had shown me once. Instead of yanking harder on the catch, I pushed and pushed until I felt a shift, the lock knocked partway out of its groove, the trunk rising just far enough for me to shove in the stick and seesaw back and forth until, even as I could feel the wood splitting, the lock clicked free, and I opened the trunk to find not Bryan, but a battered, barefoot Tessa, her mouth taped shut, her hands bound together into one broken fist. She was soaked from head to toe in sweat.

I don't think I had ever moved so fast.

ONE LAST SHOT

Another broken latch in a day of broken latches. Why should Ursie be surprised? In fact, she almost greeted the fallen screen door, the splintered wood, the break where GF Nagle's foot had pushed through. But that was only the beginning. They'd upended the house, torn it apart. A knife had ripped open the couch and chair, great piles of white stuffing littering the linoleum. The glass on their family photographs was smashed in, and torn scraps of paper had been flung from one end of the room to the other. She felt, more than saw, the disaster in the kitchen, every last relic of her mother's in shards. A long brownish smear marked the floor along the hallway and for a moment, the punch in her chest gave way to mean elation. They'd hurt themselves. They'd bled. She knelt by the stains, ran her fingers gleefully along each horrible splotch. She still had that nasty taste in her mouth from Keven Seven's cocktail. Worse, she wanted more.

Those bastards, she laughed as she sat up, she hoped they'd bled to death.

Did she think that? Whose words were those? Whose voice?

The blood on her fingers itched. Itched and burned and stank. She wiped her hands on her jeans, but her fingers remained stained and, as if punched in the chest, she suddenly remembered Tessa's little face, all those bruises and cuts.

Madeline had sworn she'd tucked Tessa into bed. Groggy

Ursie heard her aunt's singsong promise. "Yeah, sure," she said. "She's all tight and safe."

But when Ursie staggered to her room, the bed gaped empty, another center broken and streaked with more blood. And she swam again to the surface, slowly and oh so painfully. Who had done this? Where was Tessa? Where was Bryan? He must have come to the P&P to get her. Unless something had happened to him as well.

In the ruin of her house, Ursie began to shake. It was the end of days. Her mother gone. Her father gone. Her brother gone. And Tessa—Tessa, too.

When Albie had discovered that Room 11 had been occupied by a Nagle brother, she tried to imagine how Tessa had come to be in his company. Even now she struggled. And Bryan's warning began to thump in her head:

If they come here, don't hesitate. They *won't.*

If they come here, don't hesitate. They *won't.*

Amazingly, the Nagles had missed the rifles hung on the hooks behind the curtains. Ursie eased both down into her arms, checked again to make sure they were loaded, and went outside. Whatever was coming next, she wanted to be out in the open for once, ready.

The porch steps, swept just that morning, were rimmed with fresh black soot. Ursie's hands shook as she set down the rifles, and she had to steady herself, one palm on the siding of the house, as she made first one then another attempt to turn on the outside faucet. The hose jumped under her fingers, a darting snake she barely managed to hold steady as she washed the steps until the soot became a thin black stream that curled and leapt and finally arched and fell into the scabby, heat-burned grass.

Ursie struggled to follow the wiggle and dart, and then it was gone, gone, gone, a snake in the grass. She did not remember turning off the faucet, but the hose was dry, and she was sitting at full alert on the stained, damp step, one rifle across her lap, the other leaning beside her. Her heart empty, her lungs full of smoke, she waited for the devil to appear.

And she was not disappointed. Bits of captured light bounced among the cottonwood leaves, always dying, never dead. The heavy sky pressed down and she, too, might have succumbed, lying insensible, sideways on the step, if he hadn't arrived so swiftly, so clearly. Ursie's hands began to steady, that old familiar skill arriving with a rustling, a brazen animal approach through the woods. She would barely let him reach the edge of the yard. She could not stand to see him in the clearing. Oh yes, she was suddenly desperate to hurt so that the pain would never end, but linger as hers would. She'd shoot clear through his heart, she decided. Without the slightest hesitation, she raised the gun, aimed. Yes, almost as steady as ever.

A single shot, that's all it took—she truly was an excellent shot—and Markus Nagle fell, fell back into the shadows, fell away from Ursie and Bryan and their mother's prized house, where there was no more damage to be done, fell away, too, from any dreams he might have had for himself and the girl with the red shoes. For the first time since she'd left Keven Seven and the P&P, Ursie felt herself again, and calmly she left her perch on the porch step to tuck the rifles back behind their curtain. Then, without a backward glance at the figure on the ground, Ursie began walking, slowly. Her neighbors would be home by now. She would call someone from there to come and collect him. But not too soon. Not too soon. He had some suffering to do, just like the rest of them.

A TREACHEROUS JOURNEY

The roads up on the mountain, like the gnarled roots of old trees, meander into twisted mazes, dead-ends, swamp land, even sudden unreasonable uphill runs that break off as if someone had been planning an idiot run heavenward. Even the logging companies have lost track of them and have to rely on old maps and an occasional helicopter geographer. Tessa was limp. She had barely enough strength to keep her arms around me as I lifted her from the trunk and undid every scrap of the black electrical tape that held her. We were both in tears as we surveyed each other. Tessa was in worse shape than me and as disoriented and sore as I was. I felt a surge of pure rage.

"Your face," I started.

Her hand fluttered to the soiled bandage flapping on her cheek, and she peeled it free.

"Brice," she whispered. "A fit."

"Not the Nagles?"

Tessa tried to take a breath, coughing with the effort.

"The Nagles did that to *you*?" she managed. "Why?" she said. "Why would he do that? Where are we?"

"I don't know," I said miserably.

"It was at Flacker's," I tried. "And Bryan . . ." But the rest, whatever it was, made no sense to me. I shook my head. The route to this godforsaken spot was as inscrutable to me as it was to Tessa.

"My shoes," Tessa said, taking stock. "My . . ."

She winced as she searched her pockets and her sore hand emerged empty. Gingerly, she lifted her T-shirt just high enough for both of us to see the deep purple bruise GF Nagle's boot had made on her left hip. In the quiet between us, a low, distant hiss reminded us of the fire we could smell coming. There was no sky. The sky had vanished. And the two of us were shifting before each other, graying into ashy shadows. As Tessa was sinking, I managed to catch her and get her up to the car's front seat. Almost immediately, she pushed out of my arms and knelt on the ground, throwing up or trying to.

"Leo, you'll have to drive," she said when she could raise her head again.

"Drive?" I said. "Tessa . . ."

A crazy thought, but it turned out whoever had left us both here had also left the key in the ignition. The car started right up, a strange miracle. Still I couldn't imagine how I would move the car without flipping it over.

"Turn it off," Tessa commanded in her small, still voice. Then at her whispered direction, with my heart leaping, I shifted her into the driver's seat, where she held the brake with her bare toes, her leg shaking with the effort while I kicked and kicked and finally loosened the rocks shoved behind the rear tires. Almost the same moment, she slipped into the passenger seat and let her foot—bare and dirty and scraped—ease off the brake pedal, the car slid slowly backward, away from the precipice, and I dove behind the wheel and held tight.

We bounced, the car sweeping dangerously close to a cliff edge before I learned to be gentler with the steering wheel and harsher with the brake. With no place to turn around on that needle stretch, we backed down blind for what seemed like miles in that bucking car, Tessa kneeling and facing backward, holding tight to the seatback, and calling out instructions as her eyes tracked the tire marks that were our only guide. Bent sideways, I hardly saw the road through my crooked glasses as I swerved and sweated until finally Tessa yelled at me to turn the wheel hard, hard, hard to the right. I did, and we flipped left so fast, she fell into the door and the steering wheel leapt out of my hands.

"Now, stop! Stop!" Tessa shouted. And, God help me, two feet slammed on the brake pedal, I did. In another moment, we'd have lost our chance.

What I had taken for smoke cleared—an achingly slow descent of dust, and we could see that the Matador had landed on another flat precipice, hardly larger than the car itself, but this time the drop was behind us and the road lay ahead and we had a clear direction to move. Another meter backward, and we would have been lost, tumbling clear off the side of the mountain. It seemed a miracle that we had avoided that fate, I thought. Even if I had been driving forward and knew where I was going, the smoke, the dust, the curves, the broken edges—well, yes, a miracle.

"Okay," Tessa said, breathing hard, "okay, okay. Now put it into drive."

Going forward was only marginally easier. Ruts and roots and black dust. Despite the fact that only one route appeared possible, the tire marks that had led us had vanished. I kept my foot partway on the brakes, which began to emit a worrisome burning stench. Occasionally, I pressed the accelerator too hard, too fast, so that the car briefly lofted on the rough road and I had to struggle to wrestle it back. At times the track ahead vanished too, real smoke obscuring our way, and we could only inch along, scraping suspension and muffler, wondering if we were driving straight into an inferno, but then we'd make out a single curve, a bank of scrub trees emerging, and gradually we would breathe again. We passed one turn-off after another, and sometimes it seemed we weren't going downhill at all anymore, just sliding sideways on old gravel, like a slalom racer in agonizingly slow motion. Every time another narrow fork came into sight, splintering into more possible routes, we gambled against the fire's route, Tessa always calling the turns.

Be careful what you wish for, my mother liked to tell me, as if wishes must carry at least a clear inch of pain within them. For years, this was all I desired: to be with Tessa in a car almost like this—a quiet back road, with me at the wheel, Tessa's trembling hand resting lightly on my shoulder. Now, my arms ached from the effort of holding a steering wheel. The cut on my finger had opened again, stinging a slick thread of blood. My right knee jiggled uncontrollably and my foot arched painfully as I navigated accelerator and brake pedals. No wonder my mother was such a menace on the road. Driving hurt.

How long could we manage with no guarantee of escape? We might simply be weaving between the same logging roads again and again. The thought might have crossed both our minds moments before we hit what would turn out to be the last blind curve and the road opened into a dry patched lane of gravel and dirt, more groomed than anything we'd come upon before. The dead trees thinned to scrub. A tight breeze ruffled the dust beyond us as we eased into one last series of gentle switchbacks and knew we were heading downward for sure. Glimpses of a familiar sky appeared, still burdened and beleaguered, yet a harsh welcome glint. Both of us held an image of the road to the refuse station, a route we knew in our bones, and we began to relax. We could almost see the intersection ahead where, with Bryan, we'd drop off Jackie before turning right toward town. But when we finally— too fast—did come to a level stretch, we were on a far better road, one Tessa and I didn't recognize or anticipate, a road that appeared to head for a vast green plain. It was as if the world had inverted itself, and as if to emphasize that point, we were suddenly enveloped in mist, real rain, shushing across the filthy windshield, blinding me. I hit the brakes too late and too hard, and the car rolled onto that swell of endless perfect lawn even as a new wave of heavier rain tippled over us. I couldn't stop the car now, not even when Tessa leaned across and yanked the hand brake. The car pressed forward, out of our control, hydroplaning over that flawless field. We floated through an impossible rain, in one graceful twirl after another until Tessa flew, a ragdoll weight, out of her seat and landed twisted across me, her head settling against my chest.

Not for the first time, I wondered if I was already dead, in a version of heaven not even Uncle Lud could dream up. The two of us inverted, Tessa gazed down at me and with her bandaged hand touched my cheek.

"Your face," she said, suddenly tearing up.

"It's okay," I said, holding her tighter. "It's okay."

Still, it would take me several more long beats to recognize the intermittent showers as coming from sprinklers, the vast green lawn as a golf course, and, ever so slowly, even the irate figure running in our direction, and know for certain I was telling Tessa the truth: we were safe.

• • •

We had heard about the Scotsman and his private golf course, the clever network of expensive irrigation, that velvet sod. We had heard about the Scotsman, an introvert, obsessed by a game he played alone. He had wolfhounds. My mother had met one when the animal wandered away. But until we saw him approaching, a lean, livid man, flanked by a pair of equally lean wolfhounds, we had never given him much thought. Any curses he'd been about to heap on Tessa and me burbled away once he got a good look at us. His mouth gaped open then.

"Can ye walk?" he asked, his brogue purling with concern.

I had to laugh because the Scotsman sounded like none other than Alexander McAfee, the BBC fox who had so enchanted Uncle Lud.

"I mean," he continued, "if ye could get yerselves . . ."

Tessa, too, began to silently shake and for an altered moment I supposed my laughter was infectious.

"The poor little gull," the fox was saying. Was he wringing his hands? I couldn't quite tell. The light had gone dim again, the whole car shivering. A siren rounded, circling closer and closer.

"The poor little gull," the fox repeated.

Those hills are full of gulls, Hana broke in.

No, no, I protested, no, not *this one,* as doors flew open around us and Tessa was lifted out of my arms.

BEAUTY + DESPAIR
A POEM BY THE DEVIL

You cannot equate them, no formula makes sense.
So reconcile, please, the absence of solutions.
Days of computation will always return
a wound that never heals,
a wound littered with blank dust, wormed gravel,
with particles of shivered glass and, worse,
a reeking emptiness that you can subtract
or multiply to kingdom come
and never satisfy the infernal problem.

The end of the world comes not all at once
but in gasps. How grand is that?
Your real tragedy is that you can dream only
a single, shared ending, neat sums in a line
like tree after tree waiting for the saw,
the flame, or the wretched bloom
of a wheedling insect staking claim
on a girl breathing light, alone.

IN HIS WAKE: INFERENCE, INTERPRETATION

On that long July evening, Jackie's mother and Tessa's surprisingly sober sister made the rounds, with three of Jackie's sisters filling the car's backseat. The Health Centre had no news for them, and in the wake of the fires, the lumber camp had closed, its managers blotto and disagreeable down at the Peak and Pine. The women were pulling up Lamplight Hill, where my mother was keeping vigil over Uncle Lud and fuming at my absence when they were nearly run off the road by Trudy, arriving with news of her own.

Bryan had spent a frantic hour combing town for the orange Matador before returning to search the hills east of Flacker's and, not incidentally, dodge the crews arriving to deal with the new outbreak, that chemical reek. The Flacker Fire, it would be called, all blame placed on the missing Flacker's head (his meth lab, his still). It wouldn't take long for a dozen people to say they foresaw the inevitability, for warrants to be issued, Flacker declared the bogeyman of this terrible fire season. People would forget the fire had started well before that afternoon. Bryan could not stop to savor his success. He vaulted his own considerable fears and went to Trudy, who was fielding a rash of local calls in the midst of the fire brigade's own crises.

Blood along the highway.

A car flipped upside down on the Scotsman's golf course.
A concussed child.

The town's only two aid cars idled at the Flacker fire, waiting fruitlessly for survivors. Over the incoming radio static, Trudy gazed at soot-covered Bryan and ordered the aid cars back just as one last call arrived.

A shooting on the dead-end curve of Tripcott Road.

"That's your place, isn't it?" my cousin asked Bryan, who was stunned to find himself nodding.

"Hey, Kenny," she called out to the frazzled chief in the inner office. "Going now." She pushed her chair away from the desk and radio and without a backward glance, pushed past Bryan and out the door.

"And Jackie?" her mother asked hopefully as Trudy broke the news to my mother: Tessa and me on our way to the Health Centre; Marcus Nagle ahead of us; Albie Porchier wrangling with the police on behalf of Ursie.

"And Jackie?" her mother tried again.

Not even Trudy was ready to shake her head. She shrugged. "Nothing yet," she hedged.

By late the next evening, the wind had all but ceased to exist. The original fire swept farther north and was slowly, painfully contained. Still, the Flacker Fire burned in place for weeks, as if that damned soul refused to give up the Earth. Every bit of venom he'd spewed burbled back in scorching impotence as the fire tried to singe the sky, make one everlasting mark on the heavens.

Flacker was clearly dead, although it seemed to take ages to find the remains and verify. At first, no one knew what had happened to Cassie Magnuson and the little Magnuson kids and belated worry about them fueled search efforts until Cassie Magnuson was arrested for shoplifting a few towns over and the little Magnuson kids were sent, at last, to live with a grandmother who turned out to be loving and anguished on her own account.

When finally the areas up around the logging camps were declared safe, a search-and-rescue team made a desultory attempt to find Jackie and Hana Swann. No one believed they were out there. The police were positive Jackie had simply run off with her new friend, a gal most agreed now was nothing more than a troublemaking transient. Even Jackie's logging bosses suggested the two had planned and plotted an adventure well away from our small town. They might not have believed, but everyone who knew Jackie were certain she would never run away. Tessa, Bryan, Ursie, and I knew. We knew, too, that we'd failed her, failed, failed, failed to save one we loved.

Search and Rescue did unearth the remains of a jeep with two male bodies inside, not far down from the ledge that had almost claimed Tessa and me, and a few hardened old hearts leapt painfully at that news.

"What the hell were they doing up there in the fire?" GF Nagle's grandfather bellowed around town.

Mitchell Flacker hadn't a clue. He didn't even have Markus to interrogate. The single bullet Ursie fired had, of course, unerringly found its mark. Even the judge, considering the evidence, the damaged house and Tessa's bruised body, agreed it was in self-defense and marveled that Ursie was able to stop a moose of a man with that single shot.

Uncle Lud did not die that night or even the night after. For ten long days, he lingered in the twilight sleep he and I briefly shared, yet while I woke, safely back in my own bed still dreaming I held Tessa in my arms, Lud traveled on. And I sat with him. Me and my mother and Trudy and—and Tessa, too. She was still sporting all kinds of new scars, but ready now to hold my hand while we waited.

Uncle Lud died on the afternoon my mother buried one last feline victim in her animal boneyard. He died while Jackie's sisters insisted endlessly to the police that Jackie had not run away, that she would not run away, that she did not do drugs or sell herself, that she was a good, hardworking girl who had gone missing. He died as Trevor Nowicki and my father finally reached the edge of town, not knowing what they'd find as they proceeded homeward and for once, flat afraid.

He died while the rescued Magnuson kids tumbled from cot to cot, unable to calm after their rescue. Within four safe walls, in new pajamas and beds with pillows, after devouring elbow macaroni and cheese piled high on real plates, they were dazed by the sudden fullness of their existence and had already begun to believe that everything they'd known before this place had been a kind of fantasy in which, barefoot and vulnerable, they'd been carried from an ogre's palace, hidden in a giant's burlap sack.

Uncle Lud shouldn't have known about all that. But he did; I was sure he did. Just as I was sure he saved two boys from Snow Woman and heard Keven Seven instructing Ursie in dark arts. I imagined Uncle Lud in his final hours ascending his own mountain path, standing one last vigil as the Man Who Came Out of a Door in the Mountain arrived in his sights, shadowing that creature until the rock slipped back into place behind him, at least for a while. Then, Uncle Lud might have turned and faced an altogether different landscape, another sort of brilliant path finally visible.

"There is," Leila Chen wrote me in one of her last e-mails, "a clear connection between physics and poetry (as you well know, **Leo Kreutzer**) and it is this: both are links between the visible world and its vast invisible counterpart."

Quoting from a preface in the *Physics Online,* she wrote:

"Some estimates are that the universe is 70% dark energy, 25% dark matter, and only 5% of the universe is visible matter or energy."

You see, **Leo Kreutzer,** the world is mostly composed of that which acts only in reaction-to, not that which simply *acts*. Inference, **Leo Kreutzer,** and Interpretation, these are what matters and both are provinces of poetry and physics. Perhaps, one day, you will turn to poetry. I foresee that, like me, you might have some small skill in that arena.

ACKNOWLEDGMENTS

The story here was sparked by outrage over the ongoing murders and disappearances of aboriginal women along Highway 16, the so-called Highway of Tears, in northern British Columbia, a situation that needs as much light as can be shined upon it—and energy and solutions. The story veered into a more fanciful narrative after a dinner party discussion of good and evil (thank you, Tom Jay and Candy and Michael Gohn). My extreme gratitude is owed to the indefatigable Gail Hochman, who read and read and read for me with grace, honesty, and generosity; and to Maggie Riggs, my insightful editor; also Debra Magpie Earling, Germaine Harun, and my dear Peter Scovil, all of whom I've hypnotized into believing I'm smarter and better than I truly am and so are the best of listeners. I'm also indebted to Kent Meyers, who gave the novel a valuable reading at a crucial point, and Duncan Scovil, reader extraordinaire, who read, listened to, and discussed the book with me more than anyone should have. To Alistair Scovil, well, hell, Ali . . . there isn't a book big enough to acknowledge or thank you, love.